Consumed BY YOU

Consumed BY YOU

The bride is stunning. The groom is delightful. Shame the best man is a class A jerk.

When my BFF asks me to be her maid of honor, I'm, well, honored. Until she introduces me to the best man and I realize we've already met, just this morning when... wait for it...

I accidentally spilled a cup of OJ all over his pristine designer suit.

Not my finest hour, but he didn't have to be a dick about it either. And now—God help me—I'm forced to spend five days on a paradise island with a guy who's the complete opposite of me.

He's bossy, a clean freak, and hates tardiness.
I'm sassy, messy, and will turn up late to my own funeral.

But if I dig real deep, there are *some* similarities.

I loathe him, and he despises me.
He loves to win. I hate to lose.
He's a playboy... and I'm a playgirl.

Which is why it shouldn't surprise me that we're dynamite between the sheets.

Not that it matters. Life is too short to commit to one guy. Especially when that guy is Mr. Billionaire Penn Kingcaid.

A note from Tracie

Dear Reader,

Oh my. What a fun ride this book was. Sometimes characters need to be coaxed gently from hiding and encouraged to reveal their story to you. Others are ready to shout from the rooftops before you've even sat in your chair.

Gia was most definitely the latter. When I first plotted out the Kingcaid series, I intended for Johannes's story to come straight after Asher & Kiana, but Gia wasn't having any of that. She muscled her way to the front and demanded I shut up and listen.

From chapter 1, I connected with her on a deep, soulful level. Her sass, her confidence, her gives no fucks attitude impressed me from the get-go, but even more impressive was that beneath it all is a woman who cares about the things that matter. I love her deeply, and she will stay with me for the rest of my life.

And as for Penn... God, some of the banter he shares with Gia had me gasping one second and laughing out loud the next. The chemistry between them sizzles from their very first meeting and just keeps getting hotter and hotter.

As with the book prior to this one, those who loved the ROGUES series will be delighted to find another surprise contained within these pages - all I'll say for now is Pumpkin Pie. Bear with me. It's worth the wait.

I do hope you enjoy meeting Penn and Gia and sharing in their story. I'd love to hear what you thought once you've finished reading. Why not join my Facebook reader group Tracie's Racy Aces, and take part in the discussion over there.

In the meantime, turn the page and dive in to the second installment of the Kingcaid Billionaires. I am so very excited to share it with you.

Happy reading.

Love,
Tracie

Chapter 1

Gia

Note to self: Watch where you're going.

I HAD A PLETHORA OF TALENTS IN MY TOOL KIT. I WAS A FABULOUS chef, a terrific daughter, and an awesome sister to my baby brother, Roberto, I had an unshakable belief that I was meant to meet and marry Christian Bale—the issue of him already having a wife was a minor blip I hadn't quite figured out yet—and I was an absolute fireball between the sheets, according to my many lovers.

One skill I hadn't yet mastered? Punctuality.

I hurled the alarm clock across my bedroom and threw myself out of bed. Jackhammers from downing too many tequila shots at the club last night battered my skull as I dashed from the bedroom to the bathroom, leaving destruction worthy of a tornado in my wake.

I couldn't be late for work again this month.

Three strikes and Freddo, the head chef at the restaurant where I worked, would have my ass in a sling, or worse.

"Shouldn't have gone out last night, you idiot," I muttered while simultaneously drying my hair and grappling with the button fastening on my pants.

When would I learn?

Answer: Never. Probably.

Going out drinking the night before an early shift was a terrible idea, yet when my friend Ben had called and dangled the promise of meeting his new boyfriend *and* being on the guest list for Paradise Lounge, a trendy new club in the Village, I couldn't say no.

Well, I mean I *could* have.

It wasn't as if the word "no" had become impossible to say.

I just liked to have fun; that was all. Life was for living, not for holing up in my too-small apartment and burrowing under the covers before nine every night.

My little brother taught me the importance of making the most of each second. Every. Single. Day. Through no fault of his own, he'd had to overcome herculean challenges, yet he'd faced each one with the kind of courage that inspired those around him.

God knew, he inspired the hell out of me.

I sent Lorenzo, my work buddy, a text, asking—no, begging—him to cover for me. He lied like a champ. He'd come up with a plausible excuse, saving my neck for the gazillionth time.

Stuffing a banana into my backpack, I slammed my apartment door and sprinted down the five flights of stairs to the street.

The train was crammed with commuters heading over to Manhattan from where I lived in Brooklyn. This was one of the many reasons I preferred the late shift. The lunch and early dinner shift meant I had to wrestle with commuters on their way into work, *and* on the way home.

Double bullshit in the same day.

I tucked myself into a corner and wolfed down the banana, cursing that I hadn't grabbed a drink from the fridge, too. Thirty minutes later, I emerged onto the street, the air thick and humid despite the early hour.

Only the tenth of June, and already I'd had enough of summer. Fall was my favorite time of the year, when the leaves turned orange and gold, the tourists all fucked off back to where they'd come from, and the bitter winter was still far enough away to convince myself that, this year, it wouldn't come at all.

The line of customers waiting to be served at my favorite deli wasn't too long, and deciding that Freddo would be pissed whether I was fifteen or twenty minutes late, I joined the back of the line.

I ordered an OJ, the hangover cure of champions—for me, anyway—and a chicken salad on rye for lunch. I sometimes ate at the restaurant, but my hips could only cope with so much pasta before they ballooned to an unfortunate size requiring an intervention of painful proportions. Diets made me grumpy, which was the main reason that as soon as I hit five pounds over my self-imposed target on the scale, I dialed back on my Italian genes that demanded I eat everything in sight.

For a few days at least.

Peeling the plastic lid off the OJ cup, I swigged half before I even hit the street. I checked my watch. Fifteen minutes late.

Balls. Better run.

I broke into a jog, weaving in and out of commuters and tourists alike. Sweat dripped between my breasts, and damp hair clung to my forehead. I wasn't built for running. Too curvy, and my tits were way too big, the kind that risked a black eye even when hemmed in by two heavy-duty sports bras.

My phone buzzed with a text. Bet that was Lorenzo urging me to hurry, or giving me the shitty news that Freddo was already at the restaurant and my efforts to avoid getting fired were moot.

I dove into my purse. Yup. It was from Lorenzo. I opened it to reply and—

"Oof."

I slammed into a solid wall of rock. The remains of my OJ exploded out of the cup and drowned the unfortunate man in a crisp, once white shirt, a well-pressed navy suit, and a glower worthy of a fighter at a UFC pre-match face-off.

"Shit. Christ, I'm sorry."

I haplessly wafted my hand at him like that might dry and clean his shirt.

"You should be sorry."

He shoved at my flailing hands as if I were a rather annoying wasp he didn't have the patience to deal with.

"Why didn't you look where the hell you were going?"

"Orange not your color?" I flashed a grin, hoping to dial down his exasperation. "I mean, orange and blue are a thing, you know. Maybe you could start a new trend."

"Are you for real right now?" His scowl deepened. "Have you seen this?"

He pointed to himself as if I needed a signpost to notice the huge orange splotch already beginning to dry in the heat of the morning sun.

I narrowed my eyes. "I said I was sorry."

"If you weren't so busy checking the number of likes on your latest Instagram post, you wouldn't have bumped into me, and therefore, you wouldn't need to apologize. And I wouldn't have to arrive at an important meeting looking like this."

Instagram?

Okay, I'd given him the benefit of being pissy with me until now. The accident had been completely my fault, but come on, it was just a shirt. Easily cleaned. No need for him to carry on as if I'd maimed a puppy or something.

Not that I'd ever maim a puppy. God, the thought alone made me feel sick.

Focus, Gia.

Somehow, I channeled my amicable American dad rather than my feisty Italian mother and kept my voice calm.

Go me.

"I'll pay for the dry cleaning."

"You think this... this... orange mess will come out of this shirt? Don't be ridiculous."

I ground my molars. Okay, enough already. Sorry, Dad, but time for my Milanese roots to come out to play.

"Oh, bite me, asshole. It's a fucking shirt, and not a very interesting one. I apologized. You chose to be a douche about it rather than accept my apology. Now, if you'll excuse me, I have far more important shit to do with my day than stand here listening to you."

I stomped off to work, more than ready to take on Freddo after dealing with Mr. Jerkface. I ducked into the restaurant through the staff entrance and stuffed my bag into my locker, my blood pressure still hovering around "boiling point."

Some people. Honestly.

Would it really have killed him to brush it off and agree to send me the cleaning bill, or the cost of a new shirt?

The door opened behind me, and I whipped around. "Fuck, Lorenzo, you scared me. Is Freddo in yet?"

"You got away with it." Lorenzo plucked my chef's hat and whites off the coat peg and thrust them at me, a tendril of dark hair spilling out of his own hat. "Get changed and get in the kitchen before he figures out you were late. Again."

He grinned, unperturbed when I stuck out my tongue at him.

I fastened the buttons on my whites, muscled my thick, long hair into a net and put my hat on, and headed into the kitchen. Lorenzo had laid out my station with the vegetables that needed prepping for the lunch service. I rose up on tiptoes and kissed his cheek.

"You, my friend, are an angel."

"You'd do the same for me. Us workers should stick together." He nudged me with his elbow. "Right?"

"You're not wrong."

I started chopping the stack of red and yellow peppers while I told Lorenzo about the altercation with The Suit this morning. Like I knew he would, he laughed.

"Poor man. Doused in orange juice and tongue-lashed by a feisty Italian, and all before nine in the morning."

"Poor man, my ass. Shame I'd drunk half the OJ. He deserved a full drenching."

"I'd love to be a fly on the wall in his office when he tells his side of the story."

"Pah. Bet there's a description of 'stupid' in there somewhere, and a 'bitch' or two. He looked like the type to talk about women in clichés."

Lorenzo laughed again, his brown eyes twinkling. "Wanna tell me why you were late and I had to cover your ass for the third time this month?"

"My alarm didn't go off." I grimaced. "Or rather, it might have, but I didn't hear it." I peeked up at him through my lashes. "I kinda went out last night."

"Gia!" Lorenzo shook his head. "After last time, you said you weren't going to party the night before an early shift anymore."

"I know." I groaned. "But Ben called and dangled a sweet little honey-glazed carrot that I couldn't resist."

"What kind of a carrot?"

"One you'd love to take a bite out of." I waggled my eyebrows. "He took me to that new gay club in the Village."

"Paradise Lounge?"

When I nodded, Lorenzo's jaw dropped.

"You lucky bitch."

"I know. God, it was amazing. Your eyes would've bugged out the whole time. *And* he introduced me to his new boyfriend." I wafted my hand in front of my face. "Damn, he was fiiiine. What I wouldn't give to be the meat in that delicious sandwich."

"Wrong equipment, honey."

"I know." I pouted. "Why are all gay men gorgeous?"

Lorenzo ran his tongue along the underside of his top teeth and kicked out a hip. "Because we're God's gift, sweetie."

"Y'know, I think gay men are God's final 'fuck you' to women."

"How so?"

"Well, he gives us periods when we're too young to deal, then menopause when life's just getting good, and in between, he throws these stunning gay men at us with a 'Haha, joke's on you.' Ugh."

"More work, less yapping, Gia." Freddo breezed through the kitchen on his way to the dining room.

"Sure thing, Freddo." I gave him my sweetest smile, then flipped him off as he disappeared out of sight.

"One of these days, he's going to see you do that," Lorenzo said. "And then it's..." He slowly drew his forefinger across his throat.

"Nah, I'm too smart for Freddo. And besides, I'll have my own restaurant by then."

Lorenzo's eyes softened. He knew how much owning my own restaurant meant to me, but he also knew, as I did, it wouldn't be easy, or cheap, or anytime soon.

Which meant I probably shouldn't rile Freddo at every opportunity.

"It's good to have goals, Gia. And if anyone can do it, you're the girl."

"It's written in the stars, my friend." I grinned. "One day, I'll have it all."

Chapter 2

Penn

Orange juice is stickier than cum.

I LEARNED SOMETHING NEW TODAY. ORANGE JUICE IS STICKIER than cum. Not a life lesson I'd woken up this morning thinking I was about to learn, but the whirlwind of a woman who'd rounded a corner and spilled a cup of the damn stuff all over me had put a stop to that idea.

Fortunately, my favorite Tom Ford suit had escaped the worst of it. The same could not be said for the shirt by my favorite designer. And of all the days for this to happen, it had to be when I was about to break the news to my father and the entire board of directors that I'd opened my own restaurant outside of the hallowed "Kingcaid family" brand. Not only that, but it was doing a roaring trade.

Oh, and to add insult to injury, it was only two blocks from a Kingcaid hotel and, once word got around, could steal business away from there.

Asher, my eldest brother and the CEO of Kingcaid Hotels, was fully aware of my new venture. I'd told him when it was only a sliver of an idea, and Asher being Asher, he'd encouraged me to go for it and screw what Dad thought. Okay, he hadn't used those exact words. My father garnered an enormous amount of respect from us both, but Asher had been in my corner all the same.

I hadn't opened the restaurant for the money. Lord knew, between my salary as CEO of Kingcaid Restaurants and the sizable trust fund I'd gained access to last year when I'd turned twenty-five, I had more money than I'd ever manage to spend even if I found the cure to mortality. But however hard I worked, it felt as if I'd simply piggybacked on Dad's and his brothers' hard work. This restaurant was my chance to prove myself outside of Kingcaid.

But the real reason was Theo. My best friend and I had planned to go into the restaurant business together someday.

And then he'd died.

Because of me.

My gut twisted, guilt a constant companion. I rubbed it, then cursed, staring at my palm covered in orange goo. Fuck's sake. Definitely stickier than cum.

As I rode the elevator up to the office, a twinge of shame pinched at my stomach. I shouldn't have been so rude to the woman with the OJ. I'd overreacted, and it had, after all, been an accident. I, more than most, knew how those could so easily happen. If she hadn't been on her phone, maybe our coming together wouldn't have triggered me to cuss her out. She'd given as good as she'd gotten, though. She probably had hot sauce rather than blood running through her veins.

I smiled. Bet when she described what happened to her coworkers or her friends or wherever she'd been headed, "idiot" and "asshole" were sure to be among the many words used to describe me.

The elevator doors opened, and I stepped out into the reception area. Hazel, our receptionist, gave me a shocked head-to-toe eye sweep.

"Oh, hell, Penn."

I flashed her one of my famous grins. "Had an argument with a cup of OJ, and I lost. Obviously. Be a love and call Neiman Marcus and have them put a new shirt on my account and deliver it. Fast. Sixteen-inch collar. And a tie," I added as an afterthought. "Blue."

"On it."

She picked up the phone, giving me a sympathetic smile as she dialed. I entered the boardroom. Aspen, my cousin and CEO of Kingcaid Music, took one look at my orange-splattered shirt and burst out laughing.

"What happened to you?"

"Some woman decided orange was more my color than white." I screwed up my face in disgust. The acidic smell of dried orange juice had started to make me feel nauseous.

"Tell her not to get a job in fashion. The white matched far better with the blue." Aspen tapped her finger to her lips. "Another notch on your bedpost decided she wasn't all that keen on your famous 'one and done,' hey, Penn?"

"She was a stranger, actually."

"Aren't they all?" She ran a hand through her shocking purple hair, her ruby-red lips stretched into a grin. "You don't keep them around long enough to get to know them."

"Oh, what's this?" I reached into the top pocket of my suit jacket and produced a middle finger.

Aspen laughed again. "That the best comeback you've got?"

"No, but you're not special enough for me to pull out the big guns."

This wasn't at all true. I adored Aspen, and she idolized me. Our family was extremely close, but we also fought and bickered with the best of them, none more so than me and Aspen. My parents had three sons, as did my uncle Jameson. Aspen's dad, Jacob, was the only one of my dad's brothers to have a daughter as well as two sons. Suffice to say, the eight of us were enormously protective of Aspen.

Not that she needed our protection. My cousin had a mean right hook.

The boardroom door opened and Asher walked in. My brother was based out on the West Coast, in Seattle, but he'd recently returned from a trip to Grand Cayman to see my grandparents and had decided to stop by on the way home to visit me and check on the Kingcaid Manhattan hotel, the business he headed up. I wasn't complaining. I didn't get to see nearly as much of Ash as I'd like, and now that he was about to get hitched, I'd see even less of my big brother. Not that I blamed him. His fiancée, Kiana, was an absolute gem of a woman. Far too good for Asher, a point of view he'd readily agree with.

"What the fuck happened to you?" Ash pulled out a seat at the head of the table. "Have a fight with a pumpkin? It's not Halloween for a few months yet."

Aspen snickered. Ash joined in. I glared.

"Funny. An accident with a cup of orange juice. That's all."

"From a so-called 'stranger.'" Aspen air-quoted.

"Ah, that's what he's calling them these days." Ash nodded sagely. "Soon, in the not-too-distant future, little brother, you're going to fall hard for someone you don't even see coming. And I, for one, can't wait for that day to come."

I rolled my tongue around the inside of my cheek and slowly shook my head. "Not gonna happen."

Ash's expression was loaded with "Yeah, sures" as he booted up the videoconferencing system. I checked my watch, musing on how long it'd take Neiman Marcus to deliver the damned shirt.

The moment the thought popped into my mind, Hazel arrived, panting, and thrust a bag at me. "Hope it fits."

"You're an angel." I shrugged out of my jacket, wrenched off the tie, and unfastened my shirt in three seconds flat. As I tossed the ruined item onto the boardroom table, Aspen covered her eyes.

"I'm blind! I'm blind!"

"Fuck off, Aspen. I'm ripped and beautiful, and you know it. I work hard for this body."

"The problem, my darling Penn, is that *you* know it, and it gives you entirely too much self-confidence."

"Bullshit." I slid my arms into the new shirt and buttoned it up. "There's no such thing as too much self-confidence."

"We'll see about that when you tell uncle Joshua that you've dared to break away from the family business."

My stomach wobbled. Dad was a cool dude. I was ninety percent positive he'd offer his support for my new venture. But there was that ten percent, chipping away at the back of my mind, that said he'd be disappointed I hadn't told him ahead of taking the plunge and opening Theo's. I hoped I could make him understand how much I'd craved a challenge of my own that didn't come with almost guaranteed success because of my family name. I'd only decided to tell him now because the restaurant had enjoyed the kind of early success even I hadn't foreseen, and the last thing I wanted was for Dad to find out through other means.

"Okay, now that you're fully dressed, Penn, shall we begin?"

I nodded, my mouth drying up as Ash signed in to the videoconferencing software. One by one, my family members appeared on screen. When Dad's face appeared, I reached for a glass of water.

Here we go.

As it turned out, I needn't have worried. The ninety percent won. Dad and his brothers were hugely supportive of me striking out on my own, as long as I didn't slack off on my responsibilities as CEO of the Kingcaid restaurant chain. I assured him I had room in my schedule for both and that I had an excellent team supporting me.

There was one awkward moment when Dad asked why I'd called the restaurant Theo's. I managed to side-step the question and school my features, and swallow past the enormous lump in my throat. Then Aspen aimed an off-the-cuff insult at me, and the moment passed.

My family had no idea about Theo, a guy I'd met during my first week at Harvard and who'd become my best friend after approximately ten seconds. No idea that, three years ago, my stupidity had resulted in his death. No idea of the guilt that ate me up inside. And I had zero intentions of ever sharing what had happened that fatal day.

The meeting wrapped, and the tension that'd ridden me hard ever since I'd opened my eyes at seven o'clock that morning evaporated. Aspen dashed off, muttering something about "fucking temperamental rock stars."

Ash clapped me on the shoulder. "Told you he'd be cool."

"Yeah." I broke into a grin. "Smug always was a good look on you." I fastened the button on my jacket. "Well, gotta go. I have two businesses to run."

"What are you doing tonight?"

I arched a brow. "Working."

"Kiana and I are heading back to Seattle tomorrow, but we want to talk to you about the wedding."

"Oh yeah?"

"We've set a date."

"That's fantastic news."

"And..." He paused. "I'd like you to be my best man."

My jaw dropped, pride filling my chest. "I'd... I'd love to, Ash. I'd be honored." I chuckled. "Johannes might be pissed, though, what with him being second brother and all."

"He's fine about it. I spoke to him before you. It only seemed fair."

That, right there, was my eldest brother all over. There wasn't a better person on the planet than Ash, besides my parents. A genuinely good guy who deserved the greatest wedding day ever. And, as best man, I'd take my responsibilities seriously—especially when it came to the bachelor party.

"This is definite cause for celebration, Ash. Dinner, tonight, on me. At Theo's."

"Thought you were fully booked."

"We are. But I can make space for three."

"Four. I'll ask Kiana to invite her maid of honor. It'll be a good opportunity for you guys to meet. I mean, after the bride and groom, you two are the most important people in the wedding."

"Perfect. I'll look forward to it. Full-charm offensive at the ready." I ran my tongue over my bottom lip.

He brandished a finger at me. "Now listen up. Gia is extremely important to Kiana, and therefore, she's important to me. So you, best behavior. And keep your dick in your pants. No hitting on the maid of honor."

I laughed and brought my hands up in a peace offering. "Not sure getting my dick out during dinner is the right kind of ambience I'm trying to set for Theo's."

"Penn." Ash packed his tone with warning. "I mean it."

"Okay, okay. I swear my dick will remain in my pants

and will not, like a divining rod, seek out the maid of honor's pussy."

Ash groaned. "You're a lost fucking cause."

"And yet you still love me." I headed for the door, sending a wave over my head. "Text me a time and I'll arrange a table."

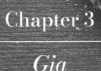

Chapter 3

Gia

The universe hates me.

By the time lunch service ended, I was a sweaty mess, my legs ached from standing all day, and I was altogether feeling the effects of last night. I just had to get through prep for dinner service, and I could go home, soak my poor shredded feet in a scalding bubble bath, and be in my bed by eight.

God, maybe this was what getting old felt like.

Twenty-five was well on the way to being thirty, and wasn't that the age when going out became a major effort and it took three days to recover from a hangover?

"Earth to Gia." Lorenzo dropped pasta ingredients at my station. "Tagliatelle, angel hair, and enough spinach ravioli for thirty-five covers."

"Who made you the boss of the kitchen?" I leaned my tired head on his shoulder. "I don't wanna." I pretended to wail. Lorenzo chuckled.

"Look at it this way. The sooner it's done, the sooner you can go home."

"Ugh. I hate it when you bring out the logic."

"And," he added, "maybe the next time Ben dangles a carrot, you'll decline."

"Depends on the carrot." I arched a brow. "I mean, if he decides to experiment and brings that new boyfriend of his along for the ride, I'm gonna have to eat the carrot."

Lorenzo shook his head. "You are incorrigible. Besides, I have more chance of enjoying a nibble on that carrot than you do."

"There you go again with that damned logic." I made a face at him. "Stupid biology."

I worked solidly for the next ninety minutes and was in the middle of cutting the last batch of ravioli when Freddo, the head chef, appeared at my side like a creepy apparition.

"You have a visitor, front of house. When you finish your prep, you can go and see them." He admonished me with a wag of his finger. "And not before."

"Gee, Freddo, you're all heart. Who's the visitor?"

"Said her name's Kiana."

I squealed, dropped the ravioli cutter, and dashed into the restaurant, ignoring Freddo's "I said when you were finished!" exasperated cry.

"Kee!" I hugged my best friend, covering her in flour. "Why didn't you tell me you were coming?"

I whipped a towel from the waistband of my whites and dusted her down with it.

She giggled, batting my hand out of the way. "I wanted to surprise you."

"Well, you've gone and done that all right. God, it's good to see you. I've almost forgotten what you look like."

"I FaceTimed you a week ago."

"Yeah, well." I pouted. "That's not the same as in the flesh. It's been too long."

"It's been seven weeks. I brought Ash to meet you, remember?"

I peered at her through narrowed eyes. "You have a tan. The sun doesn't shine in Seattle, so how have you got a tan?"

"The sun does shine in Seattle, silly. On occasion. But this... I got from spending a few days in Grand Cayman meeting Ash's grandparents."

I groaned. "God, you're so lucky. Why can't I meet a fabulous billionaire who'll take me away from all this?" I gestured around the restaurant.

Kiana grinned. "Well, his grandmother put us in separate bedrooms, so don't be too jealous."

My mouth formed the perfect "O" shape. "She did not."

"She did. We had to sneak off into the woods to get a bit of 'us' time."

"Look at you, getting all jiggy out in the open. My work here is done."

"Oh, behave."

Kee gave me one of her special looks, all lowered

brows and disapproving head shakes, but behind her despair at my devil-may-care attitude, she loved me. Just as I loved her.

"What time do you finish work?"

I glanced over my shoulder. Freddo was standing by the entrance to the kitchen, arms folded, a dour scowl on his wrinkled face.

"I've got a bit more prep to do, and then it's clean up to get ready for the evening shift to arrive, and I'm all yours." I sniffed my armpits. "After a shower, that is. Phew." I fluttered a hand in front of my face.

Kee leaned in and sniffed me, too. "Good idea. And after you've cleaned up, you're coming to dinner." She canted her head to the side. "Call it a celebration for being my maid of honor."

My jaw dropped. I covered my nose and mouth with my hands, spluttering out a muffled "OMG, you're kidding."

"No, I'm not kidding. Who else would I have other than you? But prepare yourself. His grandmother has this whole thing planned in Grand Cayman with a guest list of five hundred people, including some senator or other and the governor and Christ only knows who else." She gave a full-on body shudder. "I'm crapping myself just thinking about walking down the aisle in front of a crowd that big, catching a heel in the hem of my dress, and face-planting."

"Wait." I clasped her upper arms. "Are you telling me the wedding is in *Grand Cayman*?"

"Oh." Kee nodded. "Yeah. Ash's grandmother doesn't really like to travel."

She shrugged. I squealed. Freddo barked an order for me to get my ass back into the kitchen, pronto.

"I'd better go finish up before he fires me." I hugged Kee hard. "But I want to hear everything tonight."

"So you'll come to dinner?"

"Duh."

She grinned. "Great. We're meeting at seven at a place called Theo's. It's in—"

"SoHo. I know. Wow! That's only the hippest new restaurant on the block. The wait list for a table is, like, a gazillion years or something. Guess this is your life now that you're marrying a billionaire." I made a motion of waves parting, like Moses. "The world just falls at your feet. At this rate, you'll forget you know me. Just make it after the wedding, yeah? I need a vacay."

Kee shook her head. "Overdramatic much, Gia?"

"You know me."

"And, for your information, getting a table had nothing to do with money and everything to do with family connections. Ash's brother Penn owns the restaurant."

"Ooh, another rich, gorgeous dude." I tapped my finger against my lower lip. "Doesn't happen to look like Christian Bale, does he?"

My hero, my absolute idol, and the man I measured every other guy to. Sadly, none have met the bar, or even come close. It was the reason multiple one-nighters littered my past.

What can I say? I have high standards.

Okay, not strictly true when it comes to my colorful sexual history, but settling down with a guy who *wasn't*

Christian Bale? He'd have to be one special dude, and let's face it, those are rarer than a compliment from Freddo. Besides, life was far too short to settle down. My motto was to get my kicks while I was still young enough to wrap my legs around a guy's neck without dislocating a hip.

"Well, he's at least twenty years younger, so, not really."

"Hey. Don't you disparage my Bale. There's a lot to be said for experience."

Kee rolled her eyes. "I swear, until you drop this crazy-ass fantasy, you'll never find The One."

"Relationships are overrated."

"Gia, you want this job, you have ten seconds to get your butt into this kitchen."

I glanced over my shoulder at Freddo and made a dismissive hand gesture. "Ugh, sorry, Kee. I'd better go before his face turns that yucky purple color. No way I'm giving him mouth-to-mouth if he drops to the floor."

Kee laughed. "God, I love you." She hugged me and kissed my cheek. "Seven. Don't be late."

I grinned. "As if I would."

I tossed all thoughts of bubble baths and early nights out the window at the prospect of spending some quality time with my bestie ahead of her fiancé stealing her away.

Sore feet be damned. I was only twenty-five, and life was for living. I'd have plenty of time for sleep—and resting my feet—when I was dead.

Plus, talk about bragging rights with Lorenzo. Paradise Lounge last night, and tonight, Theo's. Two of the hottest tickets in town was the kind of news I could dine out on for weeks.

I finished up my prep, dropped in my plans for the evening, laughed at the green tinge to Lorenzo's cheeks—so not his color—and dashed home to spruce up.

I checked the dress code for the restaurant, grinding my molars at "smart casual."

I *hated* that description.

Freddo used it at our restaurant, and I often challenged him on it. What did it actually mean? Formal suit and tie for the guys, or just a button-down? Cocktail dress for the women, or would a smart blouse and dress pants pass? Google didn't help much either. Questions such as "Are jeans okay for smart casual?" with an answer of "Depends" were as much use as a man without a delicious dick.

In the end, I chose a cream sleeveless dress that finished at the knee and a pair of kitten heels. I pulled my dark hair into a high ponytail, added big-ass gold hoop earrings, and put on a set of bracelets that jangled with each flick of my wrist.

My phone buzzed, a message from Uber letting me know my driver was waiting outside. A bit extravagant, but arriving at a restaurant like Theo's after riding the subway didn't feel right.

Despite my best efforts, it was ten minutes after seven by the time I made it to the restaurant. After checking that I didn't have toilet paper stuck to my shoe, or my dress was caught in my panties, I entered the restaurant.

The inside took my breath away.

Serious cash had been dropped on decking the place out. Oak flooring laid in a chevron pattern led to a sleek, contemporary reception desk behind which a stylish hostess waited to welcome the customers. Stairs curved to the left, leading to the upper floor, and booths in a cream leather lined the main part of the restaurant, with soft individual lighting overhead.

Smart casual, my ass.

Thank Christ I erred on the dressier side.

Squaring my shoulders, I approached the desk. "Hi, I'm Gianna Greene. I'm meeting Kiana Doherty and Asher Kingcaid."

"Miss Greene, of course, welcome to Theo's. We've been expecting you. Please follow me."

I cast my eyes around the restaurant as I clipped after the hostess. The place was packed to the rafters, and I could be wrong, but I thought I saw Nate Brook, a massive Hollywood star who had roots in New York. Yep. Definitely him. Boy, his companion was stunning, with hair the color of burnt copper, athletic curves, pert boobs, and zero tummy paunch.

Still, I liked my ample curves. Skinny was overrated.

I spotted Kee before she saw me, her attention fixed on Asher. And, honestly, I couldn't blame her. The man was damned fine. He kind of took your breath away. How the hell Kee had resisted him for so long, especially after having an initial taste of the goods, befuddled me.

I wouldn't have lasted a hot minute.

Then again, I wasn't known for my ability to refrain

from the joys of sex. And I gave zero fucks what anyone thought about that.

"Gia!" She rose to greet me, and we hugged even though I'd hugged the life out of her only a few hours ago. "You're late." She wagged her finger.

"Ten minutes is good for me."

"True. You'll be late to your own funeral."

Asher stood to greet me. Kee touched his arm, and the adoration in her eyes warmed my chest. Their kind of love was special, a one-off, and while some women might have felt their jealousy bone being prodded, I only had happiness in my heart.

"Hey, Ash. Good to see you again. Sorry I'm late, but I'm sure Kee has already told you that telling the time is a little outside my skill set."

Asher chuckled, one of those low, rumbling laughs that vibrated against a girl's clit and made her want to cross her legs to get a bit of relief. I slid along the bench opposite Kee and Asher and set my purse on the table.

"Good to see you again, too, Gia."

"Is your brother still coming? I'm dying to meet him and give him kudos for this place. It's amazing."

Asher groaned. "Please don't tell him that. His ego is the size of a planet as it is."

"He got called into the kitchen just a few minutes ago. He'll be back soon. I think you two will get along." Something caught her eye over my shoulder, and she nodded. "In fact, here he is now."

I turned and—

You have got to be fucking kidding me.

My teeth gnashed together.

Well played, Lucifer. Well played.

"Penn, this is my best friend, Gianna Greene."

I scowled at the jerk from this morning. "'Gia' to my friends. Shame you won't make the cut."

"Fine by me," Penn Kingcaid drawled. "I'm choosy about my friends. I expect them to hit a certain bar." He raked me with a bored gaze. "You're some way off."

"Penn!" Asher scolded. "What the fuck?"

Kee's head volleyed between me and the man who had the balls to slide along the bench right next to me, blocking my exit.

"Wait. Do you two know each other?"

"'Know' implies interest, Kiana, of which I have none. Our one and only interaction was this morning when your 'friend' was too busy tapping on her phone to look where she was going and spilled a cup of orange juice all over a *very* expensive shirt ahead of a *very* important meeting."

He picked up a toothpick and stabbed it in an olive, slipping it between his lips.

Wonder what the rap sheet would include if I snatched that toothpick and stabbed him in the eye with it.

Asher grinned. "Ah, so you're the cause of 'Juice-gate.'"

"It was an accident." I glared at Penn. "One I can see repeated with this glass of red wine." I reached across the table and picked up Asher's drink. "Oh, oh, oh." I weaved the glass of wine over Penn's lap. "Hope I don't slip."

"Gia." Kee implored me with her eyes. Penn stabbed another olive.

"Remember the divining-rod convo after the meeting today, brother? Well, trust me, there isn't a problem on that score."

"Divining rod? Is that some kind of locker-room talk?"

"Not at all." Asher glowered at his brother. "Penn, apologize to Gia."

"What for? I wasn't the clumsy ass who was more interested in her social media than looking where she was going."

"No, but you were the rude ass who refused to accept a genuine apology," I hit back.

"Penn!" Asher slammed his fist on the table, drawing the attention of the diners at several nearby tables. "Apologize to Gia right this second, or you won't be coming to the fucking wedding."

Penn rolled his tongue around his cheek, heaved a sigh, and stabbed the toothpick into another olive. "Fine. I apologize. I accept that it was an accident." He made the entire apology without looking at me once. "Happy now?"

I huffed. "God, you apologize like a five-year-old brat who needs a good spanking."

Finally, he gave me his precious attention.

"I do love a good spanking, darling, as many of my dalliances would be only too happy to confirm. Unfortunately, I also have to like the woman doling it out, so your hand and my ass aren't likely to become acquainted anytime soon."

Might have known he was a playboy. And he liked to win, too; that much was obvious. Well, so did I. And I wasn't one for backing down easily either.

I smiled with enough sweetness to turn him diabetic. "Maybe my hand and your face will become acquainted instead."

"For God's sake." Kee put her head in her hands,

coming up for air after a few seconds. "Can we please start over? At the risk of sounding selfish, this is not about you two. This is our wedding."

She clutched Asher's hand. "We want you to be a part of our special day, an important part, but if you're going to be at each other's throats the entire time, then I don't see how this will work. So, here's what's going to happen. You two will put your differences aside until Ash and I have said 'I do.' After that, I don't care if you end up cage-fighting or ripping each other's hair out, or fucking like rabbits. What I do care about is my wedding going off without a hitch. Got it?"

My shoulders bowed. The last thing I wanted to ever do was to upset Kee, and if that meant biting my tongue and putting up with the asshole sitting to my right until Kee became Mrs. Asher Kingcaid, then I would. Well, I'd bite said tongue when Kee and Asher weren't in earshot. Outside of that, I made no promises.

"I'm sorry, Kee. Truly." I turned in Penn's direction. "I can forget this morning if you can."

He rubbed a hand over his chin, his eyes cutting over to Asher and then Kiana, and finally to me. "I'm sorry for yelling over the OJ. There's no excuse for it. My mother would have my ass in a sling if she'd heard how I spoke to you."

"True story," Asher drawled.

"I held my own."

His lips twitched. "I'll say."

I stuck out my hand. "Truce."

Penn's palm was warm, his skin soft as he accepted my

peace offering, but his eyes held a challenge that told me our sparring was far from over.

"Great." Kee, oblivious to the undertone, picked up her menu as if the entire altercation hadn't happened. "Right, shall we order?"

Chapter 4

Penn

**And the winner for the
wittiest comeback goes to...**

My future sister-in-law's best friend was a conundrum I didn't have an answer to. Now that we'd stopped arguing long enough for me to properly take her in, I had to begrudgingly admit that she was a bit of a fox. Pretty, curvy, vivacious, sharp-witted, all the things I found attractive in a woman.

Unfortunately, those positive qualities were coupled with irritating, tardy—I hated it when people were late—and outspoken, traits I didn't enjoy all that much.

Hence, a conundrum.

She closed her menu with a snap, then turned to me.

"As this is your restaurant, what would you recommend?"

Her sweet smile didn't fool me. I'd bet my first year's profits on this venture that the second Ash and Kiana weren't listening, she'd be back to sniping at me. That I couldn't wait said a lot about me. Smart, sassy women were like catnip; I found it difficult to resist biting back at every opportunity and relishing each encounter.

"That depends." I ran a palm over my jaw. "Are you allergic to anything?"

"Why?" Her full lips turned up on one side. "Are you hoping to use that against me?"

I let out a low chuckle. "Damn. You got me."

"Too bad for you, I'm only allergic to a lack of food." She ran her hands over her shapely hips. "Didn't get these by eating salad."

My eyes went there, and my dick stirred in my pants. Fuck, no.

Sorry, buddy, but you ain't getting near this particular pussy.

And not because Asher had warned me off. He and I both knew that if I wanted a woman, very little stopped me from pursuing her. But this particular woman... no, thanks. She might be hot, but the downsides far outweighed the upsides.

I tore my gaze away before she saw me ogling her assets.

Too late.

Met with flattened lips and a look that said "Check me out again and I'm having the chef cook *your* meat and two veg," I cleared my throat and opened my menu even though I knew every item on here by heart.

"Um... the lobster ravioli is a particular favorite of mine. And you can't go wrong with the filet mignon with peppercorn sauce."

"Sounds great. I'll have both."

I blinked several times in succession. "Each one is an entrée."

"I'm aware, but thanks for pointing that out. I didn't get time to eat lunch today. I've only eaten a banana, and that was on the way into work, so I'm hungry enough to chow down on this table if I don't eat soon."

"A banana *and* an orange juice," I added, arching an eyebrow. "Don't forget that."

"Half an orange juice," she deadpanned. "You soaked up the other half."

"Ah." Kiana cut in before I could offer a comeback to her friend. "You won't know about Gia's famous appetite. She could out-eat any one of these diners, and then some."

"You know that show *Man v. Food?*" Gia asked. When I nodded, she added, "Well, they're remaking it. *Woman v. Food.* And I'm the star of the show."

My dick wasn't stirring anymore. It was standing at attention. A curvy woman who also liked to eat was my fucking dream date.

Kill me now.

"I'll join you." I gestured to a server who rushed over, tablet poised and ready. "Two lobster ravioli, two filet mignons served rare with the rosemary potatoes and purple broccoli." I glanced over at Asher. "And whatever they want."

I picked up the bottle of wine and poured Gia a glass.

The heat of her stare burned my face, and as I set the bottle on the table, I gave her my attention. "What?"

"Is everything a competition to you?"

She kept her voice low to avoid drawing attention to the snippy tone to her voice. She needn't have worried. Kiana and Asher were too busy ordering their food to listen to us.

I leaned in, my mouth inches from her ear. "You'd better believe it, sweetcheeks. A word of warning. I never lose."

"First time for everything." She picked up her napkin and laid it in her lap, then went for the wine, downing a good third of the glass.

"True." I nodded. "But it'll take a better competitor than you to best me."

"How foolish of you to underestimate your opponent."

"Or maybe it's because I have more experience."

She stared right into my eyes, her cornflower-blue irises locking me in place. Damn, the woman had mesmerizing eyes, like forget-me-nots, only more luminous.

Shame she'd be all too forgettable.

"No, I'll stick with foolish."

Or maybe not.

I chuckled, readying myself for another killer retort, one that died on my lips when my phone rang and I glanced at the caller ID. I snatched up the handset.

"Excuse me, I need to take this." I answered as soon as I was far enough away from the table to ensure my conversation wasn't overheard. "Sandrine. All okay?"

Sandrine was Theo's widow, and the one woman I'd

drop everything for. She was also someone my family would *never* know about, would *never* meet. The idea of them knowing what I had done made me sick to my stomach.

I'd never forget that day, how Theo lay dying in my arms while we waited for an ambulance that arrived too late to save him. I promised him I'd spend the rest of my life making sure that Sandrine, and their baby girl, Corabelle, wanted for nothing.

And I'd kept that promise to the best of my ability.

Watching how the grief at losing him had almost killed Sandrine acted as a stark reminder of why I chose the life I did. Love hurt. Like a motherfucker. I had no intention of signing up for that.

"Yes, everything's fine. I was only ringing to remind you about tomorrow."

I cursed. Sandrine laughed.

"Exactly. I knew you'd forget."

Sandrine was moving into a new place, and I'd promised to drive up to Boston and help her get settled in.

"That came around quick."

"You're telling me. I still have tons of stuff to pack, and the movers are coming at nine in the morning. Late night ahead."

I checked my watch. Seven thirty. "I can be there by eleven tonight." Sandrine lived three and a half hours away from me. "Help you pack." I'd square it with Ash. Somehow.

"Oh, Penn, it's wonderful of you to offer, but no. I'm exaggerating. I'll have it done, no problem. Your offer to come help me sort stuff out at the other end is more than generous. I know how busy you are."

"I'm never too busy for you."

"Cora and I are lucky to have you."

My chest ached, and I rubbed it, taking a deep breath to dampen the guilt that never eased.

It. Never. Fucking. Eased.

"If it weren't for me—"

"No. Stop. Don't you dare finish that sentence." Her heavy, resigned sigh deafened me. "We love you. Theo loved you. It was an accident, Penn. You have got to stop beating yourself up."

An *avoidable* accident. If I hadn't answered my damned phone, then—

"How's the restaurant going?"

Her diversionary tactic pulled my mind away from horrors too raw to contemplate for long.

"Great guns. We're fully booked up for the next several months."

I'd tried to make Sandrine an equal partner in the business, but, proud woman that she was, she'd fought me all the way. In the end, I'd gifted fifty percent of the profits to Corabelle, which would be held in trust until she turned twenty-one. Sandrine had reluctantly conceded, but only because it gave her daughter the chance for a bright future.

And don't even get me started on the time I offered to buy her a house...

"I'm proud of you. I knew it'd be a roaring success from the get-go."

"He'd have loved it." I pinched the bridge of my nose to

ward off emotions I struggled to contain once I let them get a hold of me. "Front of house, in his element, charming the women and the men alike."

Sandrine chuckled. "Don't I know it. The man had charm for days."

"I still miss him." My voice cracked. "Every fucking day." I glanced over my shoulder and caught Ash's eye. I held up a finger to let him know I wouldn't be long. "I have to go. It's rammed in here tonight."

"Drive carefully. I'll see you at the new place around midday."

"Yeah. See you then." I went to hang up.

"Penn?"

I returned the phone to my ear. "Yeah?"

"Cora says to blow you a kiss, so here." The sound of her blowing a kiss down the phone brought an enormous smile to my face. "See you tomorrow."

She cut the connection before I had a chance to reply. I gave my chest a final rub, then wandered back to the table.

"What was all that about?" Asher tilted his head to the side, one eyebrow lifted in query.

"Nothing. Just work stuff."

"Kingcaid work stuff?"

"No." Picking up the empty wine bottle, I brandished it in the air. "Can't have an empty bottle. Be right back."

I ducked behind the bar and grabbed another bottle of red, and by the time I returned, I'd gathered myself. Or so I thought.

"Are you okay?" Gia asked as I slid along the bench and retook the seat beside her.

"Why wouldn't I be?" My voice sounded far too bright

and not at all like me. A heavy dose of sarcasm was called for, before her curiosity bone got tweaked. "And if I weren't, I'd hardly talk to you about it."

Her lips thinned. "Good, because I can't be bothered with listening to you whining."

"Good God," Kiana exclaimed. "If you two don't give it a rest, I'm going to crack both your heads together." She gave an exasperated huff. "Was I talking into the ether before?"

"Sorry, Kee." Gia lifted her hands in the air. "We're just teasing each other. Right, Penn?"

I shrugged. "Sure." Gia kicked me under the table, and I hissed. "Ow, that hurt." I bent down to rub my ankle.

"I'm thinking Johannes might be the lesser of two evils for the position of best man," Ash said. "A sentence I never thought I'd say."

"I'm inclined to agree," Kiana said. "And I don't *have* to walk down the aisle with a maid of honor, right?"

Gia gasped as Ash picked up Kiana's hand and kissed the tips of her fingers. "This is your day. Whatever you want is good by me."

"Argh, Kee."

Gia pouted, and it did funny things to my insides. Lusty things. My dick hardened.

"You wouldn't do that to me. I'm allowed one slip-up, right? I mean, come on, Penn's just got the kind of face you want to punch."

"Try it and see how far you get," I drawled.

Kiana threw her hands in the air. "I give up. You know what?" She pointed both forefingers at me and Gia, one after the other. "You two, have at it. Take chunks out of each other all day long, for all I care. But if either one of you ruins my wedding, I will drown the pair of you in the Caribbean Sea."

"We won't." Gia elbowed me in the ribs, and it wasn't playful, either. "Right, Penn?" she repeated.

This time I was more ebullient with my response. "Absolutely. I promise that nothing will ruin your day."

"Good." Kiana nodded. "Because, as best man and maid of honor, your first duty is to arrange a combined bachelor and bachelorette party."

"Wait, what?"

My jaw unhinged. "A joint party?" I shook my head. "No. At that, I draw the line."

"Finally," Gia said. "Something we can agree on."

"Well, at least we found something," Ash said.

"That's what we want and what we've decided on," Kiana insisted.

"But... but..." I huffed through my nose. "That'll ruin my plans."

"Let me guess." Gia tapped a finger against her bottom lip. "Stripper, right?" She rolled her eyes. "So predictable."

"Every bachelor party needs a stripper. You wanna apply for the job, sweetcheeks?"

"You couldn't afford me."

"Let's not be too hasty." I swept my gaze over her. "At least you're willing to negotiate."

"I never said—" She crossed her arms. "Whatever. You're an asshole."

"'Whatever' is a cop-out for when an opponent has run out of intelligent retorts."

"Must be a word you use a lot, then."

I smiled, blew on my fingertips, and rubbed them on the lapel of my jacket. "I think that round goes to me."

"I'm thinking, Ash," Kiana said, eyes on my brother. "We can probably cancel our planned entertainment for the wedding guests and just put these two on a stage."

"It's certainly cheaper," Ash replied with a smug nod as the server brought our food over. "They are quite the double act."

"But first, they have a party to organize," Kiana said, a twinkle in her eye. "Together. I can't wait to see what they come up with."

"How long have we got?" Gia asked.

"Oh, didn't we say? The wedding is on July fifteenth."

"That's only five weeks away," I said. "Not a lot of time."

"You're telling me." Kiana groaned. "Just be thankful you don't have to organize the wedding."

"Bet Gran has something to do with that." I looked at Asher, who confirmed my suspicions with a nod.

"Where do you want to have the party?" Gia asked.

"We've decided to have it in Grand Cayman so the guests don't have to travel twice."

"Makes sense." I opened the calendar on my phone. "I'm free Monday at four for an hour if you want to get started on preparations."

Gia waited for me to give her my attention before answering. The moment I did, she opened the calendar on her phone.

"Three is better for me."

I ground my molars. She was playing with me. Fine, I'd

let her have a minor win, but the major ones belonged to me.

"I guess I can move some things around. Meet here, at three."

She fired off another of her saccharine smiles. "I can't wait."

Chapter 5

Gia

**Punctuality is not my forte,
but at least I can cook.**

—

BREATHLESS, AND WITH SWEAT RUNNING BETWEEN MY BOOBS, I arrived at Theo's at ten minutes after three. The restaurant didn't open until five, and the door was locked. I swiped a hand across my forehead. Goddamn New York heat. Bring on fall.

I knocked and waited. When no one came to let me in, I knocked again, louder this time. Nothing. Surely the kitchen staff were in by now, prepping for evening service. When a third knock still brought no one to the door, I huffed and dug my phone out of my purse, bringing up the number Penn had reluctantly given me at dinner on Friday night.

It rang out, then went to voicemail. I hung up and

tried again, but when the same thing happened, I listened to the short "This is Penn. Leave a message," then did just that.

"Penn, it's Gia. I'm here, and you're not, so thanks a bunch for wasting my time."

I hung up and stomped off toward the subway, my blood fizzing at the rudeness of the no-show jerk. If he couldn't make it for some reason, the least he could have done was call me and let me know. As I passed the alleyway to the rear of the restaurant where the dumpsters were kept, Penn stepped out in front of me dressed in fitted jeans and a pale blue button-down shirt with the sleeves rolled up to his elbows, revealing the kind of forearms that were my kryptonite.

For a nanosecond, my lungs stopped working. And then my eyes drifted up over his broad shoulders and to his face, painted in annoyance, and the moment passed.

"Oh, there you are," I huffed. "I've been knocking at the front for ages."

"Define 'ages.'" He air-quoted.

"What?" I frowned. "What's that supposed to mean?"

"Well, we agreed to meet at three o'clock, correct? And I make it"—he checked his watch—"three twelve. So are you telling me you've tried to get someone to answer the door for twelve minutes?"

I gave him a flat stare. "No."

"No."

"Fine. I was late. Ten minutes isn't a big deal."

"To you, evidently not." He ran a hand through his thick, dark hair. "Let me be clear. I don't appreciate tardiness. I am running two successful businesses, which means my time is limited. So please, Gia, show me a sliver of courtesy by turning up at the agreed time in the future."

He spun on his heel and disappeared into the building while I stared after him, jaw flapping, hands clenching and unclenching by my sides, and a gazillion insults jostling for first position on the tip of my tongue. What a fucking *asshole*. It was ten minutes, not ten hours. Hardly the crime of the century.

I came so damned close to continuing my trek back to the subway and letting the arrogant bastard organize the party on his own. But then I thought of Kee and how someone had to step up and protect her interests. And that someone was me.

I swallowed my pride and marched inside.

As I passed by the kitchen, I couldn't resist taking a peek inside. It was a chef's idea of heaven, all shiny and high-tech and with plenty of workspace. Freddo had to have his arm twisted to even buy gear we needed, let alone stock the kitchen with nice-to-haves. Staff bustled around, prepping for opening time, working in synchronicity as if choreographed and ignoring the rubbernecker standing in the entranceway with her mouth hanging open, a trail of jealous drool dripping down her chin.

I dragged myself away and moved through to the dining area. Penn was sitting at the bar flipping through sheets of paper, a frown drawing his dark brows inward. I pulled out the chair next to his and hoisted myself into it, plopping my purse onto the polished surface, so glossy that I could see my face in it. He didn't even acknowledge me, his full attention taken up with whatever he was looking at.

"Hello?" I poured sarcasm into that single word and rapped my knuckles on the bar. "Anyone home?"

He gathered the papers together in a pile, tapped them like an old-fashioned newsreader at the end of the nightly bulletin, and then set them down.

"Tell me, Penn, are you always so anal about everything? Because I gotta tell you, that pole up your ass will give you piles if you don't pull it out soon."

He reached over the bar and dipped a glass into a tub of ice. Plucking out a cube, he slipped it between his lips, the crunch as he bit down on it going right through me. I shuddered.

"Your dentist must love you. Bet he's gonna retire on just what he makes from looking after your teeth."

Still, Penn didn't engage me in a single word of conversation. Jesus. On Friday night, I hadn't been able to shut the guy up. Now, it was as if he'd become mute in the last two days.

"Fine." I grabbed a piece of ice and ran it over my lips. Christ, what a relief. For a second, I thought of dropping it between my boobs but refrained. I had some decorum. On occasion.

"I'm sorry I was late. I'll try not to do it again."

"Ah, but will you succeed?"

I dropped the ice back into the glass and clasped both hands together. "He speaks. Praise the Lord."

A sigh exploded out of him, so deep that it must have started in his expensive Italian leather shoes.

"Gia, I have had a challenging weekend. I'm tired. I'm

busy. I have a ton of work to do, and waiting around for you to grace me with your presence isn't something I'm willing to do, nor tolerate. You might see time as flexible, but I do not have that luxury."

My first instinct was to open both barrels—a.k.a. my acidic tongue—and pelt him with bullets until he begged for mercy I wouldn't afford him, but as I peered closer, I noticed the dark circles underneath his startling blue eyes and how his mouth turned down at the edges. I couldn't believe it was the same guy I'd sparred with on Friday night. I shelved the sarcasm and went for contrition instead.

"I am sorry." I made the apology with a lot more sincerity this time. "Punctuality is a challenge for me, as my boss will attest to." I grinned. He didn't. "But I can and will do better. I should have at least texted you if I was going to be late."

"Or set off earlier, maybe."

"Touché." I nudged him playfully. "I promise that during our tenure as Mr. and Mrs. Party Planner, I shall endeavor to be on time for our meetings."

His look of horror wouldn't have been out of place on someone watching a ten-wheeler barrel toward a kid.

"How many meetings do you think we're going to have?"

His obvious distaste for spending time in my company should have affronted me, but all his antipathy did was make me laugh. I was well aware that my particular brand of overdramatic flair grated on the nerves of some. Hell, if I wasn't such a fantastic chef, Freddo would've cut me loose long ago.

"As many as it takes." I tapped my fingernails on the bar. "So the sooner it's done, the sooner you're rid of me."

"Hallelujah," he muttered.

"What's this you're doing, anyway?" I jerked my chin at the small stack of papers.

"Reviewing new menu ideas. We swap them out every couple of months to keep things fresh."

"Can I take a look?"

He narrowed his eyes. "Oh, that's right. Kiana said you're a chef."

"Uh-uh." I wagged my finger at him. "Not just a chef. I'm an outstanding chef. One of these days, I'll have my own restaurant, and no one will remember a place called Theo's."

He ran his forefinger over his lower lip.

Damn, he's got nice lips. Full, well-shaped, and kissable.

Wait. What the hell, Gia?

I shoved any and all thoughts of Penn Kingcaid's considerable assets into a box in my mind, slammed the lid closed, and locked it up tight.

"Is that so?" he drawled.

"Yup." I reached for the menus and ran my eye over them. "Not bad. A bit predictable."

"Predictable?" A nerve thrummed in his cheek. "Okay, Miss Cooking Genius, let's see what you can do. Follow me."

He slid off the chair and made his way through tables dressed for dinner, a confident swagger to his hips that fired up my competitive streak. Never one to step away from a challenge, I hurried after him. As I reached the entrance to the kitchen I'd rubbernecked at earlier, Penn thrust a crisp white apron at me.

"Here."

I slipped it over my head and tied the strings at the waist. The kitchen staff carried on working as if we weren't even there, bustling from the stove to the fridge to the pantry with ruthless efficiency. Penn gestured to me.

"Floor's yours. You've got thirty minutes to impress me."

A bite of anxiety nibbled at my stomach. Maybe this wasn't such a great idea. If I didn't knock it out of the park, then Penn would have even more ammunition to fire at me.

Nope, Greene. You've got this. You're fucking awesome.

I rubbed my lips together. "I don't know where you keep anything."

"That's okay. I'll be your runner. You just tell me what you need, and I'll get it for you." He folded his arms, a smug lift to one corner of his mouth.

Asshole.

"Fine." Regular go-tos like tortellini or ravioli wouldn't impress a guy like Penn. I needed to cook something he wouldn't have had before, and it had to be ready in less than thirty minutes. My mind raced. *Think, Gia.*

Aha, got it. Mom's specialty, passed down from Grams.

I ran through a few ingredients, and in less than a minute, Penn returned with every item on the list. Propping his shoulder against a gleaming silver fridge, he motioned with his hand in a "get on with it" manner.

My nerves vanished as I got to work. With a minute to

spare, I set the finished dish in front of Penn and stood back, waiting for his verdict.

I shouldn't care what he thought, but I did. Food was something I took seriously, as did the entire Italian side of my family. And this pistachio-and-honey-encrusted salmon dish with lemon and garlic aioli was an almost religious experience in our house. Whenever Mom cooked this particular dish, the whole family fell silent, too busy savoring the taste explosion on our tongues.

Penn eased a fork into the salmon, and it flaked away, as it should. He brought the tines to his mouth, holding his hand underneath. He chewed, and his eyes fell shut, a groan rumbling through his chest.

My stomach flipped, and I clenched my inner muscles on a reflex.

Oh, fuck right off, libido.

Penn Kingcaid was a looker. I'd give him that. And, yeah, that noise he just made was the kind of sound a guy made during sex—which was the *only* reason my clit perked up—but he was also a gigantic jerk and one I had no intention of sampling.

"This is divine." He went back for a second and then a third taste, dipping the salmon in the aioli. "Okay, I admit it. You're a terrific cook."

"Gosh, do you need medical assistance? 'Cause that must've *hurt.*"

He picked up the dish and cocked his head, walking away. For some weird reason, I found myself following without complaint or hesitation. I put my compliance down to his complimentary attitude toward my food rather than any desire to do what Penn Kingcaid told me to.

That sound of appreciation, though. Goddamn, my nether regions were still vibrating.

I need to get laid.

"Have a seat." He pointed at the chair I'd vacated earlier, then spread out the menus I'd found him perusing before. "Tell me what you'd change."

I widened my eyes. "I'm not giving away my trade secrets so you can get even richer. Fuck no."

He rolled his eyes and chuckled at the same time. An odd combination if ever there was one.

"I'm not asking for actual recipes, just ideas."

"It's the same thing. And besides, we're supposed to be planning a party, remember, which does not include you stealing my ideas."

"We'll get to the party in a minute." He tapped the papers. "I am genuinely interested in your ideas. And I'm happy to recompense you for your time."

I heaved a sigh. "I don't want your money."

"No?" He canted his head. "What do you want?"

Running my tongue along the underside of my top teeth, a grin stretched across my face. "You can owe me. When I'm ready to collect, you'll know." I winked. "Still want me to take a look?"

I could've sworn the look he gave me was steeped in begrudging admiration.

"Yeah," he said. "I do."

Chapter 6

Penn

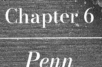

**Apparently, bodies that aren't
weighed down float to the surface.**

—

MY OPINION ON THE OUTSPOKEN, FLAMBOYANT, OVERDRAMATIC,
annoying friend of my brother's fiancée had shifted by
several degrees, and I couldn't help feeling salty about it.

Not only had she cooked me one of the best dishes I'd
tasted in years, but her ideas on expanding my offerings
here at Theo's were insightful, intelligent, and right on the
money in terms of current trends.

Gianna Greene had layers that I'd been too pissed off
to notice before.

But I noticed them now.

Still pissed me off, though. She irked the hell out of me
almost every time she opened her mouth, but I was

willing to endure the negatives for the odd glimpse of a positive, especially when it might benefit me and my restaurant.

Wherever she worked had better take advantage of her while they could, because one day soon, Gianna Greene would get snapped up by one of the top restaurants in Manhattan.

Not mine.

Dear God, no.

My blood pressure couldn't handle it, and I was far too young to turn to medication. But she'd make a terrific head chef in the not-too-distant future.

I owed her a debt, and she'd collect in a way that made me suffer—of that I had no doubt—and probably during my brother's upcoming wedding.

Well, bring it.

I had broad shoulders and a long memory.

"So, what about this party, then?" Gia pushed the papers to one side, now covered in neat handwriting where she'd made notes in the margin. "What amazing ideas do you have?"

I drew them toward me and scanned her notes. Interesting. I'd talk to my head chef and get his thoughts. She had some intriguing ideas, that was for sure.

"Well..." I tapped my bottom lip with my forefinger. "Grand Cayman looks great from the sky, so I thought perhaps paragliding, or even skydiving."

Gia's jaw dropped, and her eyelids flapped like butterfly wings. "Are you crazy?"

I twisted my lips to the side in a wry grin. "Yeah, I am.

So are most of my family. They love adrenaline-evoking activities."

"Well good for you, but I refuse to jump out of a perfectly functioning plane, and I'm pretty certain that Kee won't either."

"That's okay. My cousin Aspen can represent the girls while you two, oh, I don't know, get your nails painted or something."

I was needling her on purpose and enjoying her reaction—face turning puce, blue eyes rippling with ire—a little too much to stop.

"They want a *joint* party. That means doing something they'll *both* like."

I arched a brow. "Orgy? I'm guessing they both like sex."

She flattened her lips, and I thought she might take a swing at me, given the way her hands clenched.

"If you're not going to take this seriously, then I-I-I'll—"

"You'll what?"

"Fire your ass."

I laughed. "Sorry, sweetcheeks, but you don't have the authority."

She closed her eyes and took several deep breaths. Pretty sure she was planning a slow death, one that involved the most amount of pain—for me.

If I did go skydiving, I'd make sure to check the parachute at least ten times.

"What about a party on the beach?" she eventually said. "We could cook out, hire dancers, karaoke maybe."

"Walk over hot coals?" I arched a brow.

"Push you into them, more like," she muttered.

"Now look at who's not taking things seriously."

"Oh, I'm serious." Her eyes dug into mine. "Deadly."

I couldn't stop a smile from forming. "What about a party bus? Sightseeing, dancing, drinking, plus the happy couple can snuggle up on the back seat when the mood takes them."

She tapped her fingertips on the side of her thigh. "Y'know, that's not a bad idea, although Kee mentioned five hundred at the wedding. We'd need ten buses."

"The five hundred is mainly business associates of Kingcaid, local dignitaries that my gran doesn't want to upset, the odd politician or two. The bachelor party will mainly be close family and their plus-ones." I made a calculation in my head. "Twenty-five to thirty at most."

"So that'd work."

"It would." I dusted off my hands. "Job done. I'll make some calls."

"Hmm." She narrowed her eyes. "I'll need to see receipts. I don't trust you."

I chuckled. "What do you think I'm going to do? Arrange for a stripper to be on the bus?" I ran a palm over my chin. "Now *that* isn't a bad idea."

"My point precisely. I am here to make sure that Kee has the best bachelorette party ever, and I won't let you spoil it for her just to get one over on me."

"You have the wrong impression of me."

I smirked. She huffed.

"See you in Grand Cayman, Penn."

She slung the strap of her purse over her shoulder and

left. I watched her go, relief mingling with a kind of hankering. An odd combination. No doubt about it, Gianna Greene was a gorgeous woman with curves for days and full lips that were made for kissing, and I'd worry if my cock didn't stir to life in her company, but I'd rather dive into the hot coals she'd mentioned than fall into bed with her.

She'd drive me *insane*.

The wedding was five weeks away. By the time I saw her again, I'd have found far more pliable company to soothe the ache in my groin, and Gia would be nothing more than a distant memory.

K

"I need a favor."

I suppressed a groan. There was a hint of something in Ash's voice that experience led me to believe that I wasn't going to like whatever "favor" he had in mind.

His wedding was due to take place in eight days' time, and the closer it got, the more anxious my brother had become. Ash wasn't the panicking sort, but he was so desperate to make sure nothing ruined Kiana's day that he'd turned into a freaking nightmare, ensuring every "i" was dotted and "t" crossed.

"What now? I went for the final suit fitting three days ago, and it was fine."

My head chef appeared in the doorway to my office, and I motioned to him to give me five. He dipped his chin and backed out.

"Yeah, I know. It's not about that."

He paused. Oh, I did not like that pause.

"Spit it out, Ash."

"Well, you know that Kiana and I are flying out tomorrow so we can relax for a couple of days before the hordes arrive."

"Yes."

"And Gianna was due to fly with us."

A prickling sensation lifted the hairs on the back of my neck. "You mentioned, yes."

"Well... her boss has now decided he can't let her have time off until Tuesday of next week."

"And? That still leaves plenty of time before the wedding." I massaged my forehead. "I don't see what the problem is."

"I thought, maybe, she could fly with you. You're coming out on the Tuesday. It'd be easy to add an extra ticket to your booking."

"Oh, no. No. Four hours stuck in a steel tube with no escape? Sorry, Ash, that's where I draw the line."

"Penn, come on. She's..." He trailed off.

"She's what?"

"Nothing. It doesn't matter. Look, if you stopped needling the poor girl and took the time to get to know her, you'd realize how smart and funny and adorable she is."

"Smart I'll give you. Funny is up for debate. But adorable? Puppies are adorable. Kittens are adorable. Babies are adorable. Gianna fucking Greene is *not* adorable. She is a gigantic splinter in my ass, one I plucked out five weeks ago when we met to discuss your bachelor party. I don't intend to reinsert it until the last possible moment, which, my dearest brother, is at the actual wedding."

"Too bad. I already told Kiana you'd do it, and she let Gia know this morning. She's waiting for your call to let her know what time you'll pick her up."

"Fuck's sake, Ash." I snapped the pencil I'd used to make notes on today's specials. "What if I was bringing a plus-one?"

I'd decided not to take a date to the wedding. With five hundred on the guest list, there was bound to be someone who caught my attention. Wasn't about to curtail my fun.

"Oh, stop whining, Penn. You already told me you weren't planning to bring anyone. I have a ton of shit to get done before tomorrow, and I don't need the added pressure of you bellyaching over something and nothing. It's one fucking flight. I'm not asking you to bang the girl."

"Just as well," I muttered, tossing the broken parts of the pencil into the trash. "I'd rather bang you."

Ash laughed. "Four hours will pass in no time."

"Under torture, an hour can feel like a year."

"Overdramatic much?"

An idea sprang to mind.

Aspen.

Yeah, my cousin could act as a barrier between me and Gia. Or better still, Aspen could travel with her.

I almost high-fived myself, then I remembered that Aspen had flown to Miami a couple of days ago to try to sign some band or other and was going to travel to Grand Cayman from there rather than return to New York.

Fuck.

"Fine. I'll take her. But I'm not happy about it."

"Noted."

"At least pretend to sound like you care."

Ash laughed again, then hung up on me.

Bastard.

I grabbed my phone and called the airline. Knowing my luck, the plane would crash and the last person I'd see before I took my last breath would be Gianna fucking Greene.

K

My driver stopped outside Gia's apartment building at seven o'clock the following Tuesday morning. I sent a text to let her know I was outside waiting.

Less than a minute later—would wonders never cease?—she appeared, lugging behind her the biggest suitcase I'd ever seen, as well as a carry-on bag busting at the seams.

Dear God, hadn't the woman ever heard of traveling light? It was Grand Cayman, for fuck's sake. Couple pairs of shorts, a T-shirt or two, swimwear, and flip-flops were the only attire required. The wedding outfits were being shipped separately.

With a groan, I exited the vehicle and went to help her. I could have sent my driver, but knowing Gia, she'd accuse me of exploitation or some such crap, and I already had a pounding headache before the trip had even begun.

I could kill Ash for putting me in this position. Why she couldn't have traveled alone was beyond me.

"We're going away for five nights, not fifty," I grumbled, wrestling the large suitcase from her. "Jesus Christ Almighty, what the hell have you got in here?"

"Concrete blocks." She gave me a sickly-sweet smile. "Bodies float to the surface otherwise."

Great. Seven in the morning and already she'd turned her sarcasm up full blast.

I ignored her response, almost putting my back out as I heaved the case into the trunk. She left her carry-on by the side of the road and climbed into the car.

"You're welcome," I called out, lifting it into the trunk.

I settled into the car and fastened my seat belt. Gia's eyes were closed, and she yawned several times in succession.

"Not a morning person?"

She cracked open an eye. "Nope."

"Good. Nice peaceful journey to the airport, then."

Her body stiffened, and I readied myself for a caustic remark or two, but she kept quiet.

First time for everything.

The freeway snarled up about three miles from JFK, and from there we crawled inch by inch. Our flight didn't leave until ten thirty, which left plenty of time, but there was something torturous about sitting in a car that wasn't fucking going anywhere.

I distracted myself by going through my emails for both Theo's and Kingcaid. Not for the first time, I sent up a prayer of thanks that my deputy CEO at Kingcaid was all over shit. If it weren't for her, I'd struggle to manage my workload.

I kept telling myself it wouldn't be like this forever.

Once Theo's had traded for a year or so, I'd feel comfortable hiring a manager to take over the running of the place. But until then, I somehow had to manage both businesses without dropping a single ball.

"Finally," I muttered to no one in particular as we arrived at the terminal building. Gia still said nothing, and I began to wonder if Kiana had warned her to be on her best behavior, considering I'd let it be known how unhappy I was having to act as chaperone. Either way, you wouldn't find me complaining. Other than the veiled barbed comment she'd made about concrete blocks when I'd picked her up, she'd kept her sassy opinions to herself.

Funny, then, how I missed them.

Quiet Gia wasn't to my taste at all. Ironic, considering I'd have thought the complete opposite less than an hour ago. Maybe because she'd only ever shown me sass from the first time we'd met, but this muted version vexed me.

I wheeled her bag and mine into the departures area, leaving her to bring her carry-on. As I weaved through throngs of people lining up at the various check-in desks, a thought of how I could coax a reaction out of her crossed my mind. One I probably shouldn't act upon, but then again, I never heeded warnings, including those from myself most of the time.

Making a beeline for the first-class desk with Gia trailing behind, I waited until the perfect moment when I handed my passport to the pre check-in team for inspection. As they flicked through the pages looking for fuck only knew what, I turned to her with a puzzled frown.

"What are you doing?"

She gave me a bored stare. "Erm, checking in. Like you."

"But this is first class." I handed over her ticket. "You're in economy. Over there." I helpfully pointed.

"You... I... what?"

"You're in the wrong line."

Her cheeks bloomed with color, and she widened her stance as if preparing to take to the ring with the heavyweight champion of the world.

"Are you freaking *kidding* me? Kee said I was traveling with you, that you'd arrange everything."

"I did arrange everything. I bought you a ticket, and I gave you a ride to the airport. And I have someone picking us up in Grand Cayman. What more did you expect?"

Her hands clenched and unclenched, her nostrils flaring. "You... you... asshole!"

She snatched the handle of her suitcase and stomped off toward the long line of travelers waiting to check in at economy. I winked at the airline personnel.

"Won't be a sec."

Striding after her, I gripped her elbow. "Hold up, sweetcheeks."

"Get your fucking hand off of me right now, Kingcaid, or when you withdraw it, it'll be minus a few fingers."

Yeah, call me a masochist, but I definitely preferred this version of her. Far more entertaining.

"You are so easy to tease." I plucked the ticket out of her hand. "If you used your eyes more than your mouth, you'd see that this is also a first-class ticket. Asher would sell me for dogmeat if I let you travel in economy while I was in first."

Grabbing her suitcase again, I returned to the check-in area. One of the staff members—the guy—wore a smirk and a faint air of admiration. The other—a woman—gave me a death glare that, if looks had the power to kill, would ruin Gia's fun of getting in there first.

"Just a bit of fun."

I fired off an impish grin that had no effect in winning the woman over. She handed me my passport without a single word passing her lips, but her eyes said it all.

She greeted Gia, on the other hand, with a beaming smile as she ran her passport through the checks. Satisfied that we weren't a danger—to other passengers, if not to each other—they waved us through to the check-in desk.

I handed over both passports and our tickets to the agent and heaved Gia's ridiculously heavy bag onto the belt, my eyes widening when I read how much it weighed. Good thing the airline didn't charge an excess baggage fee for first-class passengers. Paying that would cost more than the damned ticket.

"You're in seat 1A, Mr. Kingcaid. And you, Miss Greene, are in seat 1B."

"Any chance those aren't together?" Gia ground out between clenched teeth.

The agent blinked, her gaze swinging between us both. "I-um—"

"Ignore her." I retrieved both our passports and handed Gia's back to her. "She loves me, really."

The air around us crackled, but Gia kept quiet... until we moved away, and then she let me have it.

"You are a hideous, lousy, detestable human being, Penn Kingcaid. And if I had my way, I would break both your legs, but as that'd make your role as best man"—she snorted, I presumed at the word "best"—"a little difficult to carry out, I'll refrain. Somehow. But what you did wasn't cool. Not cool at all."

She spun on her heel and walked off, leaving me, for once in my life, speechless.

Chapter 7

Penn

Miss Confident has a chink in her armor.

By the time I reached the security line, Gia had already passed through the TSA checks. Dragging her carry-on behind her, she marched off, her shoulders squared, a peeved stomp to her gait. I navigated the rigmarole of modern-day air travel, and when I finally arrived at the gate, boarding had commenced and Gia—I guessed—was already on the plane.

Wow. She really was pissed off at me. Maybe I had taken it too far, but her reaction to a bit of harmless teasing was excessive. Then again, was I really surprised? This was Gianna Greene, the queen of overdramatic responses to everything.

I traipsed down the jetway, shared a smile and a word with the cabin crew at the doorway, and made my way to my seat. Sure enough, there was Gia, seat belt fastened, earphones in, eyes closed. I purposely knocked her as I took the seat by the window, even though there was plenty of room for me to get past. She didn't even flinch, although her lips moved ever so slightly.

She was probably muttering a spell under her breath.

I plunked down in my seat and held up a finger for the flight attendant. "Could I get a mimosa?"

"Of course, sir. Miss?"

When Gia didn't respond to him, I elbowed her. She yanked her earbuds out of her ears. "What?"

I jerked my chin at the steward. "He wants to know if you'd like a drink."

"Oh." Her glower turned into a smile—for him. "I'd love a glass of champagne."

"Right away." He ducked into the galley next to the cockpit, returning seconds later with our drinks. I sipped mine. Gia... downed the entire glass without pause.

"Could I have another?" she asked the steward, who hadn't taken a single step, as she'd drunk her champers that fast.

"Yes, miss. One moment."

"Maybe sip this one," I suggested.

She ignored me, and when her second drink arrived, she downed that one just as fast.

"Jesus, Gia, take a breath. It's a four-hour flight. You don't have to drink your weight in champagne before takeoff."

"With any luck, the alcohol will help me fall asleep, and I won't have to listen to you drone on." She stuffed the earphones back in her ears and closed her eyes once more.

The woman could sulk; I'd give her that.

Within twenty minutes we were in the air. I stared out the window as we climbed, watching as the earth fell away. I adored flying. Seeing the land become a patchwork quilt beneath me was a sight I'd never tire of. In another life, I'd have loved to train as a pilot, but airlines were the one area our family hadn't moved into. Besides, I had more than enough on my plate with the two jobs I did have without adding a third into the mix.

The plane leveled out at thirty-four thousand feet. I got up to stretch out my legs. Gia still hadn't opened her eyes, but her lips had moved the entire time we'd climbed to cruising altitude, so she couldn't be asleep. She must be miming to the music or something.

The crew came around with a light snack, but when asked if she'd like to eat something, Gia refused, then returned to her virtual catatonic state.

It should please me that I didn't have to take part in firing insults back and forth, but her continued sulkiness and refusal to engage in conversation irked me. I had a long few days ahead of me if every time we were in each other's company, this was the attitude she brought. My brother's wedding was a cause for celebration, not for kowtowing to the maid of honor's hissy fits.

The plane jolted and shook. Oh, good. Turbulence. Something to take my mind off the boringness of this trip.

"What's that?" Gia yanked out her earbuds and gripped the sides of her seat.

"It's just turbulence." Another jolt came and then a third. Gia gripped my arm, her nails digging through my shirt. "Ow." I tried to pry her off, but she dug in harder.

"I don't like it."

"Jeez, you're going to draw blood in a minute."

The plane shook violently, and the Fasten Seat Belt sign came on. Gia, I noticed, hadn't removed hers in the first place. I wrangled out of her death grip and clipped mine into place. The second I did, she grabbed me again. Fuck, were those nails or talons?

"Oh God, oh God, oh God." Gia squeezed her eyes closed as a loud rattling sound came from the galley. "We're crashing, aren't we?"

I chuckled. "No, we're not crashing. It's a little bumpy airflow. That's all."

"I don't like it," she said again.

I peered closer. Christ, she was shaking more than the fuselage, and a sheen of sweat glistened on her forehead. "Are you afraid of flying?"

She swallowed and nodded, sucking in sips of air through her nose. Ah, fuck. Was this why she'd raged at me for the trick I'd played on her at check-in? Because she was dreading the flight and her stress levels had gone stratospheric?

"Why didn't you say so?"

"You'd have used it against me in some way."

Wow. She really did have a distorted worldview when it came to me. I put my arm around her shoulders and stroked her upper arm. "I'd never do that. Fear of flying, while illogical, is not something I'd ever tease someone about. But, I promise, you're fine. It'll stop soon."

"You don't know that. Planes crash all the time."

I might have known she'd bring melodrama rather than logic to the situation. "Gia, something like one

74

hundred and twenty thousand flights take off around the world every day. A minuscule number of them get into difficulties, and an even tinier amount results in a crash. It's just bumpy air. That's all. I'm sure we'll be through it soon."

"God, I hope so." She shut her eyes again, panting so fast that if I only had audio, I'd swear she was having sex. Or running. But thinking of her having sex was far more fun.

But as I studied her and saw the panic on her face, my chest tightened. A need to comfort a woman whom, until now, I'd have rather thrown myself under a bus than offered solace to, bloomed within me. She trembled, muttering under her breath. Ah. So that was what she'd been doing on takeoff and during the flight. Reassuring herself, or meditating maybe. I picked up one of her earbuds and held it to my ear, listening for a few seconds. It was one of those tapes for nervous fliers, the kind that gave strategies and exercises to do during flights to help you cope.

"Is this your first time flying?"

She shook her head, hissing when the turbulent air jostled the plane again. "Doesn't matter how many times I do it, I hate it."

"But you land safely each time, right?" I stroked her hair, squashing the thought of how soft it felt against my skin, how well she fit in my arms, how nice it was to have a break from sniping at each other.

"Stop plying me with logic, Penn."

I chuckled. "Is that your way of telling me I'm right?"

"You never let an opportunity to gain the upper hand

go, do you?"

"No."

She laughed then, and a lump of pride hit me in the chest. I'd made her laugh, which I was sure had taken her mind away from her fears, if only for a moment.

"I'm a competitive bastard, no apologies."

"You've met your match on that score."

"Yeah." I grinned. "I know."

The plane evened out and the seat belt sign extinguished, and Gia's shoulders unhunched from their new home around her neck. I removed my arm from around her, and a weird kind of emptiness came over me. "You okay?"

"Yeah. Better now that it's stopped shaking."

She picked up a magazine and brought it close to her face, almost as if her reaction to the turbulence had embarrassed her. Or, more likely, the fact that I'd been around to witness her reaction had embarrassed her. Gianna Greene wore her confidence like a well-fitting suit, so for me to see it slip, even momentarily, was the last thing she'd ever have wanted to happen.

I checked out her profile. She was a looker for sure, and when she wasn't coating every word out of her mouth with derision and mockery, she piqued my interest. And not just my dick's either. I couldn't help but wonder if I dug beneath that prickly outer shell, whether I'd find a soft, gooey center. The idea of plowing her depths was oddly attractive. So was plowing other parts of her anatomy.

"Only an hour until we land."

"Thank God." She flipped the page, and I glanced over

her shoulder to see what had absorbed her since the turbulence had stopped.

"What are you reading?"

"This girl here." She pointed at a picture of a dark-haired woman with an elfin face sitting cross-legged on a mahogany table. "She caught her boyfriend cheating, so she snuck into his apartment while he was at work and left rotting fish guts behind the air-conditioning vent in his bedroom. Took him a month to get the stink out of his apartment." She chuckled. "Giiirrrlll, kudos for delivering cold-as-ice revenge."

The idea of a smell like that turned my stomach, and the gleeful expression Gia wore caused me to ask, "You wouldn't do something that awful, would you?"

She arched a brow. "An asshole I trusted cheated on me? I'd do a lot worse." She nudged me playfully. "Not something you'll ever have to worry about, Penn, so no need to screw up your face. You'll get wrinkles."

"I can't understand why a man cheats. I mean, if you're no longer interested in the woman, just tell her. No point in dragging things out."

She arched a brow. "Don't tell me you have morals?"

"One or two." I winked. "You have to search for them, though."

"Why doesn't that surprise me?"

A smile inched across my face. "You never know, Gia, if you stop sniping at me for long enough, you might find that I'm a pretty decent guy underneath."

She closed the magazine and slotted it into the pocket on the bulkhead. "They haven't invented tools yet that'll dig that deep."

Chapter 8

Gia

**Blistering heat means chubby
thighs that chafe like hell.**

ON THE SHORT WALK FROM THE COOL AIRPORT TERMINAL TO THE
car Penn had waiting for us, I discovered that Grand
Cayman in July was more of a fiery hell than New York,
and that was saying something.

Sweat coated my neck and chest, and my inner thighs
rubbed together. I had the urge to walk with my legs three
feet apart just to stop the chafing, but I could just imagine
the ammunition that would give to Penn, and he didn't
need any help on that score.

Not that I thought Penn was one of those guys who
ran from curvy women as if they might suffocate in their
ample bosoms and rounded bellies. The man had a lot of
faults, but he'd never once looked at me as if I was less

than in the female stakes because I'd last seen a size eight in my teens. I'd even seen him rake his gaze over me once or twice, interest flaring in his electric-blue eyes. And then one of us would heckle the other and the moment passed.

I'd never tell him this, or anyone else for that matter, but the way he'd soothed me during my minor—and, frankly, embarrassing—meltdown on the plane had added a couple of ticks to his plus column.

The problem was, there were so many ticks in the minus column that I'd had to sharpen my pencil three times after I'd run out of lead.

Climbing into the cool interior of the car was heaven, like having an ice blanket draped over me. However, cold had a negative effect, too, in the name of protruding nipples as hard as diamonds. I should've worn a padded T-shirt bra instead of this balconette thing, especially when Penn glanced over, smirked, and murmured, "Cold?"

I pasted on a fake smile. "Funny, isn't it, how the cold makes a certain part of a woman's anatomy bigger and"—I lowered my gaze to his groin, lingering for a second or two before lifting my eyes back to his—"a certain part of a man's anatomy smaller. Maybe God is a woman after all."

Penn chuckled, seemingly unaffected by my jibe at his genitals. I braced myself for a typical comeback along the lines of being huge even in zero degrees Fahrenheit, but he just looked out the window, his cheeks rounded from the grin that remained in place.

I couldn't seem to stop myself from sniping at him, but soon, I'd have to swallow every potshot, or at least save them for when no one else was around. Wouldn't be easy, but I'd promised Kee I'd be on my best behavior around Penn, and I intended to keep that promise. My amazing friend was getting married, and I, for one, wouldn't be the one to spoil that for her.

But God, the thought of biting my tongue for the entire trip... I never had been very good at keeping my thoughts to myself.

The car whizzed through the streets, giving me little time to appreciate the beauty of Grand Cayman, but what I did see filled my stomach with excitement. It was so darned *beautiful* with it's lush tropical greenery and colorful flowers, and that ocean—or was it the sea?—a delicious blue-green with white topped waves that just called to me to take a dip.

I wasn't what you'd call well traveled. In fact, this was only my second time leaving the continental US—the first being a trip to Toronto in my teens—and I couldn't wait to explore some of the surrounding areas. I'd bought a guide-book and packed my comfiest sneakers, and I intended to make the most of the time here.

Sure, I had maid-of-honor duties to perform, but Kee had assured me there'd be plenty of free time, too.

Kee had booked me into a hotel a short stroll from Asher's grandparents' house. She was staying there, with them, but as the entire Kingcaid clan was descending on the island for the upcoming nuptials, she'd explained there wasn't room for everyone to stay at the house. She'd worried that I'd be upset at having to stay somewhere else, but the opposite was true. As nice as Kee had assured me Asher's grandparents were, I'd rather not stay in a stranger's home.

Besides, the hotel had a spa, a swimming pool, and a gym.

Gym. Ha! Who was I kidding? The only reason to visit the gym was to perv on muscular guys with their shirts off, looking all sweaty and delicious.

"We're here."

Penn interrupted my musings as the car drew to a stop. I unclipped my seat belt and climbed out, the heat sapping my energy. As soon as I got to my room, I planned to jump in the shower before even unpacking, and then maybe take a dip in the sea. Ocean. Whatever.

His driver hoisted out my suitcase, and I could've sworn he massaged his lower back. Hoped he hadn't put it out, but I'd struggled to know what to pack, and being so far away from home, I didn't want to find myself without something I ended up needing. Which meant I'd packed almost everything I owned.

"Better tip the valet extra," Penn drawled.

I opened my mouth to fire back a retort, but the words died on my lips when Penn removed his suitcase from the trunk.

"What are you doing?"

He frowned. "Checking in."

"You... you're staying here?"

"Yeah. Did Kiana not tell you?"

I shook my head. "She said that your grandmother's house was full and that's why she had to put me up here."

"It is full. Which is why I'm staying here, too." He arched a brow, an annoying quirk to his lips. "Problem?"

"No," I lied.

Goddammit.

I'd hoped for a few Penn-free days other than when we had to do something wedding related. And now, every time I left my room, I'd expect to see him lurking around the corner, a witty retort at the ready.

Relax, Gia.

The hotel was big enough for me to avoid him. Kee had told me it even had two swimming pools, so if I went to one and Penn was there in his Speedo with his tiny dick to offset his enormous ego, I'd move to the other one.

Why are you thinking about Penn's dick?

"Don't worry," Penn said. "We're not sharing a room."

He ambled off, and I could have sworn I heard him laughing.

With my mood in the shitter now that my plans were shot to smithereens, I dragged my cases into the hotel. Penn was already at the front desk, laughing with a smart woman dressed in a crisp white blouse and navy jacket who seemed to enjoy his attempt at flirting.

Someone has to.

A guy called me forward and I beamed at him, especially when he handed me a glass of champagne.

"Welcome to Kingcaid Grand Cayman."

Oh, for fuck's sake.

Kee hadn't told me she'd booked me in at a Kingcaid property, and I'd been too busy daydreaming to notice the signage. That meant Penn owned this hotel. Okay, his family did, but he had more than a vested interest.

God, that also meant the staff would know him and they'd probably fawn all over him at every opportunity, trying their best to impress. The whole sycophantic experience was likely to make me puke. Hopefully all over Penn's pristine shirt, or fancy Italian loafers.

"May I see your passport?"

"Oh, sure." I handed it over, rocking from foot to foot as he tapped on the keyboard.

"Okay, Miss Greene, we have you in our one-bedroom island suite on the top floor. It overlooks our wave pool and has a beautiful ocean view."

A suite. Wow.

"How many key cards would you like?"

"Just the one."

I glanced over at Penn, who was doing his best to charm the receptionist. She tossed her gorgeous, thick hair over her shoulder and laughed at something he said.

At least someone found him funny.

"Here you are. I'll have the bellhop bring your luggage straight to your suite. In the meantime, if there is *anything* we can do to make your stay more comfortable, please don't hesitate to ask."

"Thanks."

I drew the key card toward me and stole another glance at Penn still engrossed in conversation with the woman.

Good. I'd be able to sneak off without him seeing me.

I left the half-finished glass of champagne behind and made my way to the bank of elevators. I'd never been inside a Kingcaid hotel, not even when Kee had first hooked up with Asher, but my God, they oozed opulence. I swore I could smell the wealth in the fabric of the building.

I pressed the button for the seventh floor. The elevator

doors began to close, and then they sprang back open. I suppressed a groan as Penn slipped inside.

Goddamm. I couldn't catch a break today.

"Which floor?"

He jutted his chin. "Seven. Same as you."

I pursed my lips. Just my luck.

"What do you think of the hotel?"

"Well…" I glanced around the steel box. "Since I've only seen the lobby and this elevator, it might be better if I reserve judgment a while longer."

Penn chuckled. "Fair enough."

"Kee didn't tell me she'd arranged for me to stay at one of your hotels."

The doors opened, and Penn gestured for me to go first. My feet sank into the thick-pile carpeting that probably cost more than a year's rent on my apartment.

"Makes sense to keep it in the family. Besides, our hotel is the best on the island."

"Of course it is," I muttered.

Penn responded by whipping my key card out of my hand and flashing it in front of a thick wooden door with a plaque that read *Island Suite*. At the click, he opened it and waltzed in as if this was his room, not mine.

"Hey," I called out, but as I stepped inside, my intended castigation of Penn for overstepping boundaries froze on my tongue.

"Oh, wow."

I tossed my purse onto the emperor-size bed and flew over to the French doors that opened out onto an enormous wooden decking area complete with sunbeds, a jacuzzi, and a table that seated six.

But it wasn't the beautiful balcony that had rendered me speechless. It was the view.

"Gorgeous, isn't it?" His voice came from behind me.

"Stunning," I breathed, resting my hands on the wooden railing and taking it all in. The blue-green waters, white-tipped waves, golden sand dotted with beachgoers, and, below me, a sparkling swimming pool that I couldn't wait to sample.

I spun to face Penn where he loitered just inside the room. "I have to text Kee. To thank her for arranging this amazing suite. It's... luxury on another level."

"Well, you can, of course, but..." He hitched a shoulder.

My mouth gaped open. "You arranged this?"

Another hitch, this time of the opposite shoulder.

"But... why?"

"Why not? You're Kiana's friend and maid of honor, and as she's about to be my sister-in-law, I thought I should arrange the best accommodation for you."

He ducked his chin, almost as if he was embarrassed that he'd been caught doing something nice, especially for me.

I moved closer.

Our eyes locked, and a spark of... camaraderie, maybe, passed between us. It wouldn't last. Soon we'd be back to normal, sniping at each other, but right then, I almost liked him.

"Thank you, Penn. It's the nicest room I've ever stayed in."

"It's a great room." He arched a brow. "Better than mine."

He reached toward me, extracting a strand of hair that

had caught on my eyelashes. My breath hitched, and a warmth spread through my midsection.

"I'll leave you to freshen up."

He spun around and left, and just like that, the moment passed.

Chapter 9

Gia

Admitting I'm wrong hurts like a mofo.

I SHOWERED IN A STALL THAT WOULD FIT AN ENTIRE BASEBALL team, napped on a mattress made of clouds, and gorged on these delicious canapés that I found in the full-size fridge. Which, by the way, was in the full-size kitchen.

This wasn't a hotel suite. It was three times the size of my entire apartment back home, and if I had my way, I'd never leave. Still, I hadn't had this much time off work since I'd left college, and I intended to make the most of every moment.

Earlier, I'd dropped Kee a text to let her know I'd arrived safely, but she hadn't seen it yet. I couldn't imagine how much prep there was to do for a wedding of this magnitude. I shuddered. Better her than me. I couldn't ever see myself floating down the aisle in a white dress while people I didn't know watched on, like Kee would have to this coming Saturday.

Tomorrow would be her last chance to let her hair down, and I intended to make sure she had the best bachelorette party ever. When I'd told her about the party bus, she'd squealed loudly enough to pierce my eardrum and called me a genius. Was it awful of me that I hadn't told her Penn had come up with the idea? Then again, all he'd really done was take my idea of a beach party and put a different spin on it.

I wandered out onto the balcony and breathed in the sea air. Below me, a pool party was in full swing, and it made me wonder why Penn hadn't suggested having the party here. I supposed, for Asher in particular, it'd feel like a busman's holiday rather than a place he could relax and forget about work for a while. And for Penn, too, considering he ran the restaurant side of the business. Better to have the party somewhere completely independent where neither of them felt the compulsion to get involved with the behind-the-scenes goings-on.

My cell rang, and I returned inside to answer it. At last. Kee must've gotten my message.

"Hey, bride-to-be. How are the nerves?"

"Argh, don't even. I am panicking, Gia. You should see the guest list. I just know I'm going to embarrass Ash in some way, like fall flat on my face, or walk down the aisle with my dress caught in my panties."

"That's easily solved. Don't wear any." I chuckled. "And make sure you tell Ash that right before he says his vows. Problem solved."

"I'm serious!"

"So am I."

"You never take anything seriously."

"Life's too short, Kee. We're only on this planet once. Might as well make the most of it. Worrying about trivialities is a waste of time."

"Thank God for you, Gia."

"I am the gift that keeps on giving." I grinned even though she couldn't see me. "Anyway, when am I going to see you? Before tomorrow, I hope."

"That's why I'm calling. Asher's grandmother is having the family over for dinner tonight, which includes you."

I gnawed my lip. "Aw, Kee, I'm not sure. Never have been a fan of the big family do."

"When have you *ever* been to a big family do?"

She had a point. "I guess if I do something hugely embarrassing, it'll make anything you do at the wedding pale in comparison."

"That's the spirit. I'll see you at eight."

"Wait. Where is it?"

"Oh, Penn said he'll bring you."

She hung up before I could argue, or ask anything like "What's the dress code?" I tried to call back, but it went to voicemail.

Which left me only one option. I sent Penn a text.

Me: What shall I wear tonight?

He didn't reply for fifteen minutes. When my phone sounded and I read what he'd put, I rolled my eyes so hard I almost lost them at the back of my head.

Penn: Is that a come-on?

Me: Dream on.

Penn: [laughing emoji]. That'd be a fucking nightmare, not a dream. Wear whatever you're comfortable in.

His barb scored me right in the chest. It shouldn't bother me, and it didn't, not really. I wouldn't sleep with Penn Kingcaid if the future of the human race depended on it, and given I'd not had sex in weeks, that was a pretty bold statement. But most women liked to receive compliments, to think that they were attractive to another person. I might appear to others as bold and confident and larger than life, but I still preened under male attention, even if the male in question was someone I couldn't stand most of the time.

Me: Yoga pants and a muscle T-shirt?
Penn: Like I said, wear what you're comfortable in.

Ugh. The man was as helpful as a toddler in the kitchen.

Penn: And don't be fucking late. We leave at 7:45.

It took all my might not to send him back a middle finger emoji, but I decided to rise above it and refrain. Jeez. Look at me being all grown-up and everything.

I checked the time. Six thirty. I'd already showered, so that left seventy-five minutes to decide on what to wear, slap on some makeup, and do something with my hair. Plenty of time.

Famous last words.

When Penn knocked—five minutes early, I might add—I'd only put makeup on one of my eyes, which just looked weird, I still hadn't curled my hair, and I'd lost one of the shoes I'd chosen to go with this outfit, a fitted, calf-length ivory dress with a deep V-neck that showed off my ample assets. I had it, so I was going to flaunt it.

With no choice other than to open the door, I let him in and whirled around without even a cursory glance. Time was money and all that, and I still had to finish getting ready.

"Jesus Christ, did a tornado blow through here?"

Virtually every item of clothing I'd brought with me was strewn over the bed, the chair, and the writing desk, including bras and matching panties, and—what was I thinking?—pantyhose. I gathered my undergarments into a pile and stuffed them under a one-piece jumpsuit that I'd considered wearing and then realized it made my ass look so big that the local news anchor would have to report a total eclipse on the nighttime news.

"It's just a few clothes." I ducked into the bathroom to finish putting on my makeup.

"A few?" The dumbstruck note to his voice brought a smile to my lips. There was a man who lived his life with a place for everything and everything in its place. That was what I'd guess at least, especially with his penchant for punctuality.

"What can I say? I'm messy."

"This isn't messy. This is a disaster. And you're fucking late."

I glanced at my wristwatch, a fake designer number I'd gotten from a flea market on a trip upstate. "Wrong. I have one minute left."

"And are you going to be ready in one minute?"

"Will you turn back into a pumpkin if I'm not?"

He appeared at the doorway to the bathroom, our eyes

meeting in the mirror. His gaze swept over me, lingering on my hips, my breasts, and eventually returning to my face.

A sudden flush of warmth spread through my stomach. *God, it's hot in here.* I suppressed an urge to fan myself as his vibrant blue irises bored into mine. Then the shutters came down, and his brow lowered into a frown.

"My grandmother won't appreciate it if we're late, and I would think that, as you're a guest at a family dinner, you'd show a little respect."

He spun around, leaving me blinking and my jaw unhinged. And the worst part? He had a point. Christ, admitting I was wrong, even to myself, stung.

Dismissing the idea of putting a curling iron through my hair, I dragged a brush through it to dislodge most of the knots, found the missing shoe under the bed, and offered him an apologetic half smile.

"You're right. I should have started getting ready earlier. Is it far?"

"Five minutes in the car."

"Oh, so we'll make it, then."

He looked down at me and I looked up at him, and only then did I notice how *tall* he was. He had to be well over six feet, and even in these heels, he towered over me by several inches. I liked men with a bit of height to them. It always made me feel petite, in the height department if not the hip department.

"Just," he grumbled.

"I'm a just-in-time kinda girl." I nudged him and grinned.

"You're an annoying kinda girl," he replied, but he

couldn't hide the curve to his lips as he opened the door to my suite and motioned with his hand.

His grandmother's house was the sort of place you saw on *Cribs* on MTV, or in one of those magazines where celebrities had those amazing photo shoots with the women draped over leather couches, dressed head-to-toe in designer outfits, and the men stood by looking broody and holding a glass of champagne. In other words, jaw-dropping.

"Wow. This is *gorgeous*." I brushed invisible lint off my dress, more than thankful I hadn't chosen a shabby outfit just to needle Penn. He might've said to dress in whatever I found comfortable, but I already knew if I'd done that, all eyes would've been on me—for all the wrong reasons. I mean, sure, I liked to be the center of attention on occasion, but not the negative kind.

I stepped out of the car, gazing up at the wondrous house with its impressive pillars and stunning flower displays. Penn touched my elbow and cocked his head. I followed him into a vaulted-ceiling hallway, passed through a lounge, and stepped out onto a pool deck. I faltered, drawing in a deep breath.

"What's the matter?" Penn returned to me when he realized I wasn't with him. So far, none of the attending guests had noticed our arrival, and I couldn't see Kee or Asher anywhere.

"This feels weird," I replied with an honesty that surprised even me. "I mean, this is a family event, and I'm not family."

"You're family to Kiana, if not by blood, and that means you have as much right to be here as anyone.

Besides, you don't want the first time you meet everyone to be at the bachelor party."

"Bachelor *and* bachelorette party," I corrected for what felt like the umpteenth time.

Penn flashed me those perfect pearly whites. "Can't let it go, can you?"

His cocky smirk rattled my irritation bone. As my eyes cut away, I spied an opportunity to get my own back. Dearest Penn's fly was undone.

Smiling, I moved in close and pulled up his zipper.

"Probably best not to flash the worm in front of your grandmother."

His eyebrows shot up, and his chin dipped as he glanced down. For a millisecond, his customary confidence fled and he looked off-balance. If I'd blinked, I'd have missed it. He gave me another beaming grin.

"It's far from a worm, sweetcheeks. And if you want proof..." He reached for his zipper.

"Dear God, no," I exclaimed, gripping his wrist to stop him. "I'll take your word for it."

"Coward."

"Ass—"

"Penn!"

A perfectly turned-out elderly lady bustled over, her speed belying her age. She held out her arms for a hug, a request Penn obliged with the softest, most loving smile I'd seen him give. This had to be his grandmother, and Penn couldn't hide his fondness for the diminutive, gray-haired lady.

"Gran. You look amazing as always." He kissed both her cheeks.

She touched Penn's arm. "At last, you've brought a lovely lady to meet me."

"Oh, no, Gran."

"Definitely not."

We spoke simultaneously, and his grandmother frowned.

"Um, I mean..." Penn moved a good foot away from me as if he'd caught a whiff of something he didn't like the smell of. "This is Gianna Greene. Kiana's maid of honor."

"Pleased to meet you, Mrs. Kingcaid. Kiana speaks so fondly of you. Thank you for inviting me to your beautiful home." I held out my hand.

She glanced between Penn and me, curiosity dancing in her eyes as if she saw something amusing but also puzzling. No idea what that could be. Ignoring my hand, she gripped my upper arms, drew me close, and kissed both my cheeks.

"You, my dear, are more than welcome. Kiana has told me so much about you. Now come, let me introduce you to everyone."

She slipped her arm through mine, and as Penn walked with us, his grandmother shooed him away with a single flick of her wrist.

"Go get our special guest a drink, Penn. She doesn't need you crowding her."

And just like that, she stole me away.

I adored her already.

Chapter 10

Penn

Curves are the stuff of dreams.

It would have been easy to use one of the conference rooms at our Kingcaid property for Ash's bachelor party, or even commandeer one of the pools, but I knew my brother. He'd get dragged into some issue or another, disappear for hours, and Kiana would, rightly, blame me.

The party bus was different, normal, and far removed from the kind of event Ash usually attended. Which made it the perfect choice for celebrating his upcoming nuptials. My brother erred on the serious side, although since he'd met Kiana, I'd noticed a shift in his behavior. He seemed more relaxed, less at odds with himself, and happy. So fucking happy. He smiled, all the time, and he was lighter somehow, like the world he'd carried on his shoulders had lifted, leaving him freer.

I was thrilled for him, but in my quieter moments, I couldn't help sending up a prayer that he or Kiana would never have to suffer the kind of grief I'd landed at Sandrine's door. Love hurt. I'd witnessed that for myself, up close and oh-so personal. To me, it wasn't worth the risk. But to Ash, Kiana was his everything.

The upper level of the bus was decked out like a limousine with leather benches on either side, a small dance floor between, and a DJ at the rear, blasting tunes from twin decks. On the lower deck, it was far quieter. A bar had been set up at one end, and there were small tables and chairs where you could share an intimate drink or two.

I left Ash dancing with Kiana and a few other family members and made my way down the spiral staircase to grab a drink. I paused at the bottom and gripped the handrail. Propped at the bar, knocking back whiskey as if there was a world shortage, was my other brother, Johannes. And right beside him stood Gianna, sipping champagne and batting her eyelashes. Johannes said something, and she laughed.

My brother wasn't funny. Johannes was the black sheep in our family, broody and dour with a tongue that could slice through steel. Humor was not in his arsenal, yet the evidence was undeniable when Gianna laughed again, then ran her palm over his arm.

My lungs on fire, I watched a woman I wasn't remotely interested in flirt with a man who should not be left unattended with any member of the human race. And worse was that Johannes was playing along, laying on the charm and sucking her into his orbit, where, no doubt, he'd crush her, like he crushed everything.

I forced myself to walk over to the bar, schooling my features into apathy. I muscled my way between them and ordered a drink. A dick move, for sure, but the idea of Johannes and Gia wasn't one I could see myself tolerating. It wasn't a case of "I didn't want her but didn't want anyone else to have her" either. It was more like I saw myself as responsible for her well-being for the duration of this wedding, and she didn't know Johannes like I did.

"Don't mind us, Penn," Gia said. "We're only having a conversation."

"That's what worries me."

I glared at Johannes. He stared back, unblinking, an almost bored expression on his face.

"So you're not just rude to me, but to your brother as well?"

"Would you excuse us?" I grabbed Johannes's arm and hauled him a few feet away. "What the fuck do you think you're doing?"

He arched a brow. "Talking. Is that against the law?"

I shook my head. "Stop being an asshole. She's Kiana's best friend."

"You don't say?" His lips curved, barely, then flattened. "Want a crack at her yourself, do you?"

"Hardly." I snorted. "I just don't want you behaving like a jerk, upsetting her, and ruining Ash's wedding because the maid of honor is crying into her soup."

Johannes arched an eyebrow. "I thought the appetizer was salmon?"

I huffed through my nose. "Just stay away from her. Go play with someone else."

"There isn't anyone else that interests me. She's fun."

"You're not interested in fun. You're interested in destruction."

"Y'know, Penn," Johannes said, smoothing the lapels on my jacket, "it's been a minute since we spent any kind of time together, so don't pretend that you know me. We live on opposite sides of the country and have done so for years. You think you've got me all figured out, but you don't." He moved closer until our foreheads almost touched. "If I want to make a play for Gia, I will. You already said you're not interested, so what's the fucking problem? She's gorgeous, and I'm bored."

"She's not your type."

He canted his head and ran his tongue along the underside of his top teeth. "Here's a piece of brotherly advice. Stop lying to yourself. If you want her, go get her... before someone else does."

He took off upstairs. Fucking asshole. I wasn't interested in Gia. I just didn't want her to make a mistake with Johannes that she would regret. Ash always said that Johannes liked to play with his food, and I intended to make sure Gia didn't become tonight's filet mignon.

"Who the fuck do you think you are?"

I jumped, so deep in my head that I hadn't seen Gia appear beside me. I gripped her elbow and steered her back to the bar, ordering her another glass of champagne.

"Stay away from Johannes." I thanked the bartender for the drink and handed it to Gia. "He's not the man for you to scratch an itch with, mainly because he doesn't scratch. He tears, he destroys, he ruins."

"Wow. Brotherly love indeed."

"I do love him, dearly, but he's got a lot of baggage

that he's dealing with, and trust me, you do not want to climb into that suitcase."

"Think I'm fitting these hips and this ass into a suitcase?" She ran her hands over her body and laughed.

Her response startled me. It was the first time she'd mentioned her body in a negative way or shown any kind of confidence issue. Gia wasn't a catwalk model; she was far more attractive than that. Her curves were the stuff of dreams.

I should know.

The dream I'd had about her last night was downright pornographic.

I blamed the humidity.

"Please don't denigrate yourself. You're stunning, from top to toe."

She gaped at me, then narrowed her eyes. "Why are you complimenting me? What have you done?"

I chuckled. "Nothing, other than save you from Johannes, which, trust me, you would thank me for if you knew him like I do."

Asher came down the stairs looking a little worse for wear with his tie askew and his hair mussed up. He spotted us and made his way over.

"You have the best best friend in the world."

He hugged Gia and gave her a sloppy kiss on the cheek, then hugged me.

"And I have the best brother and best best man in the world."

"And I have a drunk almost groom on my hands." I stood and helped him into a chair at a vacant table. "Maybe you should go check on the bride," I said to Gia.

"Good idea." She moved away, stopped, returned, and leaned down, murmuring in my ear, "This isn't over."

Pleasurable tingles raced over my skin. Whether it was due to the alcohol, the occasion, or seeing her with Johannes, something inside me changed. I watched her sashay up the stairs and disappear, then turned my attention to Ash.

"How about a glass of water?"

"S'all good." He clapped me on the arm. "Love is the best thing in the world, Penn."

"You know you've said the word 'best' about ten times."

"I have?" He rubbed his forehead. "Well. S'true," he slurred. "Love is the best. You should find someone, like I have. Settle down. It's the best."

Now wasn't the time to tell him that a long-term relationship and I weren't in the cards.

"One day," I murmured.

Ash made a grand gesture, waving his arms about, his face shining as if he'd discovered the cure for cancer. "What about Gia? She's perfect for you."

My eyes flew wide. Despite my inner musings a few moments ago, I went straight for denial. "Gia? Jesus Christ, bro. I thought you loved me."

"Ugh. Are you two still fighting?"

I grinned. Ash had said "ugh." He never said "ugh." Kiana sure had changed my brother, and I liked this new version of him.

"Make love, not war, Penn. That's my advice."

Yeah, he's definitely hammered.

"Let me get you that water." I asked the bartender for

two bottles and made Ash drink them both. As soon as he finished the second one, he announced that he needed to pee and weaved his way down the bus toward the onboard restrooms.

I headed back upstairs, mainly to make sure Johannes and Gia weren't cozying up to one another. They weren't. Johannes was talking to my cousin Nolen, who ran our casino business out in Vegas, and Gia was dancing with Kiana, arms overhead, hips encased in ivory satin, shimmying from side to side. I couldn't tear my gaze away from her. What was wrong with me? We'd done nothing but take chunks out of each other since I'd picked her up at her apartment building yesterday morning.

Although... that wasn't true. There'd been that moment on the plane when I'd realized flying scared her. Seeing a vulnerable side to her had made me look a little deeper. Gia was too much of everything. Too exuberant, too mouthy, too opinionated, too salty. But was that a kind of armor, a way of protecting herself, perhaps? Maybe Gianna Greene wasn't as tough a cookie as she liked to pretend.

She caught my eye and waved me over to join them. I shook my head no, striking up a conversation with another of my cousins, Kadon, who was based in St. Tropez, France, where he ran our beach club business, which operated throughout most of Europe. It was rare for our entire family to get together. It didn't surprise me, though, that everyone had carved out time in their calendars to make the trip to Grand Cayman. Ash was beloved by us all. He was that kind of man, one whom people gravitated toward.

Our tour of Grand Cayman on board the party bus came to an end, but as the bus arrived back at the hotel, Ash declared that the night was far from over and corralled us all inside to continue the festivities. We ended up by the wave pool, and the next thing I knew, music was playing, the hotel guests had been invited to join us, and what had begun as a smallish family gathering turned into a full-scale party. Just as well that we'd decided to have his bachelor party on Wednesday rather than Friday as Ash had suggested. He'd need three days to get over the hangover before the wedding on Saturday.

"How about a dance with the maid of honor?"

I turned to find Gia standing beside me. I hadn't even seen her approach.

"Kee tells me it's customary for the best man and maid of honor to have at least one dance."

"In which custom?" I drawled, but I took her hand anyway and let her lead me into the throng of guests, most of which were not part of my family.

She slipped her arms around my neck, and I captured her waist, pulling her into my body. She smelled delicious, of roses and lavender, and I dared to lower my face to her neck to savor more of the scent.

What's happening?

"Did you just smell my neck?"

Busted.

I lifted my head, giving her a wry grin. "I may have."

She blinked, licked her lips, and blinked again. "I liked it."

Warmth arrowed from my belly to my groin. Was Gia

flirting with me? And if she was, did I do anything about it?

Yes! an inner voice hollered.

"Y'know, Penn, I might be changing my mind about you."

I raised a brow. "Is that so?"

"Yes. Everyone I spoke to tonight had nothing but good things to say about you."

"They're my family. They have to say nice things."

"It's because they're family that I know that isn't true." She shook her head. "And you told me earlier not to denigrate myself, yet here you are, refusing to accept a genuine compliment."

"Coming from you, it surprised me. That's all."

"Touché." She trailed a fingertip down my cheek, then ran it over to my jaw. "I may owe you an apology or two."

"Just the two?"

She narrowed her eyes. "I'm not the only one at fault."

"Easy." I ran my nose down hers. "I'm teasing you. I like teasing you, in case you hadn't noticed. And, for the record, I both accept your apology and offer one or two of my own in return."

"God, Penn, is this a real truce?"

"I think it might be."

"Kee will faint."

"She's not alone on that score."

She smiled at me, and there wasn't a hint of acerbity in it. I pulled her closer, burrowing into her neck once more. Her curves were soft, a contrast to the hard planes of my body, and I melted into her. She made a contented sound, and then she cursed and pulled away.

"What's wrong?"

"Sorry. My phone's ringing." She rifled through her purse and put the handset to her ear. "Hello. Oh, hey, Mom. What's up?"

In less time than it took a bee to flap its wings, Gia's expression shifted from happy to concerned. She whirled away, striding through the horde of dancers. I darted after her, right into the hotel. She sank into a chair, speaking rapidly into her phone. I kept my distance, unwilling to crowd her while she took a personal call, but also worried, considering how fast she'd changed. Less than a minute later, she hung up, dropping her phone into her purse.

"Are you okay?"

She steepled her hands over her mouth, pulling on her lips. "No."

I sat on the chair next to hers and rested my hand on her shoulder. "Want to talk about it?"

"Not really." She breathed out heavily. "My brother isn't well, and I worry about him. That's all."

"Oh, I'm sorry to hear that." I didn't even know she had a brother. "I hope he gets better soon."

Her eyes filled with sadness, and she shook her head. Taking a deep breath, she squared her shoulders. "Enough being maudlin. This is a celebration." Shaking herself down as if blossoms had fallen from a tree and covered her clothing, she gave me a smile as false as her bravado and stood.

"Party time."

As she walked by me, I rose from the chair and caught her wrist. "Gia?"

She stopped, turned, and kept her eyes downcast, very unlike her. "What?"

I clipped her under the chin. Our eyes met.

"What?" she repeated, a husk to her tone that the upsetting phone call she'd received could have caused.

Time to find out.

I bent my head and kissed her.

Chapter 11

Gia

Sleeping with the enemy is a terrible idea.

PENN'S LIPS PRESSED AGAINST MINE, SOFTLY AT FIRST, THEN MORE demanding when he met no resistance. He was in complete control of the moment. In complete control of me.

What the hell am I doing?

Kissing Penn Kingcaid. That was what I was doing. Or more accurately, *he* was kissing *me*. And, oh God, it was *glorious*.

Pinpricks raced through my body, lightning-fast, setting off little sparks of electricity that fired between us. He didn't hold me or thrust his hands in my hair or cup my neck. Our lips were the only part of our bodies connecting us, and it was all we needed in that moment.

The sound of a glass shattering against the floor tiles broke us apart. I pressed two fingers to my lips, still feeling him there.

"You kissed me."

"I did." He smiled.

"You did," I repeated like an idiot.

"How did I do?"

I stared at his mouth, giving his question proper consideration. "Felt a little rushed."

"Is that so?" His eyes went to my mouth, too. "How about this?"

For the second time, Penn lowered his head and tasted me. He didn't hurry or slam his mouth to mine and devour me as if he hadn't eaten in a week. He slowly explored the shape of my lips, his tongue leisurely stroking mine as if he had all day.

Penn and I were a terrible idea. We didn't even like each other, our temporary truces lasting as long as a chocolate dome with hot caramel sauce poured over the top. But as my arms snaked around his neck and I pressed myself to him as if I needed his heart to keep mine beating, I accepted the dire truth: we had chemistry that was off the charts.

We broke apart again. Penn traced his thumb over my bottom lip, his breathing uneven, his dark hair rumpled.

I didn't even remember shoving my hands through it.

"This isn't a good idea."

I shook my head, adding, "No," for added emphasis.

"Your room or mine?"

"What about them?" I jerked my head toward the pool where the party was still in full swing.

"You want to go back?"

"No."

"Then don't worry about them."

He took my hand and headed for the bank of elevators. Exhilaration, mingled with a whisper of caution, sloshed about in my stomach, and I couldn't seem to catch a full breath, my lungs greedy for more than I could give them. Maybe it was the champagne or the joy on Kee's face as she'd danced with Asher on that bus.

Or maybe it was just Penn and the anticipation of what was to come.

The elevator doors closed with a swish, and Penn's kiss swept away my worries, my thoughts, until there was only this, me and him, in a steel box, making out as if we'd die otherwise. This decision to fuck felt as if it had come out of nowhere, and yet had all our arguments and personal ire toward each other just been the buildup to this moment?

The ding signaling our arrival broke us apart again. Penn's eyes were glassy, heavy with lust, and I'd bet mine were a mirror image. He linked our fingers and towed me right past my room to his.

"What's wrong with my room?" He'd given me a choice earlier, although I hadn't answered the question.

"I remembered how you left it, and fucking on top of every item of clothing you own isn't what I have in mind."

Oh, yeah. He had a point.

His room was equally luxurious, but far neater. If I didn't know better, I'd say this wasn't his room at all but a spare one he'd decided to use rather than sully his sheets with a one-night stand.

"You are impossibly neat."

"And you are impossibly chaotic."

"Incompatible," I muttered.

"Let's see, shall we?"

Penn's hands cupped my neck, his lips locking with mine, but this kiss felt different from the previous ones. This kiss was a promise. A promise of what exactly, I couldn't say, but the tingles running up and down my spine and the flood of warmth between my legs pleaded with me to find out.

He unzipped my dress and slid it off my shoulders. It fell to the floor, gathering in a heap at my feet. Penn stood back, his eyes roving over me.

Thank Christ I went with the matching underwear set.

I couldn't help wondering what he saw. I didn't have a clue about the kind of woman Penn usually went for, but rich, successful guys were often attracted to stick-thin catwalk-model types, all sticky-out ribs and bony hips. I wasn't ashamed of my curves, and I'd had no complaints so far, but I couldn't help a snap of trepidation nibbling at my insides.

Sure, I made jokes about my ample ass and big tits, but I liked the way I looked. What concerned me was how much it mattered that Penn liked the way I looked, too.

Why did I care?

This was a one-night hookup to scratch an itch that we'd both had for weeks. If he chose to call the whole thing off right now, then he'd have shown me the person he was inside–namely, the asshole I'd made up my mind about at our first meeting.

Except... except I did care.

And that bothered me most of all.

"Say something."

Ugh, Gia! Don't beg him for compliments, or worse, reassurance. Don't be that woman.

"I can't."

I swallowed, risking another question. "Why?"

"Because I'd rather let my actions speak for me." He gripped the front of my bra and pulled me to him. Our lips mashed together, and his hands... God, his hands were all over me, caressing, pinching, exploring. My bra came off. My panties ended up around my knees, and Penn, still fully clothed in a suit and tie, knelt down at my feet.

"You're bare."

I nodded. "I don't like all that hair. Gets in the way."

"Fuck, Gia, there's no bigger turn-on than a confident woman, and you... Jesus Christ, you..."

His thought remained unfinished, but I got the picture when he traced my pussy lips with the tip of his tongue. I closed my eyes and, using his shoulders for balance, let the sensations carry me away on a blissful journey.

I loved sex.

I loved sex more than I loved cooking, and that was saying a lot. I'd had my fair share of frogs that hadn't turned into princes, but I'd also had mind-blowing experiences that I remembered to this day. Yet, with every sweep of his tongue, every caress at the backs of my knees, every nibble on my clit, Penn Kingcaid erased those experiences, one by one.

He lifted my foot and slipped off my panties, pushing

on the insides of my thighs. I widened my stance. He growled in approval, the vibrations sending violent tremors through me.

"Get on the bed. I need more."

Under normal circumstances, Penn ordering me about would result in a sharp bite of reprisal. This time, it called to a primal part of me that basked in his authority.

I did as he asked, propping myself up against a stack of plump pillows. Penn crawled after me. As he leaned over me, his tie brushed my stomach. I reached up and removed it, wrapping it around my wrists in a makeshift restraint. I lifted my arms overhead and parted my thighs.

"Let's see what you've got, Kingcaid."

His eyes widened and then closed. "You're fucking perfect," he murmured, and I preened under his praise.

I was pretty darned good at holding off my orgasm—thank you, dear vibrator—but as Penn licked and bit and petted and pinched my clit, the familiar swell in my stomach arrived far too soon. I arched my back, pushed my pussy into his face, and let my body take over.

By the time the multiple aftershocks had ebbed, I'd concluded that Penn Kingcaid gave amazing fucking head. I opened my eyes and drew in a sharp breath. While ecstasy had engulfed me, Penn had undressed faster than if his suit had caught fire.

And, oh my goodness, the worm comment I'd made at his grandmother's house couldn't be further from the truth.

Thank God.

Yup, the man was packing. Long, thick, veiny, a big crown already weeping.

My pussy pulsed in expectation, and I almost purred.

"Do you have a condom?"

If he said no now, I'd either kill him or break my cardinal rule and allow him to go bareback.

"I have several." He reached into his nightstand drawer and tossed a box at me. "Put one on me."

"You're bossy."

"And you fucking love it." He held up a hand as I opened my mouth to deny the truth. "I can read you well enough, Gia. Now shut your mouth unless you're asking me to put my cock in it, and get a condom out of the box."

A dirty mouth always got my engines fired up.

"Maybe later." I grinned as I tore through the packet with my teeth and removed the condom. Pinching the end, I rolled it onto his erection.

"There's no maybe about it." He crawled onto the bed. "Turn over."

I rolled onto my stomach. Penn gripped both my hips and pulled me up onto my knees, spreading me nice and wide for him. A low groan vibrated in his throat.

"Damn, that's a fine ass."

He slapped my right butt cheek, lined up his cock, and thrust forward.

I twisted to look over my shoulder. The sight of Penn, all hard, taut muscles and fierce concentration, stole the air from my lungs. He might irk the hell out of me most of the time, but like this, eyes hooded with desire, hips powering into me, I forgot about our spiky relationship. Lowering my chest to the mattress, ass stuck up in the air, I closed my eyes and savored every stroke of his cock.

God, I'd missed sex, too busy at work and too tired

after a long shift to bother, turning to my trusty array of vibrators to soothe the ache. But nothing, *nothing,* beat the feel of a man's cock inside me.

Penn didn't let up for a second, working me from the inside, caressing every inch of my body. He leaned over me, kissing my neck, my shoulder, rubbing my clit with blunt fingers, bringing me to the edge. Right when I crested, he stopped, and my orgasm retreated.

"You fucker," I muttered into the pillow.

He chuckled. "You'll come when I say you can."

"Don't push me, Kingcaid. I have fingers I can use."

"Touch yourself and I'll tie you up."

I growled, but the truth was that his control over my orgasm turned me on. Most of the guys I'd slept with had enjoyed the fact that I liked to top. Perhaps I'd chosen them for that reason, a primitive instinct that attracted me to men who happily acceded to my authority. Penn was a very different prospect, and I couldn't get enough.

He slowed his thrusts, building me back up with a mastery over the female body I'd never have thought him capable of. Penn Kingcaid had an ego the size of Jupiter, and in my experience, men like that often thought only of their own pleasure rather than that of their partner. But Penn was different, and as much as it pained me to admit it, there was a slim chance I'd been wrong about him.

He brought me to the cusp of climax on three more occasions, retreating each time.

On the third occasion, I screamed in frustration.

"Let me come!"

"Temper, temper, Miss Greene."

He pressed tiny kisses along the back of my neck.

Goose bumps erupted with every touch of his lips. He cupped my breasts, playing with my nipples while continuing the slow, torturous surge of his hips.

"Penn," I moaned. "Please." I fisted the sheets.

"I do like it when you beg." He kept to the same pace.

"I hate you."

"That may be, but your body *loves* me."

I couldn't deny it, much as I'd love to. Too bad for Penn that I had a few tricks up my sleeve. I squeezed my muscles as tight as I could, clamping around his cock.

And then I began to pulse.

"Jesus," he hissed. "Fuck."

I increased the pace of the pulses and reached between my legs to cup his balls. I squeezed. He groaned, his thrusts wilder now, less controlled.

"If you come before you've let me come, I will fucking kill you."

"You witch."

"You'd better believe it, Kingcaid."

He strummed my clit, and I tumbled into a climax so strong I almost blacked out. Penn let out a cry, coming seconds after me.

I collapsed to the mattress, my knees and elbows aching from being in this position for far longer than I'd expected. Penn came with me, heavy and sweaty and goddamn perfect. He pulled out, and I immediately missed him.

Correction. I miss his wizard cock. Not him. This was still the same man who'd pulled my strings and driven me mad ever since we'd bumped into each other on that street weeks ago.

The mattress depressed beside me, the sound of Penn's rapid breathing slowing along with mine. I remained on my front, too tired to move.

"Take the condom off of me."

I cracked open one eye. "Good try, Kingcaid."

He grinned. "So you'll only accept me bossing you while we're fucking." He nodded. "Good to know."

Removing the condom, he padded across the stylish wooden flooring to the bathroom. I tracked him the entire way. I hadn't gotten to appreciate him fully before, but, dear God, the man was an Adonis, a thought that if it ever spilled from my lips, I'd cut out my own tongue. Defined back muscles rippled with every step, and his firm butt should be illegal. Hell, the man even had great legs, all solid hamstrings and well-defined calves.

As he returned, I checked out the view from the front. Yup, equally delicious. Taut chest, abs for days, strong arms that could hold a woman up while he pounded her against a wall.

I had to work hard not to let the appreciation show on my face. Buzzed from champagne and orgasms, I might say something I'd lament later.

He stretched out beside me, propped up on his elbow, tracing the curve of my waist with a finger.

"Will you regret this tomorrow?"

"Probably."

He smirked, then rolled onto his back. Taking his cock in his hand, he fisted it. My gaze shifted to watch him leisurely masturbate. He must've seen a spark of interest in my eyes because he curved a hand around the back of my neck and licked his lips.

"Do you suck as well as you fuck?"

I arched a brow. "Are you always this crass?"

"Yes," he deadpanned. "Problem?"

"Not at all." I lowered my head to his groin. "Just remember, you've met your match."

Chapter 12

Gia

Morning-afters are the worst.

You know what they say about examining your actions in the cold light of day? Well, this morning wasn't cold. It was glacial.

What the hell have I done?

Fucking Penn Kingcaid had been a huge mistake, and one I'd never, ever repeat. I didn't have regrets, per se. They were pretty pointless, after all, unless I found a way to turn back time. But what I could do was remember this moment and how I felt lying beside a sleeping Penn King-caid—confused, vulnerable, and, worst of all, content—and vow never to let myself feel like this again.

I put my momentary lapse in "sleeping with the enemy" down to a mixture of too much alcohol, not enough sex, the fact that my best friend had met the love of her life, and the ill-timed call from Mom to tell me that Roberto had suffered an episode. If just one of those things had been absent, I wouldn't have lowered my guard to have sex—albeit amazing, incredible, earth-shattering sex —with the man softly snoring beside me.

Yeah, exactly. I should cut myself a break. Weddings had a tendency to create false feelings. I mean, sure, we'd connected physically, but he was still Penn Kingcaid, jerk extraordinaire and pain in my ass. He'd said some nice things yesterday, but I now knew that was only because he'd wanted to get into my panties. Today, the real Penn would make a blinding comeback, and I didn't plan to stick around to witness it.

Easing the covers to one side, I lowered my feet to the floor, glancing over my shoulder to make sure he hadn't awoken. All clear. On the balls of my feet, I tiptoed around the room, gathering my clothes. I put my dress on, leaving the zipper open at the back, and slipped out the door, making a mad dash to my suite. I expelled a sigh of relief as I locked the door. Dropping my shoes on the floor, I collapsed onto the bed, right on top of my entire wardrobe.

You complete idiot.

I let myself wallow for five minutes, then took a shower, cleaned my teeth, and dug through the piles of clothes until I found a pair of shorts and a T-shirt printed with *Hotter than your ex, better than your next* that I'd bought from Etsy.

I wandered out onto the deck. Despite the early hour, the sun beat down, glistening off the sea. People were already lounging by the pool and on the beach, and today,

I intended to join them. My sole job was to stay out of Penn's way until Saturday at the wedding.

My stomach growled. I thought about ordering room service but chose instead to duck down to the hotel restaurant. I ordered pancakes with fruit and syrup and a coffee and put in a call to Mom to check on Roberto. Relief swamped me when she said he'd had a good night and apologized for calling yesterday.

"I shouldn't have worried you, especially since you're supposed to be enjoying yourself at Kiana's wedding."

Kee had invited my parents and Roberto to her wedding, but Roberto didn't travel well, and we'd all decided it'd be better if I came alone.

"It's fine, Mom. I'd rather know if he's having an episode, not that I can do anything about it."

My brother had sustained brain damage at birth, which, as he grew, manifested itself in violent mood swings, splitting headaches, an inability to concentrate for long periods, and learning difficulties. But he was also loving and kind and fucking wonderful, and I adored him.

"Even so, I should have waited until you'd gotten home." I heard a door close and the drip of a coffee machine. "So tell me, are you having a good time?"

"Yeah, I am. We had the bachelor-slash-bachelorette party last night, and Kee looked so happy, Mom. Asher Kingcaid had better know what he's got."

"I'm sure he does. Don't suppose you'd like to snag a billionaire while you're there, Gia?" Mom chuckled. "I mean, with so many of them congregating in one place, it has to increase your chances."

If only she knew...

"Not my type, Mom. They're nice and all, but, sorry, you'll have to put off buying that house in the Hamptons for a while longer."

"Darn it." She laughed again.

"Mom, I've got to go. My breakfast just arrived. Kiss Roberto for me and say hi to Dad."

"Will do. Have a great time, darling."

She hung up, and a pang of homesickness twanged my heartstrings. I dug into my pancakes. Okay, now I felt better. Talk about melt on your tongue, although they weren't quite as good as the ones I made.

My phone rang. I swallowed quickly and answered it without looking at the caller ID.

"Hello."

"Where did you get to last night?"

Damn. Kee. "Morning! How's the hangover?"

"I'm fine. Asher, on the other hand, is still in recovery."

"He did seem on the tipsy side."

I was being kind. Asher was *hammered* the last time I saw him. Didn't think he had it in him to let go to that extent. Another plus in a column filled with pluses. Unlike Penn, although I should add "sex god" to his column.

Note to self: *Never* share that list of positives and negatives with *anyone*.

"He'll be fine. Listen, what plans did you have for today?"

"Um... sitting by the pool and reading a book."

"So no plans, then?"

"They're plans."

"Gia, you never sit on your own and read a book. Anyway, I have a much better idea."

"I thought you'd be too busy with wedding stuff."

"It's pretty much there."

"Or too busy with Asher."

She giggled, and I could imagine her blushing. "Plenty of time for that on the honeymoon."

"Go on, then. I'll bite. What's the idea?"

"Asher decided to hire a yacht. We're going to go out sailing around the island, maybe do a bit of snorkeling. What do you think?"

Sounded idyllic, except for one small problem.

"Just the three of us, or is Asher bringing the family?"

For "family," read: Penn. I wouldn't mind if any of the others came, including Johannes, whom, even though Kee had told me was an asshole and Penn had vehemently warned me off, I found rather charming, in a broody, don't-mess-with-me kind of way.

"He wasn't planning to. Why, did you want to invite anyone?"

"No," I said quickly. Too quick. I dialed back. "It'll be nice for me to spend some time with you before you're whisked into the Kingcaid family never to be heard from again."

"As if. You are such a drama llama."

"Guilty as charged. You wouldn't have me any other way."

"True story."

I suppressed a grin. Kee had picked that up from Asher. Already they were morphing into each other, like soul mates should.

"Where do I need to be and by when?"

"The marina in an hour? Or we can come to the hotel and pick you up."

"No need." The marina was two minutes from the hotel. "I'll see you then."

I finished my breakfast and headed back up to my room to change and pack a bag of stuff I'd need. I felt like a criminal sneaking down the hallway, eyes peeled wide for Penn and ready to dive into the cleaner's closet if he appeared. Or out the window. Either worked. I wasn't usually so skittish at the idea of bumping into my one-night stand the morning after, and I hadn't yet worked out why I was acting out of character this morning, but what I did know was that I lacked the energy or the enthusiasm to spar with Penn today. Therefore, avoid, avoid, avoid was by far the best strategy.

I reached my room without incident. Grabbing a beach bag, I packed a book, a sun hat, factor fifty sunscreen, my aviators, and lip balm. I wore my swimsuit underneath a flowing sundress, and after gathering my clothes into a heap and stuffing them in the closet—I'd hang them up later—I strolled down to the marina.

Yachts of all shapes and sizes gleamed underneath the bright sun. I hadn't a clue what kind of yacht Asher had hired, but when I spied Kee waving madly from the deck of a massive cruiser, I shouldn't have been surprised. A billionaire would hardly hire a dinghy. She skipped down the gangplank and dashed toward me, wrapping me up in a hug.

"You should see this yacht," she gushed. "It's *incredible*. I've hardly had a chance to explore yet, but what I have seen is jaw-dropping."

"Welcome to the world of the super-rich." I nudged her playfully. "You're swimming in different waters now."

"And as my best friend, so are you."

She took my hand and led me up the gangplank and onto the main deck. And that was the moment I regretted ever saying yes to this trip.

"Hey." Penn lounged on a white leather bench that ran across the back of the boat. The stern? Who knew? His lips formed a smile, but his eyes burned with either irritation or desire for vengeance.

Uh-oh.

"Morning." I kept my voice even. "Thought it was just us," I whispered to Kee, low enough that Penn couldn't hear.

"It was. He just turned up." Kee narrowed her eyes. "I thought you two had put your differences behind you."

"We have," Penn said.

I jumped. He'd moved off the bench and come to stand beside me. He had the audacity to slip an arm around my waist. When I tried to wriggle free, he pinched my hip. Hard.

"We finally put our differences to bed last night, didn't we, sweetcheeks?"

I widened my eyes at him, my message clear: shut your fucking mouth. The last thing I wanted was for Kee to find out where I'd gone last night. I'd avoided the question when she'd asked me earlier, and I intended to keep it that way.

I slipped my arm through Kee's, this time successfully dislodging Penn. "So, are you going to show me around or what?"

"Absolutely." As she led me away, Penn's gaze scored the back of my head. Great. What I'd hoped would be a day to relax, eat, drink, and catch the rays while sailing the Caribbean would now end up a strategy session for how to (a) avoid Penn—tricky—and (b) stop him from running his mouth about our marathon sex session.

The yacht was over-the-top luxurious, all teak boards, polished rosewood, and gleaming brass, and beyond anything I'd ever thought I'd get to see, let alone spend an entire day aboard. It had it all. Bedrooms, bathrooms, an enormous sunken living and dining room, a large kitchen. It even had a swimming pool on the top deck.

"Ash wants to buy it," Kee whispered, giving me a nudge. "He already has a yacht that he keeps in Seattle, but he's fallen in love with this one. I told him one yacht is more than enough for any man, but I don't think he plans to listen to me."

"Let the man part from his money if he wishes. It's not like he'll have to rein in on buying food or heating his apartment anytime soon, is it?"

Worry pulled Kee's eyes tight. "I still haven't gotten used to it. The wealth, I mean. It's the one thing that truly separates Ash and me. In every other way, we're so compatible, but when it comes to money, I'm not sure I'll ever understand that ease with which he looks at the world."

"I hear you." I put my arms around her and squeezed. "This is all very new, but you will grow accustomed to it. Just do me a huge favor?"

"What?"

"Don't let it change you."

"With you as my best friend?" Kee snorted.

I grinned. "That, dear beautiful, is a very good point."

We headed back to the lower deck, where Penn and Asher were deep in discussion. My stomach pulled tight as he eyed me over Asher's left shoulder, his stare flat. Fuck. Maybe I'd hurt his feelings by sneaking out like that. I immediately discarded the idea. When it came to relationships, Penn was the male version of me. One-night stands were his bread and butter. He might go back for a second bite of the cherry, but by the third nibble, his appetite waned and he moved on to the next delightful morsel.

Screw Penn. I refused to allow him to ruin my day, to spoil my fun. I was on an incredible yacht in the middle of paradise, and I intended to make the most of it. I'd bet he'd left many a woman in bed, sneaking out in the middle of the night. If he'd stayed at all. The only difference was I'd been the one to steal back to my room without waking him, and his ego was feeling all bashed up.

I'd one-upped Penn Kingcaid, and I gotta say, I was feeling pretty smug about it.

Chapter 13

Penn

She's in love with someone else? Fuck!

My dick throbbed as Gia tugged her sundress over her head, revealing a one-piece swimsuit cut high at the thigh and showing off her magnificent rack. She laughed at something Kiana said, throwing her head back and exposing her beautiful neck. I hated the fact that I found her attractive, but what I hated far more was the feeling of emptiness that had spread through my chest when I'd woken to find her gone.

Did she regret last night?

Or had it meant so little to her that she'd brushed it off as meaningless?

A feeling of being used trickled through my veins, dropping little anxiety bombs along the way. I'd had this notion of waking up, curling into her lush body, and burying myself in her heat all fucking day, and she'd destroyed that dream by leaving me with a cold mattress and a loud "Fuck you."

Sorry, sweetcheeks, but if you think you're getting away with that, you're sorely mistaken.

Sauntering over, I tossed a towel on the vacant sunbed next to hers and flopped onto it. Linking my arms behind my head, I gazed up at the vibrant blue sky, then turned in her direction.

"How was last night for you, Gia?"

She stiffened, hiding her discomfort by rustling through her beach bag and withdrawing an enormous wide-brimmed sun hat. She put it on. It hid half her face, which, I guessed, was the idea.

"The party bus was great."

"It was," I said agreeably.

"The best," Kiana chipped in. "I'd have hated some fancy-pants do. You guys nailed it."

"Yeah. Gia and I make quite the team. Perfect bedfellows, you might say."

She sucked in a sharp breath. I beamed.

"At least you're no longer arguing," Ash said as he took the sunbed on Kiana's side.

"We decided to make love, not war, right, Gia?"

Her entire body froze. She opened her mouth, then shut it.

I paused for effect. "In the nonsexual sense, I mean," I eventually added. "Imagine the bloodbath if we rolled into bed."

"I wondered for a second there whether you had

something to tell us." Kiana nudged Gia. "I mean, you did go missing last night."

"Mom called." Gia almost fell over the words. "Roberto had an episode. I didn't feel like partying after that."

Episode? She'd said her brother was unwell, which I'd taken to mean he had the flu or a stomach bug or something. What did she mean by "an episode"?

"Oh, no." Kiana sat up, crossing her legs on the sunbed. "Gia, why didn't you say? Is he okay?"

"Yeah. He's fine. I spoke with Mom this morning, and it's all good." She brandished a hand in the air. "Can we change the subject?"

"Of course."

I read Kiana's pinched expression as that she knew exactly what Gia had meant by "an episode," but if I mined for information, I doubted Kiana would tell me. Her loyalty, quite rightly, lay with her friend, but whatever it was, it caused Gia pain.

Maybe she'd left my bed this morning to call her mom, and I'd jumped to conclusions. Then again, she hadn't looked happy to see me on the yacht when she'd boarded, so there was that. Goddammit, I needed to talk to her. Alone. Not that I was likely to get a chance on the yacht. I'd have to catch up with her at the hotel.

"Hey, Gia," Kiana said. "Did you see the interview with the love of your life in *Vanity Fair*?"

I sat up straighter. *Love of her life?* She couldn't be that in love with him if she'd spent the night fucking me.

"Who's this?" I asked, straining to keep my voice on the right side of disinterested.

Gia groaned. Kiana laughed. "Didn't Gia tell you? She's saving herself for Christian Bale."

Saving herself? I begged to differ.

"Not sexually," Kiana continued, by all accounts getting into the swing of bringing the most amount of embarrassment down on her friend's head. "Relationship-wise. Gia is certain he'll come knocking one day and declare his undying love."

"You are a bitch," Gia said, tugging her hat lower over her eyes. "And Christian Bale is the epitome of the perfect man." She turned to me and lifted the brim. "They're in short supply."

Ouch.

Not sure what I'd done to deserve that. A nibble of self-doubt came at me again, and I didn't fucking like it. Before Gia, I'd had no complaints.

"Isn't he, like, twice your age?"

"So?" Gia shrugged. "Age is just a number."

"And happily married?"

"I admit, that is a challenge."

I laughed. Despite my indignation at how she'd ended our night together, Gia continued to enchant me on so many levels. This trip had opened my eyes. She was a complex woman with many layers, and after last night, I'd like the opportunity to peel back a few more. Funny how spending time with someone often kicked up a raft of surprises, and you found that what you thought you knew was, in fact, erroneous.

"So tell me, if Christian Bale turned up here, right now, what would you do?"

"With or without a wedding ring?"

"With."

She pursed her lips. "I would ask for a photo that I could keep beside my bed and pretend it was taken on our honeymoon."

I suppressed another chuckle. "And without?"

"That's easy." She sipped from a bottle of water. "I'd tell you three to fuck off, and then I'd nail him right here on the deck until his dick fell off."

Asher almost choked on his iced water, Kiana threw back her head and laughed at a decibel level loud enough to scare the birds flying overhead, and I... I burned with jealousy. What a ridiculous notion that was. To feel jealous about a situation that would never occur set off alarm bells in my head.

"Not into voyeurism, then?" I sounded as if I had barbed wire in my throat. Fortunately for me, no one seemed to notice.

"Depends." She hitched a shoulder.

"Our Gia isn't afraid to explore, are you?" Kiana winked at her friend.

"Life's for living, I say. Lots of fish out there that require catching, sampling, and then tossing back into the sea."

"While you wait for Christian Bale?" Fire scorched my chest. I covered up the discomfort with an arched brow.

"Precisely." She tugged the brim of her hat low, cutting off her eyes from me, and delved back into her bag to retrieve a book. "Now shush." She opened it. "I'm just getting to the good bit."

"Suit yourself."

I climbed off the lounger and wandered to the bow,

where I could soothe an ache I didn't understand in private. Last night with Gia had blown my mind. No, more than that. It had shifted something inside me that I'd have preferred to stay in its former position. I'd assumed I didn't like Gia, but talk about lying to oneself. I liked her. Too fucking much. Smart mouth and all.

God, her mouth. Especially her mouth.

My groin heated, memories from last night giving me a hard-on. Gia gave head like a woman truly in her element. I'd never had a blow job quite like the one she'd given me, and my dick—and I—was chomping at the bit for round two. A dream that Gia had crushed by her fast exit this morning and her clear messaging since she'd boarded the yacht that she wasn't interested in another taste.

It felt strange to be on the other side of the coin, as it were, and I didn't like it. Talk about being taught a painful lesson that I hadn't asked for, but that I'd taught to plenty of other people. Leaving a woman's bed long before dawn broke was a specialty of mine. In my defense, I'd never lied to a single one. They'd all known it was a one-time thing before we'd set foot over the threshold.

"You okay?" Ash sidled up next to me and handed over a bottle of beer.

I took it from him, nodding. "All good."

"Sure?"

A confession raced to the tip of my tongue, and I almost spilled it, swallowing the words at the crucial moment. Ash would tell Kiana, and Kiana would confront Gia, and I'd have created a fucking mess that I didn't relish cleaning up. Also, the way Gia had clutched at the arms of her sun lounger had made it clear she wanted to keep what had happened between us private, and as much as I enjoyed teasing her, I'd never set out to purposely hurt her.

"Yeah, just tired." I touched the neck of my bottle to his. "Thought you'd have seen enough alcohol last night to last you a week."

Ash chuckled. "I'll only ever have one bachelor party. Might as well make the most of it."

"Kiana's definitely The One, then, huh?"

"Yeah. She's The One."

"What's that like?"

He ran a hand over his close-cut beard. "As close to heaven as a man can get. I highly recommend it."

I snorted. "Not for me."

But was that true? Looking at Ash and seeing the shine to his eyes, the way he tracked Kiana every time she moved, the little touches and secret conversations—it pulled at my gut.

Then I thought about Theo and Sandrine, and my hand tightened around the beer bottle. I forced myself to relax before the damn thing shattered.

Nope. A serious relationship wasn't a part of my future.

Ash stared out to sea. "Y'know, when I brought Kiana here to introduce her to Gran and Granddad, we were out exploring and we stumbled upon this gorgeous little church. Kiana half joked that she'd love to get married there rather than at the huge event Gran has organized, but when I suggested that we could, she backtracked, saying she'd never do that to her family, or mine. But I can't help thinking about the look on her face that day and wishing things were different."

"They can be. You can get married wherever and however you want."

He shook his head. "No, we can't."

His wistful tone got the cogs in my brain spinning. "What did it look like? The church, I mean."

"Tiny place with whitewashed walls and a gray tiled roof, and a pretty stained-glass window behind the altar. It'd probably seat fifteen or so with standing room for a few more. Why?"

"Just curious. Sounds cute."

"Yeah. It was." He drained his beer. "Want another?"

"Sure. I'll join you shortly."

I waited until he'd gone, then got on my phone. In five minutes, I'd found the church and the name of the minister. I fired off an email, then returned to the main deck. If I was to pull this off, then I needed help.

"Hey, Gia, got a minute?"

She laid her book in her lap and shielded her eyes. "For you, Penn? No."

I chuckled. Kiana gave her a dig.

"Gia!"

"Fine." She huffed, closed her book, and dropped it into her bag. "But your timing sucks. The baddie just killed victim number five."

"Wouldn't have thought thrillers were your thing."

She peered at me through narrowed eyes. "You don't know me well enough to judge my 'things,' Penn."

Ouch. Again. I scuffed a hand over my jaw.

"True."

I made my way into the sunken living room, glad for the cool air. I dismissed the steward and grabbed a couple of bottles of water from the bar, handing one to Gia. I gestured to the couch.

"If this is about this morning, I'd rather—"

"It isn't."

She appeared startled, her head jerking back. "Oh." And then her entire body relaxed, and I realized she'd been on edge waiting for me to call her out on the way she'd left things between us. *Hmm. Interesting.* That conversation would happen, but I'd make sure it occurred at a more appropriate time. If I pressed for answers now, I'd push her further away. Besides, I had more urgent things to discuss.

"Has Kiana ever mentioned a church on the island to you? One she found the last time she and Ash visited?"

She frowned. "No. Why?"

I broke into a smile at the opportunity to bond. Gia adored her friend, and she'd do anything for her.

"How do you feel about ruining their wedding plans?"

Chapter 14

Gia

This is the best wedding EVER!

Kee strode through the hotel lobby in a flowing white sundress and glanced around. I held up a hand in greeting, and she hurried over.

"What's up? Your text said it was urgent."

"I have a surprise for you. Call it a pre-wedding gift."

"Gia." Kee sighed. "Tomorrow is my wedding day. I've finally ticked everything off of Ash's grandmother's list, and I'd planned to enjoy a nap."

"It's three thirty in the afternoon, old lady."

"I know, but I'm exhausted and panicking about tomorrow, and I didn't sleep well last night."

"Hmm, I thought you looked a bit peaked at lunch."

She squinted, looking me up and down. "Why are you dressed so smart?"

I glanced down at the turquoise, calf-length floaty dress I'd chosen, purchased right here in the hotel at Penn's insistence—and on his dime—and then shrugged.

"I spend my life in chef's whites, Kee. Sometimes it's nice to dress up a bit. Now come on, or we'll be late."

I gripped her elbow and propelled her toward the front of the hotel where Penn had arranged a car to take us to the church. All I had to do, he'd said, was get Kee there on time. He must've repeated "on time" on at least twenty occasions. In the end, I'd told him to shut the fuck up or he could figure out a way to get Kee to the church without her suspecting anything.

On spying the limo, she beamed. "Oh, please tell me it's a spa day. I'd love a hot stone massage."

"Kinda," I lied. "Now shut up and get in or you'll ruin the surprise."

I waited for her to climb in and tapped Send on the pre-written text informing Penn we were on our way. According to the message I'd received from him late last night, every single member of his family—including his fearsome grandmother—and Kiana's mom and dad and brothers had gotten on board with the plan. If even one of them had objected, then that would've been it. Over. Kaput. Finished.

My phone buzzed, the message showing on a banner across the screen.

Penn: We're all here. Ash didn't punch me.

I suppressed a giggle. Penn had worried that Asher would refuse to go through with the wedding before the wedding, so to speak, but Penn must have assured him that the families were thrilled and excited and completely on their side.

The driver nosed the car through the hotel gates and onto the main road, if a two-lane road counted as a main anything. The church wasn't far, and the closer we got to our final destination, the more I plucked at my dress with trembling fingers. What if we'd misinterpreted her wishes and she threw a hissy fit? Not that Kee was the type to do that—hissy fits were more my territory—but we had kind of hijacked her special day, assuming she still felt the same as she had when she'd told Asher she'd love to marry at this church.

"You're jumpy." Kee gave me one of her all-seeing looks. "What's going on?"

I took her hand and laid it in my lap, patting the back of it. "Relax. It's all good."

"Relax? You should take your own advice, Gia. Your legs haven't stopped twitching since we got in the car."

I glimpsed the church through the windshield. Any minute now, we'd stop, and Kee would see what I saw. My mouth went dry, and I had an urge to call Penn and ask him to reassure me that we'd done the right thing. Not that I could.

"Okay, that's it. What's going on?"

At that precise moment, the car rolled to a stop. Kee looked through the side window at the quaint old building with its scuffed whitewashed walls and ancient door. Her jaw unhinged.

"What... what's this?"

I took her hands in mine, squeezing tight. "Asher told Penn about your visit here, and Penn spoke with close family members, and they all agreed, Kee, that you should have the wedding *you* want. They're all in there. Your mom and dad and your brothers, Asher's parents and grandparents, his brothers and cousins. But that's it. Family only. No standing on ceremony, wondering if you'll trip up the aisle in front of five hundred strangers. Just you and Ash and those who love you both so much. Although..." I grimaced. "You still have to go to the big event tomorrow. I think the minister is going to perform some kind of blessing or ritual. Whatever. Something that satisfies the stuffed shirts."

"Oh God." Kee clutched the thin gold chain around her neck and scissored the pendant back and forth. "And... they're not mad?" she whispered.

"Who?"

"His gran, his parents."

"No, Kee. They aren't mad. They're happy you're having the day you want." I opened the door. "Ready to marry Asher?"

Kee's eyes filled with tears, and she made this noise at the back of her throat, halfway between a sob and a laugh.

"You took a risk."

I shrugged, grinning. "You know me, Kee."

"Yes, I do. And I love you." She hugged me.

Emerging into the brilliant sunshine, I squinted. Should've worn shades, although that would look weird as I trailed behind Kee up the aisle. I brushed a hand over her dress, straightening out the creases. Asher's gran must be a master of deceit to have persuaded Kee to wear a dress that, while not the silk number that had cost thousands of dollars, suited the Kee I'd grown up with far more.

"You look beautiful."

"So do you. And now the dress makes sense." She nudged me. "You are too good a liar."

"It's a skill."

We giggled as we made our way to the church. Kee took a deep breath and then nodded for me to open the door.

Flowers filled the old building, lined along the sides and covering the altar. So many flowers, the sweet smell invading my nostrils. Penn must've done this, although I had no idea when he could have found the time. The man was a genius, in and out of the bedroom.

Music began, and the congregation stood in preparation for the bride. Penn had arranged for an organist to play, too? My heart warmed toward the man who'd pushed every one of my buttons from the second we'd met. The whole event was perfect and thoughtful and made me second-guess myself. I'd thought Penn was self-centered and egocentric. And he was. But what he'd done here, for his brother and for my best friend, showed a different side of him.

Kee's dad hurried down the aisle with the goofiest grin on his face, ready to give her away. My gaze drifted past Owen to Penn. Our eyes met, and he dipped his chin and smiled. Everything south of my waist tensed, and my belly fluttered. *Butterflies?* I didn't get butterflies, yet there they were, flapping their wings against my insides.

It's just the occasion. That's all.

And gratitude, maybe, for the work he'd put into this.

He'd taken the lion's share of the effort required, and he'd pulled it off with panache.

I tried to concentrate on the ceremony, but my eyes kept drifting to Penn. The man looked fucking sexy in a suit. That was for sure. Whether he sensed me staring or he was just taking a mental picture, our eyes locked at the precise moment Kee said "I do." Penn licked his bottom lip and ran his gaze over me. I had enough experience to recognize appreciation and lust, and Penn's eyes blazed with both. I couldn't help but wonder if he saw the same in mine.

We hadn't spoken about my early morning exit the night after we'd slept together, and while my first instinct had been to run as far away from this man as possible, right now all I wanted to do was strip him out of his suit and scratch an itch that wouldn't quit.

The minister pronounced Asher and Kee husband and wife, and as they kissed and the congregation applauded, I sought out Penn once more. He cocked his head, indicating I should move beside him as Asher and Kee began their walk down the aisle as a married couple. Me being me, I cocked my head at him and pointed at the floor. Penn's grin lit up every nerve ending, and those damn butterflies went nuts. He joined me, sticking out an elbow.

"We did good, Gia."

I slipped my hand through his arm, basking in the joy of this moment. Of my best friend getting married. Of Penn and me taking a huge risk and having it pay off. Of the happiness on the faces of family members. But most of all, I basked in the strange yet wonderful feelings caused by this man beside me. In a single minute, Penn could make me feel frustrated, enraged, elated, and sexy. I'd never met a man like him.

And I would *never* tell him such a thing. God, imagine the smugness. It'd smother me.

I smiled up at him. "Yeah, I think we did."

K

The Kingcaids and the Dohertys—and little old me—gathered back at grandma's house, where she'd laid out a sumptuous buffet. Tomorrow's shindig would dwarf this one, but it'd never be as special. Kee must've hugged me twenty times in the last half an hour, thanking me profusely for giving her the wedding day she'd dreamed of. I kept telling her that Penn had done the majority of the organizing, but either she didn't hear me, or she was lost in the enormity of the moment, and another hug ensued.

I spied Johannes, Penn's older brother, standing off to one side, all by himself, his gaze on the stunning ocean view at the rear of his grandmother's house. He was the only male guest not wearing a shirt and tie, choosing instead a black turtleneck sweater underneath his tux. And in this heat, too. He had this distant air, as if he'd rather be anywhere than here, and although a waiter had pressed a glass of champagne into his hand, he hadn't taken a single sip.

I'd only spoken to him for a few minutes on the party bus before Penn had muscled in and gone all caveman, beating his chest and warning me off, but I didn't take kindly to being told what to do. There was a sadness about

Johannes that tugged at my chest. Not in a sexual way, but more in a sisterly way. Kiana tolerated but disliked him—that was the impression she'd given me at least—but I'd found him rather charming, if aloof.

"Penny for your thoughts." I held up my champagne glass.

He startled, then tapped his glass against mine, and still didn't drink.

"Save your money. They're not worth that much."

"Ah, I can splurge." I pretended to dip my hand in a nonexistent pocket and produce a coin. "For you."

He squinted, and not because of the sun. "You're an odd girl."

"Gee, thanks. No wonder you're standing here all by yourself."

"I prefer to be alone." He peered down his perfectly straight nose at me. "Take a hint."

"Ah, hints. Not really my forte. I'm more of a whack-'em-between-the-eyes kinda girl."

"Fine. Then fuck off." He smiled but it didn't reach his eyes. "Better?"

I beamed at him. "Much."

He sighed and shook his head. "Like I said. Weird."

"You actually said 'odd,' but who's keeping score?"

"You, apparently."

I chuckled. "Aren't you hot? In that, I mean?" I pointed at his sweater.

"No."

"Hmm. Cold-blooded, huh?"

"And coldhearted."

"You must be quite the catch." I arched a brow. "Some lucky girl is going to win first prize one day."

He breathed out through his nose, and as he opened his mouth, his eyes shifted over my shoulder.

"Brace for incoming," he drawled.

"What do—"

A vise gripped my arm and whipped me around. Anger poured off Penn, hotter than sun flares as he steered me away from his brother. I yanked my arm, to no effect.

"Get your hands off me," I hissed.

"Hand," he pointed out, you know, like the jerk he was. "I told you to stay away from Johannes."

I tugged again, and this time he let me go, but only because he caught Asher staring, his mouth flattened in disapproval.

"Something you should know about me, Penn. I don't take kindly to orders."

"You didn't mind on Wednesday night when I ordered you to get on your knees and suck my cock. In fact, you couldn't obey fast enough."

I jabbed my forefinger in his chest. "Too far, mister. Too fucking far."

I flounced off—I was in the perfect dress for it, the chiffon or whatever it was made of swishing around my calves—and headed over to Kee and Asher. I didn't have to look over my shoulder to feel Penn's furious gaze burning a hole in the back of my head. What the fuck was his problem with his brother? Johannes was a sullen bastard, but at least you knew what you were going to get. Penn made my head spin, and I couldn't be bothered with the stress of dealing with a man whose mood swings rivaled my mom's when she'd gone through menopause. Maybe I should stuff a bunch of estrogen pills down his throat and see if it had a positive effect.

"Your brother is a jerk," I announced to Asher, downing my glass of champagne and swapping it for a fresh one.

"Which brother?" He arched a brow, then chuckled.

"Both, although only one of them is likely to end up getting pushed into your grandmother's pool."

"God." Kee shook her head in exasperation. "Will you two just bang each other already and get it over with?"

Tried that. Didn't help.

Warmth crept up my neck, and I fanned myself to camouflage my embarrassment as heatstroke. "Isn't that what you two should be doing?" Master of the diversionary tactic, me. "I mean, this is nice and all, but aren't newlyweds supposed to struggle to keep their hands off one another?"

"Good point." Asher bent his knees and swept Kiana into his arms. Her squeal drew the attention of the small gathering. "Night, everyone. See you at the secondary event in the morning."

Kee waved at me, her delight at Asher's alpha routine evident to me and the watching guests. Her mom pressed a hand to her chest, her face a picture of jubilation, and reached out to take her husband's hand. I grinned until they'd disappeared, then made a beeline for the exit. Now that Kee had left, there was no reason for me to hang around, and I had a craving for some alone time. I'd struggled to shake this low mood ever since the wedding, and I couldn't figure out why I had this urge to bawl my eyes out.

Then again, I had lost my best friend, so maybe a good old cry was precisely what I needed. Well, not lost per se, but things wouldn't be the same anymore.

I thought of calling an Uber but decided to walk back to the hotel. It wasn't all that far, and I could do with the fresh air to clear my head. By the time I reached the lobby, a hot mess, I bemoaned that I hadn't taken a cab. Pushing damp hair off my forehead, I crossed the Italian marble floor and ducked into an empty elevator. As the doors closed, an arm appeared, and they sprang back open.

I groaned. "What are you doing here?"

Penn strode inside and waited for the doors to close again. As they snapped shut, he pounced. My spine hit the back wall, and our teeth clashed as his mouth took mine in a kiss filled with exasperation and impatience and longing. His hands were everywhere at once, and somehow my dress ended up around my waist.

"Jesus Christ," he muttered, nipping the skin at the base of my neck. "You drive me insane."

"Not as insane as you drive me." I tugged on his hair, pulling several strands out by the roots, and forced his mouth back to mine. We reached our floor and lurched down the hallway, kissing and touching and muttering insults at one another. Somehow, we ended up in his suite.

"I've waited two fucking days to get my hands on you, and you decide to flirt with my fucking brother. Again." In his haste to get me naked, he tore my dress. "What the hell, Gia?"

"I wasn't flirting." I shoved his jacket to the floor and

returned the favor, ripping his shirt and sending buttons flying across the room. "And I'm not interested in round two." I bent my head and kissed his chest.

"Yeah, I get that loud and clear."

He picked me up and tossed me onto the bed. Fuck, I gotta say the whole alpha routine made my lady bits tingle.

"Get naked."

He shrugged out of his ruined shirt, yanked down his smart pants, taking his boxers along for the ride, and strode, buck naked, around the bed.

"If this is how you seduce women, no wonder they never return."

He snagged the box of condoms from his nightstand and set them on top. "Gia, if I tried to seduce you, you'd laugh in my face. You like to fuck. I like to fuck, and more importantly, I like to fuck you. So while we're here, can we just stop fighting the inevitable and fuck?"

As much as it irked me to admit it, Penn had me nailed. I wasn't a hearts-and-flowers woman who needed a man to say all the right things before capitulating with a coy smile and crossed legs. I was a spread-'em-wide girl who was comfortable with my body and my sexuality and intended to have as much fun as I could cram into my life before I was either too old to get my kicks, or Christian Bale came knocking, whichever happened first.

I threw off the remnants of my dress, stripped out of my bra and panties, and crawled on all fours to the edge of the bed. Penn's cock jutted straight at me, the tip sticky with precum. I flattened my tongue over the head, lapping up the moisture. Penn hissed, his fingers threading into my hair.

"Fine, we'll fuck." I blinked up at him. "But tonight, I'm in charge."

"Whatever you want." He groaned as I took him to the back of my throat. "Yeah, whatever you want, Gia. Just don't fucking stop."

I didn't. I licked and sucked and grazed his length with my teeth. I fondled his balls and fucked his cock with my tits, and reveled in every moan, every plea that spilled from his lips. As I sensed his approaching orgasm, I stopped.

"What are you doing?" he breathed. "I'm close."

"I know." I smiled sweetly at him. "Fucking frustrating, isn't it?"

His jaw slackened. I rocked back on my heels, grinning at his discomfort. "And if your hand goes anywhere near your cock, I'll chop it off. Now get over here."

He joined me on the bed and ran a hand up my thigh. "You," he said, "are magnificent."

My smile widened. "I know."

Chapter 15

Penn

Payback is a bitch.

GIA GREENE WAS A SEXUAL GODDESS.

My dick begged for her attention, the slit seeping precum worthy of a full-blown orgasm. And the more I produced, the more she lapped it up. But every single time that tingle appeared in my balls, almost to the second, she stopped—and I howled in frustration.

She read me better than any woman I'd been with, almost as if she'd found a key to my body and was in there, with me, feeling what I was feeling.

Payback was a bitch. Her name? Gianna Greene.

"Please, Gia. Blue isn't my color."

Her chuckle vibrated against my cock. This time, though, she didn't stop. No, she... she... hummed against my shaft, and I blew.

"Fuck!" I almost blacked out, gripping her shoulders as my balls emptied of cum and my head of blood. I'd had powerful orgasms before, but this... Jesus Christ, this was otherworldly.

I sank onto the mattress, my chest powering air to my lungs, and yet it wasn't enough. I panted, like a dog made to run in one-hundred-degree heat, and more words of gratitude rushed to my lips.

"You're... fucking unbelievable."

"Thanks."

She straddled me and rubbed her pussy over my rapidly deflating cock. It didn't deflate for long. The turn-around sent my head into another spin, and I squeezed my eyes closed, hoping a lack of visuals would help.

Nope.

My dick might already be up for round two, but I needed a few minutes to recover.

I flipped Gia, tossed her legs over my shoulder, and drank from her pussy as if I'd been deprived of the taste of a woman for years rather than two days. I'd come here without a date, hoping for a hookup, but never in my wildest dreams had I imagined I'd tumble into bed with my nemesis, and that she'd be everything I could've wished for, and more.

The perfect fuck buddy to spend a few days with before going our separate ways.

I thought of denying her an orgasm, but as I'd started this and she'd paid me back, I called it even. I thumbed her clit, and she came all over my tongue, her cry of pleasure music to my fucking ears.

I reached for the box of condoms, tearing a packet with my teeth. Gia snatched it out of my hand and put it on me.

"I told you, Kingcaid, I'm in charge. Now get on your back. I need to ride you."

Yep. Fucking perfect.

"Jesus Christ, Penn." Gia whipped around my room like a whirlwind, gathering her clothes. "It's ten o'clock."

"So?" I linked my hands behind my head, taking in her fine rear end as she bent to pick up her shoes. "Can I fuck your ass tonight?"

She glared at me. "Are you for real? Wedding number two is at eleven thirty, in *ninety minutes*," she emphasized as if I didn't know how to tell the time. "We're supposed to be there at eleven, and you're talking about fucking my ass."

"It's a great ass."

She growled. "Don't test me right now, Penn." She grabbed her purse, then jabbed a finger at me. "If we are late, I'll kill you."

I chuckled. "Hold the front page. Gia Greene, the master of tardiness, is worried about being late for something." I showed my palms to the ceiling as if praying to God. "It's a miracle."

"Now is not the time for jokes. I'm going to get dressed and try to do something with my hair. Get ready, Penn."

She wrenched open the door to my suite and disappeared.

I lay there, stretching, thinking about last night. My dick stirred and I palmed it, then stopped. If I went down that road, masturbating while replaying all the ways Gia and I had fucked, I'd still be here in an hour, and I'd believed her when she'd said she'd kill me. I imagined it wouldn't be a quick death, either.

I took a shower and dressed in my tux and was outside Gia's suite thirty minutes later. I knocked and entered. Clothes were strewn everywhere, and a shoe had somehow ended up on top of the bedside lamp, balanced at a precarious angle. I crouched, picking up a pair of panties. Bringing them to my nose, I sniffed.

"Jesus, you're feral."

I looked up, and got hard. Again. Gia stomped across the room, dressed only in her underwear. She snatched the panties from my hands and tossed them onto the bed. I snagged her around the waist and kissed her, palming the ass I couldn't get enough of.

"Penn!" She shoved at my chest. "This isn't funny."

"Do you see me laughing?" I ran my gaze over her and licked my bottom lip. "What're you doing to me?"

"Nothing unless you help me get dressed and to the wedding on time."

"I'd rather get you undressed."

She fisted her hands on her hips. "I'll tell you what I've done to you. I've turned you into me, someone who is late for important events. And while I'd usually celebrate the ease with which I have corrupted you, today is not the day,

Penn." She picked up her dress from the bed and poured herself into it. "Zip me up."

I did as she asked, taking my time to caress her soft skin as the backs of my fingers traveled over each vertebra in her spine. Her breath caught, bringing a smile to my lips. I bent my head and kissed her neck, then turned her around.

"Beautiful." I tipped up her chin and brushed my lips over hers. "You'll eclipse the bride."

"Oh, stop. I'm fucking you. No need for compliments."

She pretended she didn't care, but the gleam in her eyes told me everything I needed to know. Gia acted all tough and excessive and outrageous, but beneath the surface, she wanted what most of us did. To receive praise. To matter. To be seen.

I saw her.

And she mattered to me, more than I was willing to examine too closely. I quickly diverted from unwelcome thoughts.

"So I can fuck your ass later?"

A frustrated sigh burst out of her. "Let me grab my shoes and we can go."

Thirty seconds later, she stood beside me. I held out my arm and she slipped her hand inside.

"Ready?"

She took a breath. "Yes, let's go."

A line of cars waited outside the hotel to take the guests and family members staying here to my grandmother's house.

Wonder if Gran has told everyone that Asher and Kiana are already Mr. and Mrs.

I guessed she'd have had to, especially as the minister couldn't exactly go through the entire rigmarole again. Besides, if it had been an issue, Gran wouldn't have agreed to the wedding we'd had yesterday, and if my grandmother had said no, that would've been it. No one went up against Gran. Not ever.

I helped Gia into one of the cars, waving at Aspen, London, and Roman, my uncle Jacob's kids. The others must've gone already, and I couldn't see Johannes anywhere. I wouldn't put it past him to not turn up at all, but if he did, I'd be having a sharp word about staying the fuck away from Gia.

Cars filled the driveway of Gran's house, and throngs of people made their way inside and through to the back where Gran had set up a marquee in the garden. I took Gia's hand and went in search of Asher and Kiana. No point in sticking with the tradition of not seeing each other before the wedding. I found the groom—husband— talking to Dad. There was no sign of Kiana, although with all these people, it'd be easy to miss her.

Asher's eyes lowered to where I held Gia, and he arched an eyebrow. "There you are."

I dropped her hand and hugged him and then Dad. "How are you feeling, bro?"

"Like a married man." He chuckled. "But Kiana is far more relaxed than she was about today, and that's all I care about." His eyes softened. "Thank you again to you both for what you did yesterday. It was the perfect wedding I know she wanted, but she'd never have initiated."

"Penn did all the work," Gia said. "I just made sure the bride got to the church on time."

"A miracle in and of itself." I nudged her and winked.

She rolled her eyes. "Where is Kee, anyway?"

"Upstairs. Second room on the right. Her mom and dad are with her, but I know she'll be glad to see you."

"I'll go see if she needs anything."

I couldn't peel my eyes away from Gia as she sashayed into the house. That ass. It'd be the death of me. Ash cleared his throat, bringing my attention back to him.

"Is there something we should know?"

I shrugged. "It's nothing. Just having fun."

"Is Gia having fun?" He air-quoted "fun."

I caught the hidden message and laughed. "You don't need to worry about Gia, Ash. She and I are the same person in different bodies. No one's getting hurt, if that's what you're worried about. We're both consenting adults."

"Two versions of you, Penn?" Dad chuckled. "God help us. Right, I'm off to find your mother. Last I saw, the governor had cornered her, and she'll want rescuing right about now."

He clapped me on the back and wandered off, stopping to shake several hands as he made his way to find Mom. I cocked my head at Ash.

"Shall we get wedding number two underway?"

Ash grinned and motioned with his hand. "Can't wait."

163

I scanned the dance floor, heaving with people, but I couldn't see Gia. In fact, I hadn't seen her since right after the speeches. If she was with Johannes, I was gonna lose my shit. Tension rolled down my spine, dissipating when I spotted my brother sitting by the pool, deep in conversation with my cousin Aspen. Good. That was one problem I didn't have to solve.

After I'd checked outside, I wandered into the house. I eventually found Gia in the kitchen, talking to the head chef. I caught something about seasoning for chicken. A smile stretched across my face. Gia loved food, the creativity, the pleasure it brought others, and, man, she could cook. I'd once thought I'd never have her work at Theo's, but I'd begun to question that idea, on a purely professional basis, of course. Right now, we had a full complement of staff, but in the future... maybe.

"Hey, there you are."

She glanced over at me, and I couldn't say she was happy to see me. In fact, I'd go so far as to say she was pissed. She had this pinched expression that pulled at the skin around her mouth, and her hands briefly clenched.

Okay. Yup. Pissed. Over what, I hadn't a clue.

She marched over and poked me in that soft place between my clavicle and my shoulder joint.

"Ow." I rubbed it. "What was that for?"

"You told Asher about us. You are such an asshole, Penn."

The head chef's eyebrows shot up so fast I thought he might lose them in his hairline. I gripped Gia's elbow and shoved her out of the kitchen and into a living room my gran rarely used. I slammed the door shut with my heel.

"Appreciate it if you didn't call me an asshole in front of staff my grandmother has hired. It's a small island and word gets around."

"And why would that be a problem?" She planted her hands on her hips. "It's a factual statement."

I breathed out heavily through my nose. "So Ash knows we're fucking. I don't see the problem."

"Don't see the problem?" She gaped at me. "Jesus, you are unbelievable. Asher told Kiana, and now my best friend is pissed at me because I wasn't the one to tell her."

"Oh, is that all?" I rolled my eyes. "She'll get over it. It's not as if we're about to follow them up the aisle. We're on vacation and decided to hook up for a few nights. It's no big deal."

She made this sound, kind of like I imagined a lion would right before it tore out the throat of its poor cornered prey.

"You are a prick and a jerk and… and…" Her hand flew in the air. "I can't wait to get back to New York, where I never have to see you again."

She stormed past me. I snapped out a hand, grabbing her by the wrist. I hauled her against my body and smashed my lips to hers. She pummeled my chest and scratched my neck, and still I kissed her. In seconds, anger turned to lust, her nails, rather than drawing blood, burrowed into my hair, digging into my scalp. She rubbed her pussy against me, making me hard in seconds.

"Let's get out of here." I nipped along her jawline. "I've too much respect for my grandmother to fuck you in her house."

"Who says I'll let you fuck me after what you've done?"

She grabbed my face. Our teeth clashed as she mashed our lips together. She hooked her legs over my hips, and I cupped her ass—God, I loved her ass—and slammed her into the nearest wall. My balls ached, my cock ached, my fucking heart ached because our time here was coming to an end and I wasn't ready to let her go.

I would, though. It was for the best. Even if I could bring myself to contemplate a relationship that lasted more than a few days, Gia and I would be a disaster. We worked only because we were on vacation and in some kind of a bubble. We moved in different circles, and once we returned to New York, there wouldn't be a requirement to ever see her again.

A band pulled tight across my chest, and my stomach hollowed out.

Gia biting my tongue yanked me back to reality.

"Ow." I touched it. Spots of blood dotted my fingertip. "What the hell was that for?"

"You disappeared on me. When a man's kissing me, I prefer it if he's present. Knowing you, you were probably fantasizing about some girl you banged last week."

God, I adored her. I fucking adored her.

She went to walk away. I snapped a hand around the back of her neck, yanking her to me. One hundred percent in the moment, I poured as much desire into my kiss as I was capable of, my hands exploring her tits, her waist, her hips, her face. I touched everywhere I could reach, and when a moan sounded in her throat, I knew I'd won. I clasped my hands to her face and stared right into her eyes.

"When I'm with you, you're the only fucking woman I'm thinking of. Got it?"

She panted, saying nothing for a beat, two beats. Five.

Finally, she spoke.

"Then let's get outta here."

Chapter 16

Gia

Unexpected visitors sometimes have upsides.

THE MIDMORNING SUN BEAT DOWN AS I STOOD OUTSIDE THE Kingcaid Grand Cayman hotel with a great fat lump in my throat, not at all ready to say goodbye to my best friend. All around, bright tropical flowers and vegetation contrasted with the gray funk I was trying my hardest to keep at bay.

"Oh, Kee, I'm going to miss you so much."

I hugged her again. This was our third attempt at goodbye. Asher had stuck around for the first two, then announced he had a call to make and left us alone. I sensed her slipping away into her new magnificent life with her rich, gorgeous husband, and I couldn't stop it. I didn't want to stop it, but damn, it hurt to lose her. For years, it'd been me and her against the world, and now she had someone else who'd, rightly, have her undivided attention.

I felt bereft.

She drew back, her hands on my upper arms. "I'll call you from the Maldives."

I forced a laugh. "Don't. Otherwise, I'll assume Asher isn't doing it right. I'll speak to you when you get back to Seattle."

Kee laughed, too. "I love you, you crazy bitch."

"Love you more."

The car waiting to take me and Penn back to the airport tooted its horn. I glanced over my shoulder and fired a glare at Penn, knowing full well he'd asked the driver to do that in a bid to hurry me. We had tons of time, even by my standards.

"Looks as if lover boy is anxious to have you all to himself." Kee arched a brow.

I snorted. "Let's put this down to a minor aberration. A momentary brain fart brought about by being here with you, in paradise, while you married the man of your dreams."

Kee's expression grew serious. Huh. I'd have thought the brain fart comment would've gotten a chuckle at least.

"What if it wasn't? What if Penn is your Asher?"

This time, I didn't need to force a laugh. It burst out of me without assistance. "Kee, there's as much chance of that as you returning from your honeymoon and announcing you and Asher are getting a divorce. So please, put any thoughts of matchmaking right out of your head. As soon as we get back to New York, I'll never see him again."

Kee's mouth turned down at the edges, and it was only then that I realized she'd harbored hopes of something more. Hadn't we joked about that, years ago? Me and her falling in love with two brothers and ending up as sisters-in-law? Silly dreams that wouldn't have ever happened anyway.

"Gia!" Penn's exasperated plea almost burst my eardrums. "Will you get in the goddamn car? We're going to be late."

I rolled my eyes. "And right there," I said to Kee, "is one of a million reasons we'd never work. The man is so fucking anal about punctuality."

Kee grinned and gave me a final hug and a push toward the car. "Go, before he has an aneurysm."

"If that's a possibility, I might take my time." I got into the car and wound down the window. "Love you." I blew her a kiss and waved as Penn instructed the driver to "step on it" as if we were in the movies or something.

As the car rounded the corner and I couldn't see her anymore, I clipped my seat belt into place and let depression move in. Stupid love. It ruined everything.

"Anyone would think one of you was dying after that performance," Penn drawled.

"One of us will be." I gave him one of my sugar-smile specials. "You."

He snickered. "Normal service is resumed, I see."

"Aww, Penn." I clasped a hand to my chest. "Did you think that just because you've seen my sex face and drunk from my pussy that we'd become besties?"

The driver choked. Penn glowered and pressed the button that raised the privacy screen. I muffled a laugh and stared out the window. If needling Penn lifted my spirits, then he was in for a long flight home.

A few minutes passed without a word from Penn. I glanced out of the corner of my eye, and he looked... defeated. Crushed, even, though both were impossible. His lips tipped downward and his shoulders slumped, all self-assuredness scattered in the breeze that blew through the leafy trees lining the road. A prickly feeling crept across my chest. Was he upset at what I'd said or just sorry to leave his family behind and head back to normality? Why did I feel the need to belittle what we'd had, which, let's face it, had been pretty darned good, even if it wasn't destined to last?

Kee's words came back to haunt me. *"What if Penn is your Asher?"*

No. Impossible. This weird stabbing sensation had nothing to do with Penn or the fact that we'd part ways in a few hours, and everything to do with knowing I had to return to work tomorrow while my best friend began her new life.

Satisfied that I'd analyzed the problem, I let Penn stew in his sour mood and committed the last few moments in Grand Cayman to memory.

The car pulled up outside the terminal building. Penn got out before I'd even unclipped my seat belt, and by the time I joined him, he had my suitcase and carry-on out of the trunk. The driver lifted out Penn's far smaller case, and Penn shook his hand and thanked him. We walked in silence toward the check-in desks. As we approached the first-class aisle, a male voice called out Penn's name.

"Penn Kingcaid, what the fuck are you doing here?"

Penn turned, his eyes widening. "Slade Gleason. Fuck, man, I haven't seen you in ages."

Slade? What kind of a name was that? Weren't they a band from sixty years ago or something? Then again, Slade looked a bit like a rocker with tattoos up both arms, long, luscious hair hanging halfway down his back, a thick beard, and a black T-shirt with the name of some band emblazoned across the front. Possibly his own band.

"Never mind what I'm doing here. What are *you* doing here?"

"Weekend of R and R, my friend. Headed back to Miami. Dawson's opening a new club there tonight, and I'm VIP." Slade's eyes glided over to me. "You should come. Bring your girlfriend. Dawson'd love to see you."

"Oh, she's not my girlfriend." Penn couldn't get the denial out fast enough. "We've been here attending Ash's wedding. This is just the maid of honor."

I clenched my fists so tight I'd probably lose a finger from blood loss. *This* is *just* the maid of honor. *This*, as if I were an object of some kind rather than the woman he'd spent days fucking. Sure, I'd made it clear we wouldn't be picking up where we'd left off when we returned to New York, but did that mean he had to reduce me to nothing status?

"Well, anyways, you should come, man. It's been ages since the gang got together."

Penn glanced at me. He shuffled his feet and bit down on his lip, and right then, I fucking *knew*. He wanted to go, and he did not want me tagging along.

Fine. Fuck him. I didn't need him anyway.

"Go." I flicked my wrist. "I've had enough of you to last

173

a lifetime anyway. A bit of peace and quiet on the trip back to New York is just what the doctor ordered after the last few days."

Slade barked out a laugh. "Tell it like it is, angel."

I grabbed my bags. Penn put his hand on my shoulder.

"You really want me to go rather than come back with you?"

No. That wasn't what I wanted at all, and it stung to admit it. But it didn't twist the knife in my chest nearly as much as his easy dismissal of me.

"Yes. That's what I want."

"But, what about the flight? You're scared of flying."

I forced a sneer, hiding my hurt behind bravado. "Oh, for goodness' sake, Penn, I've taken other flights without you nannying me. Don't inflate your part in this. Now go with your friend, have an awesome time, and a great life. I'd like to say it's been nice knowing you, but I wouldn't want to part on a lie."

I dragged my cases over to the desk. The backs of my eyes burned, but I'd be damned before I'd shed one single tear over Penn Kingcaid. That didn't stop me from holding my breath and hoping he'd sidle up beside me, apologize for what he'd said to Slade, and insist that he'd rather fly home with me than go to some stupid club in Miami.

He didn't, and I had to struggle to haul that ridiculous case I'd filled with too many clothes, ninety percent of which I'd never worn, onto the belt.

Guess that told me everything I needed to know.

New Yorkers sweltered in the sticky July heat, trussed up in their suits and office gear, while tourists moseyed about in shorts and T-shirts and generally got in everyone's way.

I loved New York, although I missed my hometown of Chicago, but some days I wished it wasn't a place vast swathes of the world loved to visit. Imagine how much easier it'd be to get around with half the people. *Bliss.*

I dodged around a group of people pouring out of a nearby hotel, cameras at the ready, and ducked into my favorite deli to grab a sandwich for lunch. For once, I wasn't late for work—maybe Penn had rubbed off on me after all—and I daydreamed as I stood in line waiting for my turn. I ordered chicken with mayo on rye and an OJ. I left the deli and set off for work. Halfway there, my phone buzzed, and, never the kind of person who was able to leave it until a more suitable moment, I set the OJ on the ground and rummaged through my purse.

The banner gave me a preview of the text.

Penn: Hi. How are you? Hope you...

I deleted it without reading the rest. I'd made my mind up on the plane journey home that the way Penn and I had parted at the airport had been for the best. Since returning to New York, I'd realized how much head space the man had taken up, not just during the trip, but before, and in the couple of days since landing at JFK. I thought about him entirely too much, and if I didn't quit, I was headed for disaster.

Freddo was in a foul mood when I arrived, and Lorenzo warned me to be on my best behavior or, at the very least, try not to goad the grouchy head chef. Not an easy thing to promise, so I said I'd do my best.

Somehow, I made it through my shift. Instead of heading straight to the subway, I decided to take a detour. When the only thing waiting for me at home was an empty apartment and a lousy crime drama on TV, there wasn't much point in rushing.

Whether by accident or some kind of subconscious thought, I found myself on the same street where Theo's, Penn's restaurant, was located. I stood across the road, staring at the building. Was he in there, buried in paperwork, or was today one of the days he gave his full attention to Kingcaid?

A blaze of heat flooded my stomach. As much as it pained me to admit it, I missed the sex. I missed the banter.

But most of all, I missed him.

I lost track of time, only jerking back to the present when a taxi driver leaned on his horn for a good five seconds, shaking his fist at the car in front. Mortified at finding myself brooding outside Penn's restaurant, I dismissed all thoughts of him and set off for home.

My small apartment felt emptier than ever as I trudged through the door and hung my purse up on a coat hook. I opened the fridge and cursed. I was supposed to go to the grocery store on the way home, and the thought of going out now that I was home did not appeal to me. *Guess it's mac and cheese for dinner.*

I peeled back the film and put it in the microwave. As I watched the digits count down, my phone pinged with a text. Another message from Penn. This time, I tortured myself and read the entire message.

Penn: Can we talk? I miss you. Weird, I know. Call me.

My chest hurt, and I rubbed it. I missed him, too. There, I'd admitted it. We sniped and battled and provoked each other, yet whenever I thought about our time in Grand Cayman, all I could recall was his kindness, his humor, how he'd arranged the wedding Kiana had dreamed of, how highly his entire family had spoken of him. And the sex. God, the sex. I'd had my fair share of experiences, some good, some bad, some fabulous, but none had come close to what I'd had with Penn. But great sex was one thing. Opening myself up to the idea of *more* wasn't something I was ready for. Maybe I would never be ready.

Besides, Penn had humiliated and belittled me in front of that Slade guy, and I couldn't forgive him for that. He didn't have to introduce me as his girlfriend—I wasn't— but he could have given me a higher status than *just the maid of honor.*

I deleted the text. I almost deleted his number, too, but my finger hovered over the delete button for so long that I had to reheat the mac and cheese after it went cold.

I couldn't do it. I couldn't take that final step to cut myself off from a man who, as much as I loathed to admit it, had burrowed beneath my skin.

The soles of my feet burned as I trudged down the hallway toward my apartment. These goddamn fourteen-hour shifts were killing me, but with three vacancies at the restaurant and Freddo struggling to recruit even half-decent staff, I didn't see an end to it for a while.

A week had passed since I'd heard from Penn, and good riddance to him. So much for missing me if two ignored texts put the man off. If he was that interested, he'd have bombarded me with flowers or gift cards to a spa or, oh, I don't know, a voucher for a freebie dinner at Theo's. Something to remind me he still existed.

Not that I'd forgotten he existed. Too many sleepless nights and unfulfilling sessions with one of my good old vibrators were all the proof I needed that the man had fucking ruined me—in the sexual sense at least. I often used vibe time as a stress reliever when I was too tired to bother with an actual man, but the orgasms came too fast and didn't come close to scratching what amounted to a permanent itch. Maybe I needed to seek medical help to cure that.

I flicked on the living room light and—

"Jesus Christ, Penn!"

My heart rate rocketed, adrenaline shooting through my body, and my purse dropped to the floor with a thud. I stared at the uninvited guest sprawled out on my couch, remote control in hand, flicking through the TV channels.

"What the fuck? It's one o'clock in the goddamn morning."

"I'm aware," he drawled in that lazy way of his, his eyes still fixed on the TV.

I poked my tongue in the side of my cheek and inhaled a long breath through my nose, irritation a swarm of prickles along the back of my neck.

"Did you break in?"

"Hardly."

He turned off the TV and tipped up his chin, his blue eyes piercing mine. A perverse sense of relief coursed through my veins, which annoyed me even more. Why was I bothered whether or not he looked at me? I'd spent days promising myself he meant nothing to me, and now here I was, all gooey inside because the great Penn King-caid deigned to give me his attention.

"Your neighbor, the one across the hall, let me in." He flashed a broad grin that made my belly flip. "She couldn't resist my charm. Most women can't."

"More fool most women," I muttered. "What are you doing here?" I flopped into the chair by the window and kicked off my shoes, groaning at the relief.

"Long day?"

Digging my thumbs into the soles of my feet, I shot him a withering glance. "What do you think?"

He threaded his fingers and linked them behind his neck, extending his legs out in front of him as if he lived here.

"Make yourself comfortable, why don't you?"

"Thanks. I have."

"No shit," I grumbled. "Again, why are you here?"

"Have you missed me?"

"No."

He arched a brow. "Liar."

A smile threatened, and I shut it down, but my lips weren't happy. Penn irked the shit out of me ninety percent of the time, but the other ten percent made me want to jump his bones until my pussy begged me for a time-out. And after a nine-day hiatus, my libido jump-started like it'd been jet-fueled.

Guess there isn't a requirement for medical intervention after all. Just a burning need for Penn Kingcaid.

I still hadn't worked out why he, of all people, had this effect on me, only that it was stronger than with any other guy. And, weirdly, I got off on the banter almost as much as the sex.

"I missed your dick. Maybe you could leave it behind after you get off my fucking couch and leave?"

"Sorry, sweetcheeks. We're a package deal."

"More's the pity."

He chuckled. "If I thought for one second you really believed that, I'd leave. But as much as you hate to admit it, I know you better than you think I do. You're tired and irritable, and it'll take you hours to drop off to sleep because you're too wired from a hectic shift at the restaurant. The only way you'll get more than two hours of sleep before Groundhog Day arrives is several orgasms, courtesy of yours truly."

God, he was an arrogant prick, but he'd also homed in on the issue with the precision of a laser-guided missile.

"You missed my dick, Gia? It's right here. Come get it."

His deft fingers, the same fingers that he'd stuck inside me, repeatedly, in Grand Cayman, reached for his belt. My core clenched as he unbuckled it, my eyes watching his every move. He flicked the button, tugged down the zipper, and reached inside, releasing his cock. Thick veins stood out along the shaft, the slit already weeping with precum.

Lots of women sucked cock because guys liked it, but

me, I sucked cock because *I* liked it. The power it gave me turned me on. When a guy's dick was in my mouth, and I cupped his balls in my hands, right before he came, he'd agree to anything. That was what I got off on.

Women spent their lives fighting for equality, yet in that moment, we had the upper hand, the guy little more than Play-Doh for us to manipulate and control and maneuver in whatever way we chose.

Heady shit, right there.

"Get on your knees." Penn's hooded eyes locked on me as he gently stroked his dick. He reached behind him and tossed a pillow at his feet.

"Gallant of you."

He smiled a little. "I love your sassy mouth, Gia. Now bring it over here and put it to good use on my cock."

I wanted to resist, to argue, to refuse his demand. I truly did. But did I?

The hell I did.

Chapter 17

Penn

Turns out orange juice isn't stickier than cum.

"WHY DID YOU IGNORE MY TEXTS?"

Gia ran her fingernail around my nipple, then drew figures of eight on my chest. "I've been busy."

"Too busy to take five seconds to reply?"

"Yes." She snuggled closer and yawned. "How was Miami?"

Diversionary tactics. Fine. I'd bide my time, but if Gia thought I was letting her slip through my fingers because she had some kind of an issue with relationships, she had a wake-up call coming.

I almost laughed aloud at the thought. *Both of us* had issues with the idea of relationships, but since returning from Asher's wedding, not a second had passed by when I hadn't thought of her. And not just her pussy and her tits and, *God*, her ass, but *her*. Funny, mouthy, argumentative her. I missed it all, and as she'd refused to reply to my olive branch, she'd given me no option other than to come to her.

It stung. I didn't chase women. Ever. But for Gianna Greene, I wasn't only prepared to bend the rule, but snap the fucker in two.

Besides, I owed her. After the way I'd left things at the airport in Grand Cayman, I'd spent the flight to Miami kicking my own ass for leaving her. In my defense, I'd been tense at the prospect of parting ways with Gia while at the same time wrestling with my burgeoning feelings, and when she'd acted as if she'd rather lie in a coffin with ten thousand cockroaches than travel back to New York with me, I'd chosen to go—and regretted it from the moment I'd stepped on the plane with Slade.

"Okay, I guess."

"Just okay?" She tipped back her head and looked up at me. "You were mighty keen to go. I'd have expected an 'awesome' at least."

"Who said I was keen to go?"

"You did."

"No, I didn't. You were the one who said I should go. I'd have rather traveled back to New York with you, but you made it clear." I laughed and it sounded bitter. "Crystal clear you wanted me nowhere near you."

She shifted out of my arms and onto her back, eyes fixed on the ceiling. I rolled onto my side and played with a lock of her hair.

"Want to tell me why you pushed me away when I thought we'd made a peace deal? And I'm not just talking about what happened at the airport, but also what you said to me in the car."

She might as well have stabbed me right through the heart when she'd belittled what we'd shared with that comment she'd made—and in front of a local driver, too. The whole island would've heard that tasty tidbit before the plane had taken off. Hell, there was probably a local entrepreneur printing T-shirts with a picture of a cat and underneath in bold black font *Wanna drink from my pussy?*

"You made it clear from the start that it was a vacation thing and nothing more."

I clasped her chin. "No, Gia. We both made it clear that was all we wanted. But things changed. Or at least they did for me. Am I alone in experiencing a shift, one that made me thirst for more?"

She gnawed at her lip. "I don't know, Penn. I've never had a relationship, and I'm not sure I'd be that good at it."

"Not sure I will be either." I chuckled. "Look, you have to admit we are dynamite between the sheets. Why don't we just agree to have fun, until it's not?"

"Like friends with benefits but without the friend part?"

I shook my head. "With the friend part. It's been a blast pretending we don't like each other outside of the bedroom, but that just isn't true." I lifted an eyebrow. "Right?"

"Exclusive?"

I noted that she'd ignored my question, but I let it go.

"Yeah. Until one of us decides it doesn't work anymore."

"So it's not a relationship per se?"

"No. It's a fuck-a-thon."

She burst out laughing, and the strings that tied my heart together twanged. "Fine. But know that you drive me insane, and I can't see it lasting."

"You drive me insane, too, so we're even on that score. And it lasts as long as it lasts. Life's too short not to indulge the inevitable."

"Y'know, Kingcaid, that might just be the most truthful thing to come out of your mouth."

I pinned her beneath me. "Did you just say to come in your mouth?"

She laughed again. "You're the male version of me."

Lowering my head, I captured her lips. "No, sweetcheeks, you're the female version of me."

K

The sound of water running woke me. I checked the time. Eight thirty. Sunlight peeked through a gap in the drapes, and I stretched my arms overhead, working out the kinks in my body caused by a night in Gia's bed. She and I were so alike that it both scared and excited me. Perfectly matched in every way. Yet her reaction to our conversation last night—or rather, early this morning—told me that if I wanted to prevent her from ending this before it had begun, I'd have to tread carefully.

I threw back the covers and padded into the bathroom. Opening the shower door, I stepped into the stall and wrapped my arms around a soaking-wet Gia, her soapy body making it easy for me to explore every inch.

I kissed her neck, shoulder, spine, lowering to my knees to lap between her legs. She opened them, giving me full access. Gia's body confidence turned me on to such an extent that I often had to think of other shit, such as taxes or food orders for the restaurant or the next Kingcaid board meeting, just to stop myself from coming in ten seconds flat.

Her palms hit the tile, and she pushed back, moaning, opening her legs even wider. "Close."

I eased two fingers inside her, grazing her inner walls, and slowly pumped them in and out, swirling my thumb over her clit.

"God." She shuddered, tipping her head back so far that the tips of her wet hair tickled my nose. "Fuck."

I kept up the pressure until I'd wrung every pulse from her and she stopped clenching around my fingers. She twisted to face me and tipped up my chin.

"Kiss me."

I rose to my feet, put my mouth on hers, and caressed between her legs, coating my fingers in her desire. My dick brushed against her belly, the friction a killer to my hanging-by-a-thread control. Gia made no move to touch me. When I urged her to take me in her fist, she moved her hands behind her back.

I broke off our kiss. "What's the matter?"

"Touch yourself." She leaned against the tile, water

bouncing off of her tits. "I want to watch you make yourself come."

Already close to orgasm with little encouragement, I didn't need her to ask a second time. I gripped my cock, groaning at the momentary relief. My eyes closed, the pleasure intense, electrified tingles shooting up and down my spine.

"Eyes on me."

I obeyed her—a new experience but one growing more prevalent since this incredible woman had burst into my life and tossed a cup of OJ all over me. She cupped both her tits, running her thumbs over nipples so hard I imagined they could cut glass.

"Faster, Penn."

I pistoned my hips, fucking my hand, balls squeezing tight against my body. Gia ran the flat of her palm over her rounded belly, widened her legs, and fingered herself.

I came, the sound in my throat a mixture of a groan and a cry of pain. I muttered several "Fucks" under my breath, panting as my body took over and did what came naturally. My head rolled back on my neck, and I whacked it on the tile.

"Ow." I rubbed it.

"You're such an idiot." Gia grabbed a cloth and squeezed a dollop of soap into the middle, then lathered it and ran it over where my cum had splattered her stomach. "Christ, you'd have thought God would have made this less sticky."

"Stickier than the OJ you tipped over me the day we met?"

"Much stickier. Cum and water do not mix, my friend.

It's like goddamn glue. You should know this. You must've whacked off in the shower a gazillion times."

I burst out laughing. I'd thought it before, and no doubt I'd think it many more times in the future, but Gianna Greene was unlike any woman I'd met in my life. Unique and utterly bewitching.

"Can't say it's ever crossed my mind. Besides, I usually aim for the spray." I took the cloth from her. "Here. Allow me. It's the least I can do."

"I should say so."

I washed every inch of her, then myself. I turned off the water and helped her out of the shower. Wrapping her in a huge towel, I grabbed a second one and fastened it around my waist.

"What time's your shift today?"

"Ugh." She shook her head. "Late shift. Again."

"You don't like it there?"

She hitched a shoulder and squeezed a dollop of toothpaste onto her brush. "It's a job. It's not my dream job, but it pays the bills."

Turning toward the mirror over the sink, she brushed her teeth. I stood and watched her, an idea nudging me. Once, I'd thought the notion of Gia working at Theo's, of me having to see her every day, as some kind of medieval torture that only a crazy man would sign up for. But, like I'd said to her last night, things had changed. Now, it was more the idea of *not* seeing her every day that felt like a razor blade to my heart, tearing it to ribbons.

She ran the toothbrush underneath the tap and dropped it into a glass. I picked it up and added a dollop of toothpaste. Gia's hand on my wrist stopped me midway between brush and mouth.

"What are you doing?"

"Brushing my teeth?"

"With my toothbrush?" Both her eyebrows arched.

"You're right." I pretended to put it back. "I'll just grab my wash bag from the overnight case I didn't bring."

I stuck the toothbrush in my mouth. She made a frustrated sound and flounced out of the bathroom. I grinned. Good to know that my shift in feelings hadn't altered my love of teasing her.

Gia wasn't in the bedroom when I came out of the bathroom. I dressed, ran my fingers through my damp hair, and went in search of her. She'd made coffee and even poured me a cup.

"Is it safe?" I lifted the cup to my lips and winked.

"Don't worry, Penn. I'm reliably informed by my potion specialist that the amount of arsenic I've added to your coffee kills fast."

"Potion specialist?"

"Every girl should have a potion specialist on hand to rid themselves of men after they've fulfilled their usefulness."

I was enjoying this game enough to keep it going. "And how long does it usually take?"

She gave my question full consideration. "Couple of days."

"Wow." I sipped my coffee. Tasted like coffee. Although, did arsenic have a taste? Wasn't that the entire point? "I'm doing pretty well, then."

"Don't get cocky." Her hand came up. "Wait. Too late."

"Har har." I set down the cup on the kitchen countertop and captured her around the waist. As I nuzzled her neck, the words spilled out.

"Resign from your job and come work at Theo's."

Even I was shocked, although I'd mused on the idea, so it hadn't come entirely out of the blue. But my surprise paled in comparison to Gia's. Her jaw hit the floor, and her eyes widened to such an extent that I could see the whites all the way around.

"What?"

"The restaurant is crazy busy, far busier than I'd anticipated when we opened. My head chef has raised the issue of understaffing with me several times, and I'd hate to lose someone of his caliber over a failure to take his concerns seriously."

It wasn't a complete untruth. Pierre had mentioned how busy the kitchen staff were, although he hadn't suggested another chef. But now that I'd said it, I wanted her to say yes almost as much as I wanted to fuck her over the tiny kitchen table butted up against the wall.

"Oh, Penn, I'm not sure." Gia repeatedly grazed her top teeth over her bottom lip. "We're not exactly... stable together. And I have been known to throw a fit in the kitchen if things aren't to my satisfaction."

"You, throw a fit?" I feigned shock. "Surely not."

She flicked me. "Stop it. I'm serious. Anyway, I'd rather hoped my next move would see me running my own kitchen, rather than working beneath another chef again."

"Not to blow my horn here, sweetcheeks, but Theo's is a far bigger restaurant than where you currently work. Besides, you could learn a lot from Pierre. He's worked in some of the best restaurants in the world. I poached him from Kingcaid Paris."

"You did not?"

"Yep. Gotta be some perks to running the restaurant side of the family empire." I pressed my fingertip to my lips. "Not a word to Asher, though."

She chuckled. "You are a maverick."

"Charming, isn't it?" I clipped her under the chin. "So, what do you say?"

She rubbed her lips together, taking far too long to give me an answer.

"I have conditions."

"Of course you do." I gestured to her. "Shoot."

"When we're at work, it's strictly business. No slapping my ass as you pass by or making inappropriate comments."

I pressed my palm to my chest. "What do you take me for? I'm the consummate professional."

"Hmm."

Grinning, I said, "Go on."

"I want our... relationship"—she screwed up her face as if she'd bitten down on a lemon—"or whatever this is to remain private. Otherwise, people will think I got the job through nefarious means."

"'Nefarious' is an awfully big word for this time of the morning."

"Penn! I'm serious."

"I know you are, sweetcheeks. Is that it? No ass slapping at work and no blabbing about how many times I made you come the previous night?"

She rolled her eyes in exasperation. "That's it. For now.

But I reserve the right to add more codicils to a formal employment contract that you *will* have to me by the end of the day."

"Jesus, is this how it's going to be?"

"Yes. Having second thoughts?"

"Never." I sealed our deal with a kiss. Now she truly was mine, and I had no intention of ever letting her go.

Chapter 18

Gia

**When your lover messes up,
make them grovel.**

—

THE FOUR WEEKS I'D BEEN WORKING AT THEO'S HAD FLOWN BY.

It turned out that having Penn for a boss wasn't nearly as difficult as I'd anticipated. Each time our paths had crossed, he'd behaved impeccably, treating me the same as any other employee. Besides, he'd hardly been here, too busy juggling his other full-time job—namely, CEO of Kingcaid Restaurants.

Outside of work, things were going well, too, although I still couldn't quite believe I was in a real relationship. Sure, we'd begun by agreeing it was only a fuck-a-thon, but what Penn and I shared had become so much more.

I couldn't deny how fiercely I missed him when he

wasn't there, my mind drifting to the moments we'd shared.

Or how my chest twisted when, through work commitments, a few days passed by without us seeing each other.

Even so, the thought of Penn and me dating made me screw my face up in disgust. Me. Gianna Greene, granting my pussy to only one man and having zero regrets.

Not that I would *ever* tell Penn that. The man wouldn't ever let me forget it.

He'd spent the last few days traveling with Asher. The Kingcaid ever-growing empire had opened a new hotel in Edinburgh, Scotland, and as it had an adjoining restaurant, Asher had expected Penn to attend also. He was due back Sunday afternoon, and I planned to spend the morning buffing and shaving and pouring myself into a brand-new set of lingerie I'd splurged on to celebrate his homecoming.

God, I missed him.

The next forty-one hours were going to be a hell of a slog. Still, one more shift, two more sleeps, and he'd be home.

Jesus fucking Christ, Gia, what the hell has happened to you?

I'd gone soft in my old age, pining for a man I'd despised two and a half months ago.

I blamed Kee and her loved-up status. If I hadn't gone to her wedding, I wouldn't be sitting here dick-whipped.

This state of affairs was completely unacceptable. Yet if a genie appeared and offered to grant me a wish, I wouldn't change a single thing.

My phone rang. Perfect timing. I answered, glowering at Kee's exquisite, shining, all-loved-up face.

"You are in so much trouble, Kiana Doherty-hyphen-Kingcaid."

Her head jerked back. "What have I done?"

"You've hexed me with all your lovin'."

Kee beamed, her grin wide enough to split her face in two. "Will there be another wedding soon?"

I snorted. "Not likely. In fact..." I looked up at the ceiling, pretending to think hard. "Never."

"Me doth think the lady protest too much."

I chuckled. "Shakespeare never was your forte."

"Or yours, as I recall."

"You heard from Asher?"

"You heard from Penn?" she countered.

"I asked first."

"He called this morning to say he's going to try to leave earlier. No promises."

Hmm. Penn hadn't called to tell me the same thing. The heat surging through my chest was a surefire sign I wasn't too happy about that. I tamped it down with a swig of water.

"Here's hoping."

"Seriously, though, how are things going with Penn?"

"You mean Asher hasn't conveyed all the gory details?"

"As I have intimate knowledge of your past sex life, the details are sure to be dirty. But no, he hasn't said a word. In fact, if you hadn't told me you were dating—"

"We're not dating."

"Fine. Fucking, then. If you hadn't told me you were

still fucking Penn weeks after Grand Cayman, I'd have been none the wiser."

More heat.

This time it burned.

So Penn wasn't just keeping our liaison—ugh, I hated that word but couldn't come up with a more suitable one—secret from my coworkers at the restaurant. He wasn't talking about me to his brother, either.

Was he ashamed of me or something, or had he taken my warnings of secrecy to the extreme?

"I told him I didn't want anyone knowing."

"Well, he's heeded your request. Either that, or Asher is keeping quiet about anything Penn shares. Bro code and all that."

"Yeah, probably."

Unlikely.

Asher told Kee everything.

"Ooh, I've got to go," Kee said. "There's a delivery person in the lobby with today's gift. Wonder what Asher has sent today?" She giggled. "He's so resourceful."

Penn hadn't sent me anything.

Okay forget burning. There was an inferno spreading through my chest.

"Go. Call me next week. Love you."

"Love you."

She cut our video call. I sank onto the couch and tossed my phone into the space beside me. Penn had been the one to suggest this... thing. Yet I was starting to wonder if, to him, it was just a fuck-a-thon as he'd told me, and therefore, the idea of gifts hadn't crossed his mind.

Funny how I'd been the one to set the rules, and now I was bitching about the consequences.

I heaved myself off the couch and made a cheese sandwich. I wasn't that hungry, but if I went to bed without eating, I'd regret it in the morning when not even half a cow would satisfy my raging appetite. I knew my body—in every way—and it did not react well to hunger. Hangry Gia greeting Penn wasn't a good idea, especially when I was feeling salty about the lack of gifts arriving at my door.

I'd taken a single bite when my phone rang again. If this was Kee calling back to brag about what Asher had sent her...

It wasn't Kee.

A coldness hit my core, and I wrapped one arm around my stomach, answering the phone with the other. "Mom?"

My mother never called this late unless something was wrong.

"Oh, Gianna. I'm at the hospital with Roberto."

My mouth went dry. "What is it?"

"They think he's got some kind of fluid in the brain. They're doing a scan now."

When Roberto was younger, he'd had a couple of episodes where fluid had built up between his brain and his skull, but he hadn't suffered from it for years. I'd thought he was over the worst of it.

"I'm on my way."

I grabbed my purse and keys and sprinted out the door. I made it to the children's hospital inside thirty minutes, and after butting in line to speak to the receptionist, she directed me to the third floor.

"Mom! Dad!" I ran down the hallway, hugging them both. "What have the doctors said?"

"He's having the scan now. If it's fluid, they're going to take him into surgery to drain it."

My mom looked at least ten years older, and I swore Dad's hair was grayer than when I'd had dinner with them last week. My parents doted on Roberto to such a degree that once he'd been born, and the full extent of his health challenges had come to light, they'd pretty much left me to raise myself from that point onward, their time and attention, rightly, directed toward my brother. It still stung, though, to know I wasn't a priority in their lives. Not that I would *ever* share such a thought. They did their best, and Roberto needed them far more than I did. And I'd turned out all right. Kind of.

"He'll be okay. He's tough." I squeezed her cool hand. "How about I get you a cup of coffee, or some soup?" Not that the watery broth that came from a vending machine could pass for soup, but that was what it said on the label.

Mom shook her head. "I'm okay."

She wasn't. None of us were. What if this fluid, if that was what it was, made Roberto's brain damage worse? What if he lost the ability to talk, or walk, or be the funny, kind, amazing boy he'd grown into, despite all his challenges.

I missed Penn. I wish he were here with me, comforting me, holding me. Not that he would be here, even if he was only across the river in Manhattan rather than thousands of miles away in another country. We didn't have that kind of relationship. He hadn't even asked about my family, not since the night of Kee's bachelorette party when Mom had called about Roberto. I'd brushed off his questions, and he hadn't inquired since.

Yet more evidence of what we were to one another. Fuck buddies. Friends with benefits. But not partners, not the person we turned to when times were tough.

This is what you wanted, Gia.

True. It was. But did I still want that, or was I ready for more? And more importantly, was Penn? Somehow, I doubted it.

A doctor approached, and we all stiffened, but he walked right past. Thirty minutes went by before another doctor strode down the hall.

"Mr. and Mrs. Greene?"

In synchronization, Mom and Dad shot to their feet. I wasn't far behind.

"Yes."

"We've completed the scans on Roberto. He does have a small buildup of fluid, so we're prepping him for surgery now."

"Is he..." Mom's voice cracked.

"He'll be fine. You did the right thing bringing him in. I promise, before you know it, he'll be in recovery."

My knees buckled and I sank into the chair. My heart skipped, feeling as if it missed every third beat.

"Can we see him?" Mom reached for Dad, who squeezed her shoulder.

"Of course."

We all piled into my brother's hospital room, crowding around his bed. Mom did her best to hold back her tears, failing miserably. I hugged my baby brother, his body so slight against mine.

"Am I gonna be okay, Gia?" His bottom lip wobbled. God, I'd give anything, *anything,* to take his place. Why him? Why did this have to happen to someone so pure and innocent and *good?*

"You'll ace this, Roberto," I whispered in his ear. "Like you ace everything."

My sweet little brother came out of surgery at two in the morning. Mom and Dad went to see him first, and thirty minutes later, I was allowed to visit. He managed a smile and a wave, and I kissed his forehead and his cheek and stroked his hair as he fell asleep. If anything happened to me, my parents would go on. But if anything happened to Roberto, it'd rip out the heart of our family, and none of us would make it. Dramatic thoughts, maybe, but I truly believed it.

For Mom and Dad's sake, I hung around the hospital, despite Mom urging me to go home and get some sleep. As dawn broke, I eventually capitulated, falling into bed a few minutes before six. The sound of my phone snapped me from a fitful sleep a couple hours later. A text from Mom letting me know that Roberto had had a good night and was awake and eating. He'd demanded Froot Loops, apparently. I sagged against the pillows, exhausted and groggy, but relieved beyond words, and promptly fell back to sleep.

I returned to the hospital at noon to relieve Mom and

Dad so they could get something to eat and maybe sleep a bit, but knowing Mom, she wouldn't. Dad, though, yawned seven times as he said goodbye. He'd probably fall asleep in the cab on the way home.

I played cards with Roberto and chatted about school and video games, and he, for his part, showed no outward signs of the trauma he'd suffered. Kids were so resilient, but none more so than my brother. In my eyes, he was a hero.

My parents returned to take over just before five, looking far more rested than they had a few hours ago. I promised to come see Roberto—hopefully at home—tomorrow. As I left the hospital, my phone vibrated.

I read the text, and my stomach flipped. It was from Pierre, asking where I was. Fuck. I'd forgotten all about work. I hadn't even called in to let them know I couldn't work tonight's shift. I was so tired, I'd probably chop off a finger or two, but to not even text...

I typed a message, keeping the details brief but citing family issues, along with a groveling apology and an assurance that I'd be there on Monday without fail. Pierre responded, telling me not to worry and he hoped my family issues weren't too serious. My heart expanded with gratitude for his understanding. I could only imagine what Freddo would have done in the same circumstances. Fired me, probably.

My stomach growled the second I stepped into my apartment, but sleep was calling me more than hunger—for once. I fell on top of the bed and passed out.

A hammering on my door woke me from a slumber I

wasn't ready to leave. I squinted at the clock. Thirteen minutes after ten. I rubbed my eyes as the banging continued.

"For fuck's sake." I stuffed my arms into a robe and tied the belt. "The building had better be on fire." I wrenched open the door, and my eyebrows shot up my forehead. "Penn?"

My pleasure at seeing him didn't last long. He muscled past me, the skin crinkled around his eyes, his mouth mashed into a thin line that screamed disapproval.

"Why aren't you at work?"

I sensed the tone and batted it back. "Why aren't *you* in Scotland?"

He shook his head as if ants had crawled into his ears and he was trying to get them out. "I thought when I hired you, wrongly as it turns out, that you'd knuckle down and quit with this tardiness you seem to think is appropriate. But when it comes to my business, Gia, I have zero tolerance for slackers."

My jaw hit the floor at the same time anger swelled in my chest. I ground my teeth. How fucking dare he?

"I am *not* a slacker."

"Really? Then why aren't you at work when you're supposed to be on shift?"

"Have you spoken to Pierre?"

"No. I turned up at the restaurant, hoping to surprise you, and Angie told me you didn't show up for work today."

Angie was one of the hosts who greeted the guests at the door.

"Angie doesn't know what the fuck she's talking

about. Pierre is well aware of why I'm not at work, yet you..." I jabbed a finger at him. "You take Angie's word for it, march over here, and yell at me? For your information, dickhead, my brother is in the hospital, and I spent most of last night and today at his bedside."

My eyes pricked with tears. I wasn't sure if they were caused by tiredness, fear for Roberto, or blind fury at Penn's shitty attitude.

I stomped to the door. "I'm not in the mood for your bullshit, Penn. Get out."

He blinked several times, the dawn of realization that he'd screwed up inching across his face. His annoyance vanished, replaced by contrition. Too fucking late.

"Shit, Gia, I'm sorry. Is he okay?"

"He will be. We hope his doctor will release him today. Now go."

Penn's face bled with relief. "Thank goodness."

I glowered. "Did you not hear me? I said go."

He stayed right where he was. "Gia, I'm sorry I jumped to conclusions. I wanted to see you so badly, and then when Angie..." He blew out a breath between pursed lips and raked a hand through his hair. "I'm sorry," he repeated for the third time.

"I don't care, Penn. You and your goddamn restaurant are not my priority." I motioned with my hand. "I want you to leave."

"No."

"I said get out."

"And I said no."

"Then I'll call the police." I wouldn't call the police.

"Do it." He sat on the couch and folded his arms. "But I'm not leaving until we've straightened this out."

"Straightened it out? This isn't a fuckup on a food order, Penn, where I cooked salmon instead of red snapper. You made your mind up about me before even giving me a chance to state my side of the story or, I might add, talked to my fucking boss and see what he had to say."

"I'm your fucking boss."

I snorted. "You're an asshole."

His lips quirked up, and I had to shove my hands into the pockets of my robe to stop myself from punching him.

"I adore you."

"I hate you."

"Please, Gia. Forgive me." He held out his arms. "I've missed you so fucking much."

My resolve weakened. Last night at the hospital, I'd have given anything to hear those words from Penn, to have him reach for me and comfort me, stroke my hair, and tell me everything would work out. And now, here he was, offering what I'd craved. He'd jumped to conclusions, sure, but it wasn't like I didn't have form. My propensity toward unpunctuality was well documented, although I hadn't been late once since I'd started work at Theo's, mainly because Pierre, though supportive, scared me more than Freddo ever had.

"You hurt me."

His face crumpled, and he dropped his arms. "I'm sorry."

"That's four times, Penn. I bet that's a record."

He smiled, faint and brief, but a smile nonetheless. "I'll

apologize all night if it means you'll forgive me in the end."

He opened his arms again, and this time, I folded myself into his embrace, seeking his warmth, his solace, his smell. His solidity.

"I missed you, too, jerkface."

He kissed my hair. "Now I know I'm home."

Chapter 19

Penn

Morning-afters are the best.

IF I COULD KICK MYSELF IN THE ASS, I'D DO IT SEVERAL TIMES over.

What a fucking idiot.

Why hadn't I sought out Pierre and asked him if he knew the reason Gia wasn't at work? I could blame jet lag, or the fact that I'd barely slept since leaving the United States a week ago, too busy missing Gia lying beside me to fall into a deep sleep, but there were no excuses for my behavior.

Gia and I had started this journey as enemies, then fuck buddies. But somewhere along the way, our relationship deepened, although neither of us had voiced that out loud. Yet I'd never even bothered to truly get to know her outside of the bedroom, and that made me the jerk she often accused me of.

Time to begin putting that right, this second.

I kissed her hair. "Tell me about your brother."

She took a deep breath, her grip on my shirt tightening. "Roberto suffered mild brain damage due to a lack of oxygen at birth. I was fifteen at the time. Mom really shouldn't have had any more kids after me, and she hadn't planned to. Roberto kind of surprised us all."

She looked up at me, her eyes sad yet filled with love for her brother.

"He suffers terrible mood swings, which occasionally turn violent, and he has difficulty concentrating on anything for too long, and he faces complex learning challenges. But he's super bright and kind and loving and funny, and I adore the bones of him."

"He sounds like a great kid."

"The best. I just wish we could do more to help him. His school does a fantastic job, but what he really needs is one-on-one tutoring to help with his learning difficulties. The problem is the fees for his day-to-day schooling are so high that my parents just can't afford it."

She sighed, the heavy kind that came from many years of struggling.

"A few years ago, Roberto had a couple of episodes where the space between his skull and his brain filled with fluid, but he hasn't had anything like that happen in a long while."

"And last night, it did?"

"Yeah. They operated and drained the fluid, and he's

fine, but it gave us all a scare. Luckily, Mom watches Roberto like a hawk, and she saw the signs and got him to the hospital early."

"Your mother sounds like a remarkable woman."

"She is. Dad, too. I'm lucky to have them." Her eyes took on this faraway look. "They kinda checked out when it came to parenting me after Roberto was born. Not that I blame them," she hurriedly said. "He needed enormous amounts of care, and still does, although not quite as much now that he's a bit older. But..." She shrugged.

"A teenage girl needs her mom."

"Yeah." She sighed. "Still, it made me strong and resilient and self-sufficient."

"And mouthy and opinionated, and fucking awesome."

"That, too. Especially the awesome."

I grinned, but my mind whirred. Could this be why Gia was so outspoken and outrageous, almost as if she'd been using that as a way to garner attention from her parents?

It made sense on a psychological level. Fifteen was a tough age for anyone, but if Gia's parents had been, understandably, caught up with a younger sibling who'd demanded swathes of attention, she must've felt abandoned and alone, and that could have manifested itself in this larger-than-life attitude she had.

I almost asked her, but she spoke first.

"Y'know, after Roberto was born, I craved my parents' attention, then I'd feel guilty for dragging them away from my brother to deal with me. I became more and more outrageous, and the madder they got, the more antics I

211

threw down. I look back at that time now, and I'm ashamed."

Bingo.

"Nothing I did ever felt good enough, so I rebelled."

Double bingo.

"You were just a kid with a lot of pressure piled on your shoulders. I dread to think what I'd have been like if my parents hadn't kept a close eye on me."

"A rebel, then?"

"Yeah. Ask Ash. He has some stories that'd make your hair curl."

She chuckled. "I'd have said Johannes was the rebel."

"You'd think, but as a kid, he was a model child."

"What happened? 'Cause he's a dick as an adult." She nudged me in jest and grinned.

My chest tightened.

To this day, I still remember getting the call from my parents to tell me they were on their way to England and that Johannes was in the hospital fighting for his life. The clammy fear of losing my brother had stayed with me for a long time. Fortunately, he'd survived—and had changed beyond all recognition.

"He was attacked in his hotel room while in England by four, five guys. He can't really remember. They slit his throat and left him lying there in a pool of blood. He was lucky to make it."

"Jesus." Gia scrambled upright. "That's awful."

"It was a scary time for our family."

"Is that why he wears those sweaters with the high neck all the time?"

"Yep. He hates the scar and what it represents."

Gia frowned. "Survival?"

You'd think.

I shook my head. "No. Weakness."

Her eyes widened. "Wow." She rubbed her lips together. "Poor Johannes."

"Don't ever say that to him. He does not react well to pity."

"I'll bear that in mind." She yawned and stretched. "God, I'm exhausted. I need sleep. I haven't had more than a couple of hours."

"Want me to stay?"

Please say yes.

She caressed my face in a very un-Gia-like way.

"That'd be nice."

My chest tightened again, but for a very different reason.

Yeah. It fucking would.

K

Clattering noises from the kitchen woke me. Sunlight streamed through the window, and I squinted as I swung my legs out of bed.

I pulled on my jeans and yawned as I made my way to where chaos ensued. I'd once voiced the thought that Gia was the female version of me, and it was true—except when it came to neatness and punctuality. There, we violently diverged.

Case in point—the sight that greeted me.

Pots and pans sat piled up in the sink, the kitchen countertop wore a blanket of batter, and flour decorated the side of Gia's face. For a chef, she was darned messy, although I hadn't witnessed this amount of chaos at the restaurant. Perhaps in her professional life, she managed to keep her true self under wraps, only to unleash the beast in her home environment.

"God, you look sexy all covered in flour."

She glanced over her shoulder. "I dropped the damned bag. It went all over the floor. And then I dropped the frying pan on my foot. I'm surprised you didn't hear my cussing."

I sidled up behind her, slipped my arms around her waist, and rubbed my cheek against hers. "There. We're both covered in flour now."

She peered at me. "I hope I don't look that ridiculous."

I chuckled. "Good morning to you, too." I slapped her ass and pulled out a chair at the tiny kitchen table. "Now get my breakfast on the table, wench."

She arched a brow. "My, my, Kingcaid. You're brave this morning."

"Or stupid." I gave her a goofy grin.

"That goes without saying." She slid three pancakes onto a plate and set down syrup, a bowl of berries, and a pile of crispy bacon. "Eat. I have to go to the hospital soon."

"Can I come?"

My request surprised me, but not as much as it surprised Gia. She took a step back, and her gaze wandered as she looked anywhere except at me.

Ah, she wasn't ready to introduce me to her parents yet.

Fair enough.

"Um. I'm not sure it's the best time."

"No, you're right. They have far more important things to concentrate on. Another time, maybe."

"Yeah, perhaps."

She set down a plate of pancakes equal to mine and sat on the only other chair. Our knees touched and we played knee wrestling for dominance, both of us chuckling. In a move very unlike me, I gave in.

"Ha. Knew I'd win."

"I allowed it."

"Keep telling yourself that, Kingcaid."

She drowned her pancakes in syrup and dug in. I couldn't take my eyes off her. There were many things I adored about Gia, but her unashamed, voracious appetite was right up there with her curvy, gorgeous ass and fabulous tits as my favorite things.

Oh, and her wit and humor and cooking skills.

I took a bite of my stack, groaning in pleasure. "Fuck me, these are amazing."

"Well, I am a chef."

I shoveled another forkful into my mouth. "An amazing chef."

She fanned herself. "Stop with the compliments, Penn, or I might think you're sick."

I grinned, forking a stack of bacon onto my plate. "I'll dial it back."

"That'd be best."

We finished breakfast, and I offered to clean up and

wash the dishes so that Gia could make her way over to the hospital to see her brother. She accepted my offer without argument. Would wonders never cease? She declined my offer of a ride though, saying that it was just as quick to ride the subway.

I watched her from the window as she made her way down the street, only moving away when she disappeared out of sight. It took me an hour to clear up the mess she'd created in the kitchen, but by the time I'd finished there wasn't a single trace of the disaster zone I'd woken up to.

After locking up, I headed down the stairs to my car. But as I started the engine, Gia's comment last night about Roberto's schooling came back to me.

Her parents might not be able to afford a tutor, but I could.

Gia would fight me on it, but as it was for her brother and not herself, I bet I could convince her to accept the help.

I hadn't a clue how to go about finding a suitable tutor, but Sandrine would. She worked with special needs kids up in Boston. Surely she'd have contacts. I put in the call, and five minutes later, she'd emailed me a list of providers right here in New York that came highly recommended.

I drove home and researched every one, making copious notes about their skills, success stories, and testimonials.

In the end, it came down to a choice between two, both highly qualified experts in their field. I rang them both and, after a long conversation, chose the second one.

Mrs. Hunter had adopted two dyslexic children and had "ologies" coming out of her ears.

Now all I had to do was convince one of the proudest women I knew to accept my interference, and not murder me for it.

Chapter 20

Gia

Turns out I like praise.

"You've what?"

I stood with my mouth hanging open—*attractive, I know*—as Penn confessed what he'd done. A part of me wanted to fling my arms around his neck and hug him until he suffocated in my ample bosom. The other part wanted to tell him to back the fuck off, that we didn't need his charity, that he was overstepping on our agreement. We were fuck buddies. That was it. Not boyfriend/girl-friend. Not partners. Not "in a relationship" that, yeah, I felt the need to air-quote myself every time the thought came to my mind.

"Hear me out." Penn showed me his palms. "I know what you're going to say, and you're right. This may be seen as interference in something that isn't any of my business. But, Gia." He curved his hands around my face. "Let me do this. Don't toss a kind gesture in my face over some misplaced sense of pride. I'm not known for them."

He flashed me one of his impish grins that often melted my panties right off. And it had the same effect on me now, making me squirm to stave off the growing heat between my legs.

"I don't know what to say."

"Say yes." He planted a hard kiss on my lips. "Or if you can't go that far, at least say you'll come and see Mrs. Hunter with me. On paper, she's perfect, and she sounded lovely on the phone."

"Oh, Penn." I rubbed my forehead, taking it all in. This would be amazing for Roberto. The school was marvelous, but the teachers only had so much time and attention to share between all the kids. Everyone at Roberto's school had special needs. But, God, I hated the charity of it.

"Gia, this isn't about you and that stubborn pride of yours. It's about your brother and getting him the help he needs to live his best life. Don't we all deserve that chance?"

Ah, fuck. The man knew just the right things to say at the perfect moment.

"If I don't like her, that's it."

He nodded sagely, but Penn being Penn, he couldn't hide the triumphant look in his eyes, the spark of "I've won." And on this occasion, maybe I shouldn't look upon it as a competition, but more that we'd both won. If additional tutoring helped Roberto, then I'd won the fucking lottery.

"If you don't like her, then we keep searching until we find someone you do like."

"Christ, Penn, stop pretending you're so perfect. It's grinding my wheels."

"I love grinding your wheels." He bent his knees and rolled his hips, rubbing his cock against my clit.

I groaned. "When are we going to see her?"

He spun me around and bent me over the arm of the couch, gathering my hair in a ponytail. "Right after I've ground your wheels to dust."

Sitting in the passenger seat as Penn drove us to Mrs. Hunter's apartment, I stared out the window, trying to manage the multitude of feelings hitting me from all sides. Gratitude, worry, irritation, satiation. Hope. All vying for examination, and I didn't want to evaluate any of them. This—driving along as Penn hummed to a song on the radio—felt normal, like the kind of activity those in deep and meaningful relationships did all the time without even thinking about it.

But Penn and I were different.

Are we, though? Sure, we still fucked more than we talked, but the balance between the two had shifted from a ninety-ten situation to a sixty-forty. If those digits reversed, then what would I do? Was I ready to be in a real relationship, and, equally as important, was Penn?

I cast a glance at him out of the corner of my eye, and my insides tossed around as if all the bits had come loose.

Penn wasn't just handsome and great in bed with a dick I salivated over, but also funny and thoughtful and kind-hearted, and a myriad of other positive things that far outweighed his negative traits. If we were making a list about me, my negative column would extend for pages, so I couldn't sit here judging Penn for his annoying tidiness, his propensity for punctuality, or his fondness for bossing me around.

God. Me, in a serious relationship. The idea alone scared the shit out of me. It wouldn't last. It couldn't. Somewhere along the line, I'd fuck it up. Penn and I were on opposite sides of the tracks, too different to sustain this for long.

He was a playboy, and I was a playgirl. He had more money than he could spend if he lived to a thousand years old. I struggled to pay rent most months. I couldn't hope to compete. The playing field was too uneven, manageable only between the sheets. And even passion waned eventually.

So lost in my thoughts, I missed the point where he caught me staring. His lips tipped up, and he reached across the seat to take my hand. He brought it to his thigh and left his resting on top.

"It'll be okay, Gia."

I frowned. "What will?"

"Us. I feel it, too. Try not to panic."

What? I felt seen, and all I wanted to do was hide. How unlike me. I usually sought the limelight, craved being the center of attention.

"I'm not panicking."

I was totally panicking, especially now that Penn had called me on it. Could the man read minds?

"Liar." He brought my hand to his lips and kissed each one of my fingertips. "We're here."

I hadn't even realized he'd stopped the car.

"Come on. Let's put Mrs. Hunter through your special brand of interrogation and see if she passes the test."

He climbed out of the car. I joined him on the sidewalk.

"You make me sound like the CIA or something."

"The CIA has nothing on you." He took my hand as if it was the most natural thing in the world. "Let's see what my girl can do."

I lit up like Times Square on New Year's. *My girl.*

Guess I'm in a relationship.

Mrs. Hunter was perfect, if such a human being existed. Patient, understanding, and so damned knowledgeable about the kind of challenges Roberto faced because of that and his other problems. After ten minutes of chatting with her, I hired her on the spot, pending approval from my mother, whom I had yet to break the news to. Mom had the same prideful gene as me—or rather, I'd caught it from her—and I wasn't yet sure how she'd take to the idea. But if I could put aside my beliefs to help Roberto, then so could Mom. Dad would be cool. He'd go along with whatever Mom decided.

God, the difference this might make to my darling

brother. One-on-one tutoring could change his life, improve his future prospects and his chances of landing a good job.

I told Mrs. Hunter that I'd be in touch real soon, and Penn drove me home, leaving me to my thoughts and rather disgusting nail biting. I never bit my nails, but in this instance, it helped me concentrate. By the time Penn stopped the car outside my apartment building, I had the words in the right order. Now I just had to make the call.

"Do you mind not coming up?"

"Yeah, I do." He leaned across to my seat and kissed me. "But I get it. Call me when you've spoken to your mom. Please tell her that I'm not an asshole and I only want to help."

"I'm not lying to my mom." I feigned shock. "You *are* an asshole."

He chuckled. "You're dating an asshole, so what does that make you?"

My girl. Dating. Crap. We're really here.

"A philanthropist. Someone had to take you on."

I got out of the car to the sound of his laughter echoing in my ears. I grinned the entire elevator ride up to my apartment, and I was still grinning when I called Mom.

"How's Roberto?"

"He's fine. I managed to get hold of his doctor after you left earlier, and he said Roberto should be able to come home tomorrow."

"Mom, that's great."

"It is. That boy is such a worry."

"But amazing."

"So very amazing." I heard the awe in Mom's voice.

"And brave. The way he takes all this in his stride while the rest of us are falling apart."

"He's a champ." I took a breath. "Mom, listen. I've found a tutor who's willing to work one-on-one with Roberto."

The line went silent. I refrained from filling it, as was my way. Let Mom process in her own time.

"Oh, Gia. I know you want to help, darling, but we can't afford it. Not on top of the school fees and the medical bills. Your father and I are working all the hours we can, as are you. As much as it kills me that I can't give Roberto everything he needs, it's just not possible."

Okay, here was the moment I had to walk the line between a lie and the truth. I wasn't ready to tell Mom about me and Penn, and at first, I'd considered telling her I'd gotten him the funding through some program or other. But Mom would see through that story in an instant, and I hated lying to my parents. Semi-truth it was, then.

"You know that my new boss is rich," I began.

"Yes." Mom sounded tentative.

"Well, he's also a good guy, and when I told him about Roberto, he offered to help."

Another long pause ensued, this one so long that I thought she'd hung up on me. I checked. She hadn't. The line was still open.

"And why would he do that?" she asked quietly, disbelief in her tone.

"Because I'm a terrific employee and chef." I laughed to show her I wasn't being serious. "Mom, he's a nice person who wants to help. That's all. And he has more money than he can ever spend, so it's not like he'll miss it."

I cringed even as I said the words. I'd never be able to repay Penn for his generosity, and the fact that he was wealthy didn't mean he owed me or anyone else a damned thing.

"That's not the point, Gia."

No, it wasn't, but I couldn't let Mom refuse this major opportunity by standing on the proud step.

"I refused at first, Mom, but then I thought of Roberto and how much of a difference this could make to him."

"It would indeed make a huge difference, but I'm not comfortable with this, darling. Hold on. Let me ask your father."

I heard muffled voices and then Dad, clear as day, say, "And what does the rich dude want in return?"

I smiled. Just like Dad to think like a man. Well, he was one, so it shouldn't come as a surprise.

"Tell Dad he wants nothing," I called out, although I wasn't sure she'd heard me.

Mom came back on the line. "You father would like to meet this mysterious benefactor."

Ah, crap. I had a feeling they might say this. How would Penn feel about a "meet the parents" moment, especially when I told him I didn't want my mom and dad to know about us, and he'd probably get a grilling about what was in it for him? And if he replied to that question with "Smoking-hot pussy," I'd kill him.

"He's a busy man, Mom. He's responsible for the running of hundreds of restaurants."

Worth a try...

"Well then, if he's too busy to meet the mother and father of the boy he professes to want to help, then tell him thank you for his offer, but the answer is no."

Shit.

"I'll talk to him."

"You do that. Oh, and, Gia?"

"Yeah?"

"Please be careful."

I almost laughed at her hidden message of the rich guy taking advantage of the poor girl. If only she knew.

"I promise. Love you. Give Roberto a kiss for me."

I hung up before she decided to bestow more sage advice on me, and called Penn.

"Brace yourself," I said the moment he answered the phone. "My parents want to meet you."

Chapter 21

Gia

Why does he have to be perfect?

"Can you pull over here for a minute?"

Penn frowned at my request. He stopped the car outside a scruffy tattoo parlor with a pizza place next door advertising two for the price of one. A balding fat man whose T-shirt was at least three sizes too small and had ridden up to reveal a rounded stomach was leaning against the doorframe smoking a cigarette. He reached down the back of his pants to scratch his ass.

Lovely.

"What's wrong?"

I twisted to face him, wearing a serious expression, unsure of how he'd take the next thing I said.

Only one way to find out.

"I don't want my parents to know about us."

"I see." He tapped his fingers against his thigh. "Are you ashamed of me?"

I suppressed a laugh because it was a ridiculous thing to say. How could anyone be ashamed of a man like Penn Kingcaid? He was perfection, pure and simple.

I stilled the drumming by putting my hand over his. "I'm not ashamed of you, or of us, but this is all so new, Penn, and I'm not ready to tell people until I've come to terms with it myself." I shook my head. "Wrong thing to say. That's not what I mean. It's just... If I tell my parents I'm in a serious relationship, one of two things will happen. Either they'll ask when the wedding is"—I screwed up my face—"or they'll make you their new best friend and tell you all kinds of things about me I'm not ready for you to know. So please, you're just my boss who's a nice guy and wants to help my brother."

Penn ran a hand over his chin, his eyes doing that twinkle thing that told me he was about to have some fun —at my expense.

"What's it worth for me to play along?"

"Your dick stays attached to your body."

He laughed. "You'd never detach my dick. You love it too much."

Couldn't argue with that assessment.

"Hmm," he continued. "Sex on the balcony of my penthouse?"

I almost stopped breathing. This was the first time Penn had mentioned going to his place, although that could be because he always drove me home and walked me to my door, and, well, neither of us was good at delayed gratification.

"Are you overlooked?"

"There's a building across the street, and if someone had a pair of binoculars, they'd get an eyeful, I suppose." He twirled a lock of my hair around his finger. "What say you, Miss Greene? A price worth paying for my silence?"

Hardly a chore to have sex with Penn on his balcony.

"I suppose."

"Such enthusiasm." He brought my face to his and kissed me. "Can we go now? I'm anxious to meet the parents who brought you into the world and therefore into my life."

I waited for a punch line that never came. Warmth flooded my stomach, and my skin tingled all over.

"You old charmer. Use that on my mom and you're in"

He grinned. "Thanks for the tip."

"Wait. No. Don't use that on her, or the deal's off."

He chuckled. "Are we going?"

"I guess."

I directed him the rest of the way. There wasn't any parking right outside the building, but Penn found a spot one street over. He grabbed the bag containing a bottle of wine—impolite to turn up to dinner without one, he'd said—and we made our way to my parents' building. My palms were damp as we stepped into the elevator. I ran them over my jacket, sucked in a breath, and held it.

"Shouldn't I be the nervous one?" Penn arched a brow. "Breathe, Gia, before you pass out on me."

"Don't fuck this up, Penn, or I'll never forgive you."

"And risk not having anal sex on the balcony? Not likely."

"I never agreed to anal."

231

"You didn't specify either way, which leaves the contract open to interpretation." He encircled my waist with his free hand and ran his nose along mine. "Don't pretend you're not turned on by it. I've seen your toy drawer, remember."

"Showing you that was the biggest mistake of my life."

Penn laughed. "Maybe we should stop by your place on the way to mine and pick up a few items."

"With all the women you must have taken back there, surely you have a drawer of your own."

He grazed a finger underneath my chin. "I've never brought a woman into my home. It's my private space and I guard it fiercely. You'll be the first."

My mouth popped open. "You're kidding."

The elevator dinged and the doors opened. Penn took my hand.

"Which way?"

I pointed, speech difficult to come by after his revelation. Oh God, this was moving so fast, a runaway train with failed brakes. Penn had *never* taken a woman back to his home, and yet he was taking me. I wanted to question him further, but we were here already. I slipped my hand from his and smoothed my hair. "That conversation isn't over."

Penn shrugged. "I'm happy to have it. The question is, are you?" He lifted his hand and rapped twice on Mom's door while I floundered, unable to come up with an answer to an impossible question.

"Darling." Mom hugged me to her. "Come in, come in." She let me go and turned her gaze on Penn. "You must be Mr. Kingcaid, Gia's boss. I'm Bianca, Gia's mother."

I groaned. "Think he can figure that out, Mom."

Penn handed over the bottle of wine. "Penn, please. For you, to thank you for having me over."

"Oh, you shouldn't have, but thank you." Mom ushered him in and introduced him to Dad. "Simon, this is Penn."

Dad shook his hand and I saw Penn wince. I withheld a chuckle. Dad was doing his manly routine.

"Good to meet you."

"Where's Roberto?" I asked.

"In his room playing video games." Dad rolled his eyes. "I swear that controller is glued to his hands."

"I'll go pry it from him."

"May I come?" Penn asked, his manners on full display in front of my parents. They'd choke if they'd heard the anal sex conversation in the elevator.

"Sure." I crossed the living room into the tiny hallway, rapping once on the door at the end. "Roberto, it's me. Can I come in?"

"Gia!" I heard scampering, and the door wrenched open and my brother threw himself at me as if he hadn't seen me in weeks, despite me visiting every day since he'd left the hospital on Monday.

"Whoa, bud, take it easy." I ran a hand over his dark, curly mop of hair that Mom tried—and failed—to tame.

He gazed up at me, his huge hazel eyes brimming with adoration. "I thought you weren't coming."

God, I adored this little dude. "Why would you think that? Of course I'd come. I promised, didn't I?" I eased myself free. Roberto, who hadn't noticed Penn until that second, widened his eyes and clung to my arm.

"Who's this?"

I beckoned Penn forward. "This is Penn Kingcaid. He's my boss at the restaurant."

"The new restaurant?"

"That's the one. Are you going to say hi?"

"Hey, Roberto." Penn held out his hand. "I've heard a lot about you."

Roberto stared at Penn's hand, then looked up at me and back at Penn's hand. He shook it, then yanked his hand to his chest and giggled.

"So, your dad said you're into video games." Penn inched inside Roberto's room. "What are you playing?"

He eyed Penn warily. "*Avengers.*"

"Ohhh, I *love Avengers*. It's my favorite game."

I had no idea whether or not that was true, but the way Roberto's eyes lit up, I hoped it was, for my sake, and Penn's. When it came to video games, my brother would sniff out a liar in five seconds. They were his passion, and he knew every detail down to the minutest level. If Penn was bullshitting him, we risked a meltdown.

"It is?" Roberto gave Penn another wide-eyed stare, this one tinged with intrigue.

"Absolutely. Can I play with you for a bit? Maybe until dinner?" He looked at me. I nodded, curious as to where this would go.

"Can I, Gia?" Excitement filled his tone, his smile wide.

"Go for it."

I stood with one shoulder propped against the door-jamb and watched, transfixed, as Penn Kingcaid became my brother's newest best friend. If I hadn't seen it with my own eyes, I wouldn't have believed it. The two of them chatted and laughed and played *Avengers* as if they'd known each other all their lives. And me? I fell a little bit harder. My brother was my light, my life, and anyone who showed him kindness and understanding and made him laugh shot to number one in my book of perfect people.

"What's going—"

"Shhh." I interrupted Mom and jerked my chin. She followed my gaze, and seeing what I saw, her face went all gooey. She pressed a hand to her chest and sighed.

"What a shame he's only your boss," she whispered, giving me a nudge. "He's just about perfect."

"Mom." I shook my head. "Stop. You barely know him."

She showed me both palms in conciliation. "Fine. But don't berate me for hoping that one day you find the right man for you."

"He'll have to be a saint," I muttered.

"Oh, shush." She elbowed me. "Dinner in five minutes."

I grinned. "It might be dinner for three."

In the end, all five of us made it to the dining table, although Roberto grumbled and groused the entire time until Dad gave him a sharp reprimand. He then pouted and sulked.

When the time came to say goodbye, Roberto hugged Penn the longest and made him promise he'd return soon to play video games with him. Penn, after shooting a look at my mother and gaining her approval—hell, she couldn't nod fast enough—promised that he would.

"So we're good to go with Mrs. Hunter?" I whispered to Mom.

"We're good to go." For the first time in ages, a weight seemed to lift off her shoulders. My parents tried so hard to give Roberto everything he needed, but they were aware that they fell short in several areas, constrained by money and time and the difficulties of life in general. That Penn had done what I couldn't, what *they* couldn't, made me even more determined to one day have my own restaurant, to build a secure financial future not just for myself but also for Roberto.

I wasn't an idiot. I knew that restaurants failed all the time, often under immense competition and escalating debts, but it could be done. I'd seen it, not only with Penn, who had the benefit of enormous wealth and a renowned family behind him, but with people who came from nothing and built an empire. One day, that would be me. I had all the motivation I needed in my beautiful brother, who would need support for the rest of his life. I would not let him down.

"I'll set it up." I kissed Mom and Dad and gave Roberto a hug. "Be good, kiddo." I ruffled his hair because he hated it. Sure enough, he gave me a glower.

"Stop it. I'm not a kid."

"No, bud. You're an Avenger!"

He beamed and made some movement that I guessed was right out of the game or the movie that I still hadn't seen.

"Thank you for a wonderful dinner, Mrs. Greene. Maybe I should have you working in one of my restaurants."

Mom blushed. My mother *never* blushed. Penn had

charmed my entire family so much that it wouldn't surprise me if Mom asked to adopt him, and disown me.

"Oh, no. Our Gia is the cook."

Penn's gaze alighted on me, his eyes soft and warm with a hint of lust. "And what a cook she is."

I bustled him out the door before he blew our cover. As soon as we were out of sight, he knitted our fingers together and gave my hand a squeeze.

"Thank you for playing with Roberto. It will have meant a lot to him."

"I can't believe he looks so well, considering he only got out of the hospital five days ago."

"He's resilient."

"Yeah, and terrific. I enjoyed myself."

I arched a brow. "Really?"

"Really. You have a wonderful family, Gia."

I did. I truly did. And Penn Kingcaid, somehow, had become a part of it.

Chapter 22

Penn

There's a first time for everything.

I HAD THIS EMPTY FEELING IN THE PIT OF MY STOMACH AS I NOSED my car into my personal parking space beneath my building. If someone had told me a couple of months ago that Gia Greene would be the first woman I brought back to my home, I'd have laughed in their face. I knew what this meant for me.

The question was, did Gia know?

Was it time for "the talk," the one I'd never had but had heard about? Where two people admitted that their futures were entwined, that they were meant to be together.

The funny thing was I hadn't planned this, yet it felt so fucking right, and not because I'd bartered for sex on the balcony. I wanted to be able to look back on this night and call on memories of Gia sitting on my couch, writhing naked in my bed, eating breakfast in the kitchen as the morning sun rose over the towering buildings of Manhattan, lighting them in oranges and yellows and golds.

I wanted the smell of her on every surface in my home.

We rode the elevator in silence, our eyes on each other, tension building with each floor that passed. I could've pushed her against the wall and fucked her right here, but that was so cliché. Besides, I was enjoying the way she kept shifting her weight and pressing her thighs together, her gaze flitting over my face, my body, down to my groin, and back up to my face.

She jumped at the sound of the elevator arriving at my floor. It wasn't like Gia to be so nervous. Maybe she felt the shift, too, the momentousness of this evening.

Her taking me to meet her parents, if under a blanket of dishonesty.

Me inviting her back to my home and the connotations that brought.

I led her through the foyer and into the living space. A bank of floor-to-ceiling windows with an unrivaled vista of Manhattan drew her gaze, and her jaw dropped.

"Wow, look at that view." She wandered over, pressing her nose to the glass. "If I lived here, I'd spend hours just gazing at it. I'd never leave."

"It's beautiful." I sidled up behind her, encircling her waist, and laid my chin on her shoulder. "Just like you."

She twisted to face me and wrapped her arms around my neck. "So where's this balcony? And you'd better have lube if you're thinking of shoving your dick up my ass."

I chuckled. Trust Gia to take a sensual moment and dirty it up. I mused whether that was her defense mechanism, something she turned to whenever she felt uncomfortable. I unwrapped her arms from around my neck and took her hand.

"Come with me."

I led her into my bedroom. Her eyes went straight to the enormous window that overlooked the Hudson, the New Jersey coastline on the opposite side of the river.

"Where's the balcony?" she asked again.

I drew her into my arms. "Forget the balcony. We'll do that another time. For now, I want to worship every stunning inch of you."

"But you said—"

I pressed a finger to her lips. "Gia, shush. For once in your life, shut your mouth."

"Can't shove your dick in it if it's closed." She grinned.

"Gia." I brushed my fingers along her neck, flicking her light brown hair over her shoulder. "Things have changed. I feel it in here."

I pressed a closed fist to my chest, my mind flipping to a conversation I'd had with Sandrine when I'd helped her move apartments.

I'd asked her how she stayed so upbeat and positive, especially considering what she'd been through. She'd told me that the heartbreak Theo's passing had brought was worth every splinter, every shard of glass stabbed through her chest because she'd gotten to love him and experience his love for her. That she wouldn't hesitate to do it all over again if the right person came along, because there was nothing greater than to love someone unconditionally and have them love you back.

At the time, I hadn't understood. I'd been so entrenched in the idea that avoiding a relationship would protect my heart from the kind of agony I'd witnessed Sandrine endure, but I'd been wrong. The risk was so worth it.

Gia had shown me that.

"I know you feel it, too. So please, Gia, stop with the quips. Don't belittle what's happening between us. Show me your heart. By bringing you to my home, I'm showing you mine."

She went completely still, her lips parted an inch, and she stared at me, unblinking. "I'm scared," she whispered. "Sarcastic retorts are all I know."

"I'm scared, too. A lot of firsts are happening, for both of us, but if we don't take a risk, then how are we ever going to move forward?"

"I don't do relationships."

"Neither do I. Yet here we are, in a relationship, and I'm so fucking happy, Gia. You make me so fucking happy. The question you have to answer is whether being with me makes *you* happy."

She licked her lips. "It does. You do."

My breath hitched, and my hands trembled, the relief intense. She could have balked, and a part of me had expected her to, but we'd been leading to this place for weeks, and one of us had to be brave enough to step into the unknown and bare our soul.

It wasn't love, for either of us. Not yet. Gia and I had

begun this journey so far apart that edging toward one another had started with baby steps, but we'd taken an enormous leap this evening.

"I mean, I'm no Christian Bale but..." I shrugged.

"Now who's making jokes."

"I play by my own rules."

"Typical."

I caressed her smooth cheek and cupped a hand under her chin, bringing her lips to mine. She arched into me, pressing her tits to my chest. Her arms wound around my neck, her fingertips playing with my hair. Usually, by now, I'd have her stripped naked and on the bed or bent over a table or the arm of a chair, but tonight had to be different. Our mutual honesty demanded a different approach.

This was a big deal, and I couldn't fuck it up.

I skimmed my hands over the flare of her hips, the curve of her ass, my mouth and tongue worshipping her. She trembled in my arms, the moment as big for her as it was for me. A trace of her perfume lingered, and I breathed in the scent of roses and lavender and Gia. I committed every morsel to memory.

The feel of her in my arms, the soft, pliability of her body, the taste of coffee lingering on her tongue. The beat of her heart and hitch to her breath.

She palmed my dick through my pants, unzipping me to allow her hand to slide inside. I felt her weight shift, her knees bending, and while fucking Gia's mouth was my idea of heaven on earth, I stopped her.

"No."

A flash of hurt raced across her face, her eyes darkening. She dipped her chin to her chest. I rushed to reassure her.

"Let me take care of you."

I picked her up, hooking her legs over my hips, and gripping her ass, I carried her over to the bed and gently laid her on it. She tilted her pelvis as I bunched her dress around her waist. I kissed her pussy through her lace underwear, then drew them down her legs.

I grabbed a pillow. "Here. Put this under your ass."

"Ah, so close to seduction, but you fell at the final hurdle."

A chuckle vibrated my chest. "Must try harder."

I tormented her with my tongue and lips and hands until she begged me to let her come. I thought of re-creating that night in Grand Cayman, but considering how she'd exacted payback, I relented. Blue balls weren't a whole lot of fun.

Opening my nightstand drawer, I grabbed a condom, shucked off my pants and shirt, and sheathed myself. But as I pressed the head of my cock against her bare pussy, I paused. Lying there, sated, her hair mussed, her cheeks flushed, her dress clustered around her waist, she was, undoubtedly, the most beautiful woman I'd ever had beneath me. This was a moment to savor, to take a mental picture of and commit to memory.

A frown drifted across her face. "What's the matter?"

"Nothing. I'm just... enjoying the view. You enchant me, Gia. I'm consumed by you. You're exquisite, and I'm so fucking thankful we met."

I witnessed the internal struggle play out, the impulse for her to belittle the moment potent. And I also witnessed the moment she dismissed the idea and embraced the shift in our relationship and paid me the biggest compliment she ever could.

"It's true that you're no Christian Bale, Penn. You're so much better."

K

I slept like the dead, waking to the sound of trance music somewhere in my apartment and the space beside me empty and cold. I glanced at the clock on my nightstand. Nine thirty-two. I rolled out of bed and padded into the bathroom. My toothbrush was damp. I grinned, squirted toothpaste on it, and scrubbed my teeth. Grabbing a pair of boxers and a T-shirt from my closet, I wandered into the living area and drank in the sight greeting me.

Gia, wearing a shirt she must have taken from my closet, had a mixing bowl tucked into the crook of her arm and was furiously beating something—I hoped pancake batter—and dancing around my kitchen. She wiggled her ass and snaked her hips and sang out of tune while I let my adoration for her envelop me. She was utterly magnificent.

I waited until she put down the bowl—knowing my luck, if I surprised her, she'd drop it on the floor and redecorate my walls—and made my way over. She still hadn't seen me, and as she bent over and reached inside one of the lower cabinets, I grabbed her hips and pulled her against my groin.

She shrieked, twisting out of my hold. "Fucking hell, Penn. You scared the shit out of me."

"Little tip, sweetcheeks. Bend over and show me that ass, and you're gonna get felt up. It's just a fact of life." I slid my hand around the back of her neck and kissed her. "What's cooking?"

"Crushed almond pancakes with eggs and smashed avocado."

My mouth watered. "Almost as delicious as you." I nuzzled her neck. "Spend the weekend with me, and we can fuck and cook and eat and binge-watch crappy TV."

"I'm on the schedule at your restaurant tonight, and we're fully booked."

"I hereby grant you the weekend off." I squeezed her ass. She slapped my hand away.

"I can't leave Pierre and the other chefs shorthanded."

"I'll send someone from the hotel."

"You have an answer for everything, don't you?"

I grinned. "Pretty much."

"Except you've forgotten one minor detail."

"Oh yeah?"

"You agreed to keep our personal life separate from our professional one. And therefore, you can't pull rank." She dipped a finger in the batter and dabbed the end of my nose. "Too bad, mister. You're gonna have to find a way to amuse yourself."

I returned the favor. "Fine. I'll trawl the internet for sex toys."

"Creeper." She snagged a towel off the counter and wiped the batter from her nose, then wiped mine, too.

"You won't say that when I test them out on you."

"Meh." She hitched a shoulder. "I've tried them all."

"Not with me you haven't." I waggled my eyebrows.

"Fine." She stood on her tiptoes and kissed me. "Let's see what you've got."

I grinned. "Challenge accepted, Miss Greene. Challenge accepted."

Chapter 23

Gia

Going out was a colossal mistake.

PENN HAD HIS ARMS AROUND ME BEFORE WE'D SET FOOT OUTSIDE the rear entrance to the restaurant, which the staff used to come and go. I wrestled out of his grip, flashing him my best "hands off" glare when he'd rather I flashed him my panties. Probably.

"What are you doing with your night off?"

After five nights straight working at the restaurant, I was ready for a break. I'd come in this afternoon to help with prep only because we were two staff members down and Pierre had asked, and, well, on the QT, I had a bit of a crush on the enigmatic, gifted chef. Not in the sexual sense, but in the creative and professional sense. The man was a genius in the kitchen.

And Penn was a genius in the bedroom.

I had the best of both worlds.

"Well, since you're dumping me for a boring business meeting tonight, I'm going to break out my best vibrator, the one that works underwater, soak in the bath, and give myself several orgasms while drinking wine and eating cheese."

Penn groaned, tugging me down a narrow passageway between his restaurant and the designer clothing store next door. "Stop tormenting me." His hands roved over my hips as he dove in for a kiss that broke all the PG-13 rules, and then some.

"You're the one who blew me off, not the other way around," I reminded him. "You'd better not blow me off tomorrow night, too." I also had Saturday night off. To get a Friday and a Saturday night off in the restaurant business happened about as often as Halley's Comet passed by the Earth, but that was how the schedule had fallen. Wouldn't see me complaining.

"I wish you were blowing me off." He grinned in that way he had that I'd begun to recognize as Penn thinking of something rude. "As long as you're super quiet, I can sneak you underneath the table and you can keep me entertained."

I laughed. "What a tempting offer." I pretended to consider it, my thumb and forefinger cradling my chin. "No."

"Ugh. Fine. I'll go to the boring meeting. Expect me hopefully sometime before midnight."

I shook my head. "Oh, no, you don't. No booty calls tonight. I'm catching up on my beauty sleep. I'm not having you stagger into my apartment stinking of booze and cigar smoke and expecting sexual favors."

"You don't need to catch up on beauty sleep. You're already stunning."

"And compliments will not encourage a change of heart."

"Worth a try." He shrugged and gave me another of his brilliant smiles. "Want a ride home?"

"God, yes. My feet are killing me."

Penn dropped me right outside my building, and after kissing him for a solid few minutes, I tore myself away and traipsed inside. The relief when I kicked off my shoes resulted in an orgasm-sounding groan. I collapsed onto my sofa and massaged the soles, digging my thumbs into the knots. I wasn't sure whether feet got knots like backs did, but whatever. It felt good.

Dinner consisted of leftover pasta I'd brought home from the restaurant last night. I ate it cold—still delicious—tossed the dirty plate into the sink to clean up later, and padded into the bathroom. The tub took ages to fill, but sinking into the bubbles and bath salts eroded the aches that seemed to be everywhere. I loved being a chef, but fuck, it was backbreaking, feet-swelling work.

An idea curled in my mind, inching a smile across my face. Perfect. If Penn wanted a little entertainment at his boring business dinner, then that was what he'd get.

I got out of the bathtub, sloshing water all over the floor. Meh. I'd clean up later. Leaving a trail of wet footprints to my bedroom, I opened my toy drawer and plucked out a large purple vibrator—waterproof, of course. Next, I grabbed my phone and a small tripod I had bought once with the idea of recording myself cooking and uploading to Instagram. I think I'd thrown up two videos before I'd decided it was a terrible idea and buried it deep underground where all bad ideas went to die.

I returned to the bathroom, quickly set up the phone, and sank back into the warm water. I pressed the remote, and the phone began recording. I gave the camera a sultry smile, brandished the huge vibrator in the air, and switched it on. Lowering it into the water, I pressed it inside me and bit my lip.

"Enjoy the show, Kingcaid."

In a performance worthy of a porn star, I groaned and moaned and gasped and totally hammed it up for the camera. I played with my nipples and ran my hands over my body, a permanent smile in place as I thought of Penn's reaction when he received this.

Except. Shit. What if he opened it right there at the table and whomever he was sitting next to copped a view?

Ah, fuck it. So what? I wasn't exactly shy in the sexual department. Besides, as soon as Penn realized what the video was, he'd either shut it off and watch it later in private, or he'd make an excuse to leave the tedious dinner and maybe give himself a treat.

One thing was a hundred percent certain, though: he'd watch it.

Heat built in the base of my spine, and it wasn't coming from the rapidly cooling water. Sparks of pleasure ran up and down my vertebrae, and my pussy grew heavy with arousal. Seconds. I was seconds away from exploding, and I intended to make it loud.

"Fuck!" I cried out as I crested, my clit pulsing through

my climax. Nowhere near as good as with Penn, but it worked for my purposes. I pulled out the vibrator, gave the tip a lick, and with a wink at the camera, I switched it off.

Laughing to myself, I wrestled the phone free of the tripod and sent the video to Penn.

I climbed out of the bath and emptied the water, wrapping myself in a fluffy towel. I hadn't even dried off when my phone dinged with a text. I snatched it up.

Oh. It isn't Penn.

I opened the message from Lorenzo, my old coworker at Freddo's restaurant, a flash of guilt shooting through my chest. Despite my promises to keep in touch after I'd left to work at Theo's, I'd failed on a spectacular level. Not because I didn't want to, but rather, I was *terrible* at this whole keeping-in-touch thing. I had good intentions, then life swept me up and all those good intentions went out the window.

Lorenzo: Yo, biatch. You still alive?

I grinned, tapping out a response.

Me: No. This is my corpse talking.

Lorenzo: Ha! Still a dick, I see.

Me: [winking emoji] It's good to hear from you. Sorry I'm a shitty friend.

Lorenzo: Nah. We're cool. What you doing tonight? You working?

Me: Night off.

A banner flashed up on my phone. Penn had replied. As much as I itched to open it, I read Lorenzo's next message instead.

Lorenzo: Good. Get your clubbing gear on. We're hitting the dance floor.

My aching feet wept, but I owed this to Lorenzo.

Me: Fine. But I have to be home by midnight.

Lorenzo: Fine, Cinders. We'll leave just as the club is heating up.

He sent me a time and a place to meet. I replied with a thumbs-up emoji and seven hearts, then jumped to Penn's message.

Penn: WTF! I just spat soup all over the table.

Me: You're welcome, Kingcaid.

Penn: I'm groaning here. They think I'm ill. I might feign sickness and hotfoot it over to your place.

Me: No can do, amigo. I have a better offer.

Penn: Hope it's fully charged.

I chuckled.

Me: I'm going out with a man. We're off clubbing.

Penn: You'd better fucking not be.

I shivered in delight. Loved a bit of possessive talk. It got my engines firing.

Me: Are you telling me who I can and can't go out with?

Penn: Damn fucking straight. You're mine.

My ovaries did a little dance.

Me: Ah, Penn. As much as I'm enjoying this display of masculine possessiveness, I have a slutty dress to pour myself into.

Penn: Gia. I'm fucking warning you.

Me: [laughing emoji] Better work on that game face, Kingcaid. I'm going out with a coworker from my old restaurant. And for the record, he'd much rather go down on you than on me.

Three dots appeared. Then disappeared. Eventually, a message came through.

Penn: Prepare for payback. I fucking growled at the dinner table. Growled, Gia! My associates must think I'm a complete weirdo.

Me: I'm laughing so hard I might have peed myself.

Me: Toodles, gorgeous. I have to go.

Penn: This isn't over.

Another shiver trickled down my body.

Me: Bring your A game.

Penn: Bank on it.

I tossed my phone onto the bed. It'd be too easy to trade texts with Penn all night and miss seeing Lorenzo, but I owed my old buddy a fabulous night out, and a fabulous night out was what I intended to give him.

"I'm drunk."

I leaned against Lorenzo as we staggered out of the club just as it was getting going. Usually, I'd have stayed, despite telling Lorenzo I had to be home early, but my feet were killing me, and sitting down in a club to rest my aching limbs rather than shaking my booty on the dance floor wasn't something I'd ever do. God forbid. Lorenzo would give me shit for months over that.

"Good thing we were only out for a couple hours. And may I remind you that you were the one who insisted on a last round of shots."

"Ugh. Stop pointing out all my failures."

Lorenzo laughed. "I've missed you, Gia. Let's not leave it so long next time."

"Ten-four." I frowned. "Why did I say that?"

"Because you're drunk."

I pointed at him. "You always were smart."

We went our separate ways with promises to meet up again in a couple of weeks. As I crossed the street to my subway station, lights from a coffee shop caught my attention. *Caffeine. Good idea.* Might take the edge off tomorrow's inevitable hangover. I tottered over, my eyes drifting to a couple sitting in the window. They were engrossed in each other, the man leaning forward, giving the woman his undivided attention while she drew her teeth over her bottom lip again and again, looking stricken.

Yikes. Hope it's not bad news.

I peered closer—y'know, like rubberneckers unable to tear their eyes away from a car crash. And then it hit me, a lump of ice to my core. I stumbled and caught my heel in a grate, saving myself only at the last moment.

Penn.

What the actual fuck?

What was he doing here at this time of night with a woman I'd never seen before? Unless...

No.

Penn had a lot of faults, just as I did, but cheating? He wouldn't.

Would he?

Was this a case of me not being worthy or able to hang on to a rich, successful, beautiful guy? No. Fuck that. I might've struggled for parental attention after Roberto was born, but I knew my worth. Sure, I had a vulnerable bone, like everyone, but I kept mine well hidden. I refused to allow any man to expose it to the elements, to poke at it and make me feel less than.

Not even Penn Kingcaid. *Especially* not him.

Penn straightened, running his hand through his hair, his lips moving as he spoke to the woman.

Maybe she'd been at the meeting and they were finishing up some business? He hadn't said he was dining only with men. She could be one of Kingcaid's senior managers.

Yeah, that had to be it.

Maybe I should go inside and introduce myself. Of two minds, I hesitated. If Penn was cheating on me, then the bastard deserved to wear the contents of the cup he was warming his hands on. But if he wasn't, and I turned up, eyes blazing with accusation, I might just ruin the best thing that had ever happened to me.

I walked away, legs shaking, and not from inebriation this time.

Next time I saw Penn, I'd ask him about the business meeting and watch carefully for his reaction. If he lied to me, I'd know.

The question remained, what then?

Chapter 24

Penn

True love is *wonderful*. According to some.

Thirty minutes earlier...

I pushed open the door to the coffee shop where Sandrine had asked me to meet her, worry curdling in my gut. I'd been surprised, to say the least, when she'd texted as I was leaving my business meeting to let me know she was in Manhattan and wanted to meet.

For one, Sandrine lived in Boston, which wasn't exactly drop-in distance away.

And for another, it was eleven thirty, hardly a normal time for a social call.

Sandrine waved at me as I entered, pointing to a

waiting cup of coffee to let me know she'd ordered. As I made my way over, a prickling crept up the back of my neck.

Something was off.

I couldn't put my finger on it exactly, but she looked... nervous. She smoothed her hands over her skirt as she stood.

"Hey, beautiful." I clasped her upper arms and kissed her cheek. "This is a surprise."

"Yeah, sorry for the late hour. I meant to text earlier, but time kind of got away from me."

"Is Corabelle in the city with you?" I slid onto the bench opposite hers.

She shook her head. "She's spending a few days at my mom's."

"Ah. Next time, maybe." I loved my goddaughter to the stars and back. "Give her a big kiss and cuddle from uncle Penn."

"She'll send them right back." Her face softened, and she reached into her purse, retrieving her phone. "Look at this picture I took last weekend at the park."

She turned the phone toward me, and I melted.

Corabelle, braids flying, was in mid-flight as she skipped headed for the slide. Sandrine had caught her exalted expression to perfection, her eyes bright and excited, cheeks flushed through happiness and exertion.

Every day, she grew to look more and more like Theo.

I clasped a hand to my chest almost as if I was trying to hold my heart together. Theo should be here, watching his daughter grow into the angel she was always destined to be. And it was my fault that he wasn't.

"Stop." Sandrine's hand covered mine and she squeezed. "I know where your mind has gone, Penn. Just stop. Please."

"He should be here." My voice cracked and I cleared my throat. "It kills me that he'll never see what she'll become, or watch her first recital at school, or warn off her first boyfriend. Or walk her down the aisle on her wedding day."

"I know." Sandrine got up from the table and came around to my side to give me a much-needed hug. "But for the love of all that's holy, you have to stop with the guilt. Accidents happen. We've had this conversation a hundred times, yet still you put yourself through this torture."

"I looked down at my phone, Sandrine." My voice came out strangled, an outer sign of inner turmoil. "I looked at my phone rather than the road. If I hadn't, then I might've been able to avoid that car hitting us. I might've been able to do something."

"Penn." She sighed heavily, resting her chin on the top of my head. "He was a drunk driver. He came out of nowhere. Even the police said that you wouldn't have been able to do anything."

"They weren't there," I whispered. "I could have braked, or accelerated, or swerved. I could have acted, but I let the phone distract me."

"Penn, sweetheart, don't." She squeezed me extra hard. "I hate seeing you like this, and so would Theo. In fact, he'd probably whoop your ass."

I smiled, though it felt forced. "You know I could take him."

261

She laughed. "Yeah, I do." She pressed her forefinger to her lips. "But let's whisper that so he doesn't hear us."

I gazed at her, this wonderful, forgiving woman who'd propped me up when it should have been the other way around. She'd never judged me, not for a single second. Wasn't required, really. I judged myself.

Harshly.

"He was so lucky to have you."

"Oh, I know." She blew on her fingertips and rubbed them against the pale blue fitted shirt she'd paired with a gray skirt. "I was far too good for him."

A chuckle burst out of me, unforced. "Truth."

She moved back to her side of the table, and as soon as she did, her nerves returned, her fingers plucking at the gold chain around her neck.

I reached for her hand, giving it an encouraging squeeze. "What's going on, Sandrine? Why are you in Manhattan, and why are we sitting in a coffee shop at close to midnight on a Friday night?"

She blinked several times in quick succession, her dark eyelashes gracing her cheeks only for a microsecond, and she avoided my gaze as she wrapped her hands around her mug of coffee.

"Don't hate me, Penn."

My forehead wrinkled. "Hate you? I could never hate you. What's this about?"

Grazing her teeth over her lip, she lifted her chin, and it wobbled. What the fuck?

I leaned in, waiting.

"I've met someone. His name is Kyle. I'm in love, Penn. He's asked me to move in with him, and I've said yes."

Every syllable was delivered at lightning speed, fast enough that she tripped over one or two words, making them sound slurred.

Christ, only last week, when I'd taken Gia to my home —the first woman who'd ever stepped over the threshold —I'd thought about the conversation I'd had with Sandrine regarding the possibility of finding someone else. But it had happened so fast.

A thousand questions assaulted me at once.

In love?

Where did she meet this man?

Who is he?

What about Corabelle?

In the end, I settled on, "Move where? You only recently moved."

Really, asshole? That's the question you chose to ask?

She smiled softly. "I know. Bad timing, right, but life doesn't always keep to straight lines. We have to bend and flex along with it. And we're moving to..."

Pausing, she grinned.

"Go on," I encouraged.

"Manhattan." She squealed. "Kyle's company is transferring him, and it's a promotion, too. We came down a couple of days ago to look for apartments, and tonight, I finally agreed to move with him, and that's when I messaged you. It means Corabelle and I will be closer to you. We can see you all the time. Won't that be great?"

My mind said, *Yeah, sure.* A red-blooded male happy to let his woman spend time with another guy who just happened to be the best friend of her deceased husband?

No guy was that laudable.

Her eyes beseeched me to accept her. To accept him. To accept them together, and what cut me the most was that she cared what I thought. I had no rights over Sandrine or Corabelle, yet the first person she'd chosen to tell such monumental news to... was me.

God, I loved her. She was like a sister to me.

Better than a sister.

I stood up and held out my arms. "Come here."

She scrambled upright, throwing herself at me. I hugged her almost to the point of cutting off her ability to breathe, evidenced by her squeak of "You're squishing me." I loosened my hold and knocked her chin up until she met my eyes.

"I could not be happier for you. If anyone deserves this, it's you. Of course, I will have to meet him and assess his suitability for you and for Corabelle."

I winked, but I meant every word. If he didn't treat Sandrine and Corabelle right, I'd cut the fucker off at the knees.

"I told him you'd say that." Sandrine's eyes twinkled, a wide grin creeping across her face. "He's prepared for a grilling."

"He *thinks* he's prepared. He isn't."

She palmed my shoulder. "Don't you scare him away."

"If I can do that, he wasn't worthy of you."

Her smile grew coy. "He's worthy."

She retook her seat and I did the same.

"I almost told you about him when you came up to Boston to help me with the move, but I hadn't fully committed to the idea of *us*, then, you know? It's taken me a long time to agree to move in with him. For a while, dating Kyle felt as if I was cheating on Theo, but looking at it through clear eyes, I think he'd want this for me, and for Corabelle."

"He would," I agreed. "The only thing Theo ever wanted was for you to be happy. And you are, right?"

She nodded. "Ecstatic."

"Then you're living the life he wanted for you." I nibbled on the corner of my lip. "I've met someone, too."

"You have?" Sandrine's eyes danced. "Who?"

I told her about Gia, about our "interesting" meet-cute. About Ash's wedding and our sparring and how our relationship slowly changed into something more, something deeper.

"For years, after watching you break apart when Theo died, I refused to consider the idea of a long-term relationship. If that was what love did, who needed it? Not me. Even when we had that talk up in Boston and you told me that the love Theo had showered you with was worth the risk, but I didn't believe you. I'd seen the agony, the heartbreak, and there was no way I'd voluntarily take such a risk. But Gia..."

I chuckled, shaking my head. "She's something else. A force of nature. Messy and chaotic, and fuck, she's never on time for *anything*, but she's beautiful and smart and funny and has a kind heart. She's also an amazing chef. Seriously, she makes my mouth water."

"In more ways than one, hey?" Sandrine canted her head.

"Yeah."

My eyes glazed over, the image of Gia pleasuring herself in the bath drifting through my mind. Talk about a tease. And she'd denied me the chance of a booty call, too. I'd make her pay. Not sure yet how, but it was coming.

Like me, hopefully.

"If this girl sends you to wherever you just went, hang on to her with everything you have. Because the bliss on your face, Penn, that's priceless." She squeezed my arm. "I'm glad you found her. True love can hurt, yes, but it's too wonderful to miss out on for fear of what *might* happen."

True love? No. That's not what this is. True lust, maybe.

"We're not in love. We're in 'like a lot,' though."

"Sure." Sandrine nodded. "I can't speak for Gia, but I can for you. And you are a hundred percent in love with that girl. Fight me."

A flare of adrenaline set fire to my bloodstream. Sandrine couldn't be right. I'd know if I was in love.

Wouldn't I?

"Does she know? About me? About Theo?"

I shook my head. Sandrine disagreed with my determination to keep what had happened away from my family, but she'd always supported my decision.

Until now.

"Keeping secrets isn't a good idea, Penn, especially from the woman you love. They have a tendency to explode in your face."

"I can't." My voice broke. "I just can't. If I blame myself, then why wouldn't she?"

Sandrine gave me one of her sympathetic head tilts.

"To quote back at you, Penn, if she doesn't understand, then she isn't worthy of you."

"She's worthy."

"Then tell her."

I scrubbed both hands over my face. "I'll think about it."

Chapter 25

Gia

Penn's a good person.
Apparently.
Although, coming from a ROGUE,
is that reliable information?

—

PENN: BE THERE IN THIRTY.

Thirty? That couldn't be right. I wasn't even showered yet. I'd whiled away hours of my Saturday thinking about what I'd seen last night on the way home from the club, and I'd decided there was nothing in it. Penn hadn't been holding the woman or kissing her, or even sitting beside her, and I refused to turn into one of those women who felt threatened by their man spending time with another female.

I trusted Penn.

I did.

He was allowed to have female friends. I had male friends. Okay, most of them were gay, but not all. And if Penn got all up in my face over me sharing a cup of coffee with one of them, it'd piss me off, and rightly so.

He deserved the same treatment from me.

There. Done. Over.

Time to get fucking ready.

The anticipated knock at my door came after twenty-five minutes, not thirty. I still had sopping-wet hair, a towel wrapped around me, no makeup, and several dresses scattered all over my bed. Penn was taking me to the Kingcaid New York hotel tonight to eat in their restaurant. I'd not eaten there before, but the idea of tucking into the kind of food served at a three-Michelin-starred restaurant made my mouth water.

Not that I'd ever eaten at a three-Michelin-starred restaurant, but I'd seen enough TV programs to know it was on another level when it came to cookery.

I flung open the door. "I know, I know. I'm not ready." I whirled my hand around in the air like some kind of lunatic. "Make yourself comfortable. I'll be fifteen minutes."

Penn chuckled. "No, you won't. You'll be at least thirty."

"Ugh. You're right."

Penn flopped onto my couch. "Take your time. I booked the table for eight forty-five."

I paused, pivoted, and narrowed my eyes. "You told me we had reservations for eight."

"True, but I knew you'd be late, so I lied." He flashed me one of his panty-melting grins. "I know my girl."

I hid the fuzzy feeling his words caused to flood my chest with a heated glare. "That's a sneaky little game."

He tapped his temple. "I'm learning."

I used two fingers to point at my eyes, then swiveled them to point at Penn. "I've got my eye on you, Kingcaid."

"Hopefully after dinner, you'll have your hands on me, too."

"You have a one-track mind."

"I'm on the same track as you, sweetcheeks."

I huffed and trotted off to my bedroom, his rumbling laughter following me. God, I loved him.

Wait.

What?

No, I didn't.

I liked him. A lot. He did it for me in the bedroom department, but love wasn't in the plan.

Neither was a relationship, but here we are.

I plunked myself onto my bed and stared at the wall. What about my beliefs? Why had they deserted me right when I needed them? Life was too short to fall in love, to commit to one guy, unless he was Christian Bale, and Penn Kingcaid was no Christian Bale.

No. He's better than that. So much better.

I clamped my hands over my ears and only just stopped myself from screaming, "Shut up!" I didn't want to hear it, not even from myself. I wasn't ready to acknowledge the awful creeping feeling that the blind truth was staring me in the face.

I was in love with Penn Kingcaid.

"Gia?"

My head snapped up. Penn had his shoulder propped

271

against the doorframe to my bedroom, his arms folded over his taut chest, a quirk of amusement lifting his lips on one side.

"Why are you sitting there staring at the wall?"

Because I've had an epiphany that terrifies me.

I forced a grin and hoped he didn't see the falsehood in it. "Sorry. Daydreaming."

"We don't have to go." His eyes roved over me. "I can think of far more thrilling things to do with our Saturday evening."

I snapped out of my funk. "Oh, no, you don't. I've been looking forward to this all damned day. I've hardly eaten all day to prepare my stomach for the gastronomic delights it's about to enjoy." I leaped to my feet and grabbed my hair dryer. "Now shoo. I don't need you distracting me."

He kissed my neck, then left. I put all thoughts of love out of my mind and managed to finish getting ready in thirty-two minutes. Which, considering he'd arrived five minutes earlier than he'd promised, meant I was only twenty-seven minutes late.

See, I could do math.

"Ready," I announced with a curtsy followed by a twirl. "Will I do?"

Penn ran his eyes over the maroon dress I saved for special occasions. It clung to my ample curves, finished just below the knee, and showed off a hint of cleavage, but wasn't slutty by any means. Not exactly classy either, but with this ass, hips, and boobs combination, it was kind of difficult to pull off the demure look.

Penn stared like he wanted to devour me. He made a move. I held out my hands.

"No. We're late enough as it is."

"But that dress," he groaned. "That body. You're torturing me."

"Good." I slipped the strap of my matching purse onto my shoulder. "Feed me now, and I'll feed you later."

"Pussy for dessert. I'm in."

Penn often drove himself, but as we arrived outside my building to a uniformed driver waiting beside a limousine, I raised a hand to my mouth.

"A limo? For me?"

"No, for me. I'm in the mood for wine."

His eyes twinkled, and I gave him a dig in the ribs.

"You're an ass."

He angled his head and checked out my rear. "Talking of asses..." He ran his hand over mine. "Time to get your fine derriere into the car."

A girl could let the kind of adoration in that man's eyes go to her head if she wasn't careful. I was even more convinced now that the woman I saw him with was no more than an associate or a friend. No one was that good an actor.

Except, maybe, Christian Bale.

Didn't stop me from inquiring, though.

"How did last night's business meeting go?" I asked as he climbed in beside me and fastened his seat belt. "Anything interesting come up?"

He pressed the button for the privacy screen, cutting us off from the driver. "Yeah, my fucking cock when you sent me that video."

I laughed. "I thought you'd like that."

"Lucky for you, I had my phone on silent. If I hadn't, the entire table... no, strike that... the entire *restaurant* would've thought I was watching a porno."

I laughed again. "You watched it to the end, though, right?"

"So far, I've watched it seventeen times." The engine fired up, and we pulled away from the curb.

"Seventeen?" I gaped at him.

"Yeah. I've had a hard-on for most of the day." He took my hand and pressed it to his crotch. Sure enough, he was rock hard.

"Oh, dear." I stifled a grin as I unzipped him, slipping my hand inside his pants.

"Gia." He gripped my wrist but didn't stop me.

I tugged down his boxers, freeing his erection. "Can't have my man sitting there all night with blue balls."

Penn's groan as I lowered my head was music to my ears.

"Wow, this place is beautiful."

I'd never visited the Kingcaid New York hotel, let alone their exclusive restaurant, but the opulence took my breath away. Chandeliers hung from the ornate ceiling, the linens were crisp and white, and I'd bet I could see my face in the polished silverware. A man in a tux smiled wide as we approached, and he even did a little bow.

I only just managed to swallow a giggle.

"Miss Greene." He bowed again. "Mr. Kingcaid, how wonderful to see you here this evening. Your table is ready. Please come with me."

Spine straight as an arrow fired from an Olympic archer's bow, the host—or did they call them maître d's at posh restaurants?—weaved his way between the widely spaced tables, stopping beside an intimate table for two set back from the rest of the diners in its own little nook. As we sat, a voice called out Penn's name. He turned and smiled, his ass never quite hitting the chair.

"Oliver Ellis." Two strides brought him face-to-face with a tall, broad-shouldered, impossibly good-looking man with a close-cut beard, twinkling navy-blue eyes, and the kind of jaw that cut glass. He had his arm curved around the waist of a pretty, slender woman with thick, wavy hair almost touching the crack of her ass, a rack to rival mine, and friendly hazel eyes that were flip-flopping between Oliver and Penn as they spoke.

"Gia." Penn beckoned for me to join him. "Oliver, Harlow, this is my girlfriend, Gia. Gia, this is Oliver Ellis, a business associate of mine, and his fiancée, Harlow Winter."

A stray thought came to me. Was Oliver one of the associates Penn had had dinner with last night? Had he gotten sprayed with the soup? A sidelong glance at Penn, whose lips twitched as he shook his head, gave me the answer.

"Nice to meet you."

"And you." Oliver's smile was unforced and friendly, and I instantly took to him. "Would you like to join us for dinner? I'm sure we can squish two tables together. I'd like to talk more about that proposal we discussed last month, Penn."

Harlow dug him in the ribs and jerked her chin at our table. "Oliver. I think they may have planned a more private evening, and one that doesn't involve work."

"Sorry, buddy, I promised my girl my full attention tonight," Penn said.

A chance to see a different side of Penn nudged at me. I'd seen him operate as the owner of Theo's, of course, but Kingcaid was a different prospect altogether. I'd admit that I was intrigued to watch the CEO at work. And I hadn't missed the brief expression that had crossed Penn's face at Oliver's suggestion. He wanted us to have dinner with them. Maybe he'd been struggling to arrange another meeting, or they kept missing each other.

"It's fine, Penn. I don't mind at all. It's nice for me to get to know your friends."

I had no clue whether Oliver was a friend or not, but the two men had seemed happy to see one another, so they weren't enemies. Following my statement, Penn wasted no time in instructing the guy who'd seen us to our table to arrange one suitable for four diners. In less than thirty seconds, we were shown to a table on the other side of the restaurant.

Turned out both Oliver and Harlow were fabulous company. I discovered that Oliver ran a global conglomerate called ROGUES with five of his friends, the size of which rivaled Kingcaid, and he'd met Harlow when he'd employed her as a nanny. That told me a lot about him. Oliver Ellis might be a billionaire, but his feet were firmly on the ground.

"When are you two getting married?" I asked Harlow.

"October ninth." She grimaced. "There's still so much to do and less than a month to do it in."

"Relax." Oliver clasped her fingers, giving them a squeeze. "You worry too much. All that matters is us. I've told you a hundred times, if you want to run away with just us and the kids and have a ceremony for four, that's good with me."

Penn glanced at me out of the corner of his eye, the parallel to Asher and Kiana's wedding passing between us, and how arranging the more intimate ceremony had brought the two of us closer together, too. For once, we'd stopped bickering and sniping at each other and worked together to bring happiness to a couple we adored. Who knew, if it hadn't been for that, Penn and I might never have gotten together.

Perish the thought.

"How many children do you have?" I asked Oliver.

"Two girls. Annie and Patsy." He set his blue gaze on Harlow. "One day soon, we hope to add a third and a fourth to our family."

"Pray for boys," I said with a laugh.

"Oh, I don't know. Girls are pretty fabulous."

"Yes, they are." Penn's hand traced up my thigh. I slapped him away, catching the grin Oliver tried to suppress.

As the dessert menus were brought over, Penn excused himself, leaving me with Oliver and Harlow. The second Penn was out of sight, Oliver leaned forward, smiling.

"I bet it'll be you two walking down the aisle soon."

I blinked five times in succession, my lips parting. "Oh,

no. We're nowhere near that. Seriously, a few weeks ago, we were at each other's throats. It's all very new."

"Love doesn't abide by the rules of time." Oliver looked adoringly at Harlow, then returned his attention to me. "Penn is a good person, and that's not something you can say about many businessmen in this town. Hang on to him."

"Oliver!" He received another sharp nudge in the ribs from Harlow. "It's none of your business."

My worries about Penn and the mystery woman further faded. I didn't know Oliver Ellis, but I wasn't a bad judge of character, and he seemed like the kind of guy who didn't dish out praise like confetti. If he thought Penn was good people, then he was. Of course, I already knew that. I'd had a wobble, that was all. My equilibrium was back in full working order.

"It's fine. I appreciate straight talk. Penn's probably in shock at how well behaved I've been tonight."

"What's this about shock?" Penn slid into the seat beside me.

"I was just telling Oliver about the video I sent you last night."

Guess being well behaved couldn't last forever.

Penn's jaw unhinged, and his cheeks reddened so much that I worried there'd be no blood left to keep his dick alive.

"You didn't," he croaked.

"Ha! No, but now he's intrigued, right?" I grinned at Oliver. "Right?"

"Very," Oliver said, those eyes of his twinkling like Orion in the night sky. Okay, that made me sound like I knew the constellations or something. I didn't. Probably should have left it at "twinkling," but I loved a bit of embellishment.

"Aww, I'd love to share, Oliver, but I've probably said too much already."

I winked at Penn. He shook his head as if I were an errant child he'd given up trying to tame.

Probably for the best.

"Shall we order dessert?" Penn stared at the dessert menu, his complexion gradually returning to a normal skin color from the earlier beet red.

"I thought we were planning to have dessert back at my place." I blinked at him innocently. "Didn't you say something about eating my pu—"

"Okay, time to go." Penn shot to his feet, gripping my elbow while Oliver and Harlow couldn't hide their amusement.

"What? I was going to say 'pumpkin pie.'"

Oliver burst out laughing. Harlow pressed a fist to her mouth. Penn muttered something about getting their assistants to set up a meeting and bustled me out of the restaurant.

"Here, bend over," I said, chuckling as we made our way through the lobby toward the street. "Make it easier for me to remove the pole from your ass."

Penn's earlier horrified expression dissolved, leaving the two of us laughing loudly enough that we drew the attention of his driver standing beside Penn's car. "You are unbelievable."

"I know. You're lucky to have me."

We chatted about dinner in the back of Penn's limo,

and I let him know I'd really enjoyed Oliver and Harlow's company and didn't mind at all that our planned night had been somewhat hijacked. Business was business, after all, and men like Penn and his entire family didn't become as wealthy as they were without putting business affairs first.

As we pulled up outside my apartment building, I ran my hand up his thigh. "I suppose after my performance this evening, you're going to make me edge all night, aren't you? I deserve it, I guess."

Penn grimaced. "Do you mind if we take a rain check? I need to set a few things in motion after chatting with Oliver tonight, and update my dad. I don't want him hearing through the grapevine that we've moved closer to a potential joint venture." He yawned. "And I am pretty wiped."

"Oh." Jibbed twice in a row for business reasons. Or so he said. Maybe he was meeting that woman again. Despite my earlier promises to let it lie, I couldn't help giving him an opportunity to tell me about her. "Did you get in late from your business meeting last night? Is that why you're tired?" I took the edge off my questions by following up with a joke. "Or maybe you just can't keep up with me."

He grinned, pulling me into his arms and kissing my neck. Goose bumps pebbled my skin where his lips trailed to my shoulder. "I can keep up. I promise I'll make it up to you. I know I owe you orgasms after what you did in the limo earlier this evening. Why don't you come over to my place for lunch tomorrow? Say, one o'clock?"

He didn't answer my question about last night's

dinner and what time he'd gotten home. I thought about pushing it, but it'd look odd. But that niggle I'd thought I'd put to bed reappeared.

Was I losing him? Maybe a girl like me wasn't destined to hang on to a successful billionaire, although Harlow had obviously managed it. But I wasn't Harlow. I was me. A girl who was well versed in being pushed into second place.

But not this time. I deserved more than that.

Tomorrow, I'd ask him outright who the woman was. No more avoidance. I'd told Oliver I appreciated straight talk. The time had come for me to be straight with Penn and uncover the truth. I'd thought ignoring it was for the best, but no. I deserved answers.

And I was going to get them.

Chapter 26

Gia

**As my namesake, Rachel Green, would say,
"Isn't that just kick-you-in-the-crotch,
spit-on-your-neck fantastic?"**

PENN SENT A TEXT THIS MORNING OFFERING TO PICK ME UP, BUT I said I'd make my own way to his place. Riding the subway over to Manhattan gave me time to work through how to approach the thorny subject of the strange woman. I mean, wouldn't he find it weird that I hadn't said a thing before now? I'd seen him at the coffeehouse on Friday night, and now it was Sunday. If we hadn't spent last night together, then maybe I'd have an excuse, but we had.

God, this was precisely why I'd avoided relationships. They just brought angst and heartache, and only psychopaths enjoyed having their hearts ripped out. Or was it that they preferred ripping hearts out? Either way, the ripping of hearts featured front and center.

Maybe I was getting a teeny-tiny bit ahead of myself, letting my fertile imagination run away with me. I could hear Kee now. "Not like you to be dramatic, Gia." And then she'd grin and nudge me, and we'd fall about laughing.

Okay, here was the plan. Let him serve up lunch, or at least wait until he wasn't busying about doing... stuff. And then come straight out with it.

"Hey, Penn, so, on my way home from a club I went to with my old buddy Lorenzo Friday night, I passed this coffee shop en route to the subway, and there you were with a woman. Was she at the business dinner, too?"

Ugh.

That sucked. Too sycophantic.

"Hey, Penn. Are you cheating on me, you bastard?"

Nope. Too confrontational.

"Hey, Penn. Saw you with that cute blonde Friday night. Fancy a threesome?"

Terrible idea. *Abort!* Not that I was averse to three-somes. I'd prefer two guys, though.

Guess I'll have to go with my usual approach. Just say the first thing that comes to mind.

I covered my face and scrubbed it, ending up with most of my carefully applied makeup all over my palms. Which, because this was me, I then rubbed on my white jeans.

Fuck. My. Fucking. Life.

My groan alerted the guy sitting opposite who, spotting a beige smudge on white jeans, helpfully offered a scrappy tissue.

I shook my head. For all I knew, he'd blown his nose on it, or worse, used it to catch his jizz. Having a potential cheating conversation with Penn with my jeans covered in another man's jizz didn't place me in a good light.

Jesus, Gia. Cheating, jizz, made-up shit. *Just stop.*

I got off the subway and ducked into a CVS. Armed with water and wet wipes, I managed to clean the worst of the makeup stain off my jeans. Just my luck, I had a big wet patch in its place, but at least it was on the thigh and not at the crotch. The sun would soon dry it off. Besides, I was forty minutes early. I had time.

In the end, my jeans dried in ten minutes. Rather than walk the streets—in the non-hooker sense—I headed over to Penn's apartment building. It wasn't like a half hour made much difference either way.

Wait. Oh. My. God.

I was early.

For the first time in my life, I'd arrived ahead of schedule.

I might faint. Penn probably *would* faint.

Sheesh. I was kind of proud of myself.

I took out my phone and sent Kee a text, plus I put up a post on Instagram, congratulating myself for such a momentous achievement. Something this big required capturing on socials for posterity.

The grin remained on my face as I trooped up the stairs and into the vast lobby of Penn's building. As his was the penthouse, you couldn't just make your way up there. The elevator had a code, and you had to pick up a key card thingy from reception. How the other half lived. A serial killer could wander into my apartment building brandishing a machete, and no one would bat an eye.

I'd taken two steps toward the opulent, sleek glass-and-chrome reception desk when laughter from the other side of the lobby caught my attention. I looked over at the precise moment Penn put his arms around a blonde woman and drew her tight to his body.

The same woman whom he'd been at the coffee shop with on Friday night.

I stared, unable to look away as they broke apart. Penn leaned in and pressed a kiss to her cheek. She rubbed her hands up and down his upper arms, then ran her hand through his hair.

I ducked behind a tall, bushy potted plant as the woman finally took her hands off of my *fucking* boyfriend and made a move toward me.

It might still be innocent. It might still be innocent. It might still—

"Love you, Penn Kingcaid."

Oh God.

"Love you, too. Call me."

My heart shredded as if it'd been put through a cheese grater, the tattered remnants floating around my chest. I grasped a handful of my shirt. I felt rudderless. Empty. Broken.

I waited for her to pass by, my eyes scorching a hole in the back of her head as she tossed her hair over her shoulder and bounced down the street. I dashed down the steps to street level and set off in the opposite direction. With no idea of a final destination, I broke into a run. My lungs burned, my legs ached, and my knees hurt, but none of it mattered. I'd given up on my entire belief system for a man who'd so wantonly cast me aside as if I meant nothing.

Well, screw him.

I meant something. I *mattered*.

Fuck Penn Kingcaid and his lies and his cheating. If he thought he'd get away with this, I had a surprise in store for him. Sure, I might not have confronted him right there, in the moment—which, by the way, I always assumed I would have—but if he thought I'd meekly disappear into the ether... not a chance. I hadn't a clue yet how to get my revenge, but I would.

Forced to stop when I couldn't catch my breath, I collapsed onto a bench. A jogger ran by, helpfully throwing out a "Maybe wear different attire if you're gonna try jogging."

Fucker.

I flipped him off, not that he'd see me, but who cared?

Not me.

I couldn't bring myself to care about anything right now, other than coming up with a plan to stick it to Penn Kingcaid.

My phone buzzed. I rifled through my purse. A text from Kee.

Kee: OMG! Penn is having the best effect on you.

My eyes stung with unshed tears, but I wouldn't allow a single one to fall. Not for that fucker. I sent Kee a winking emoji, only because she'd think it weird if I didn't reply, and I wasn't ready yet to tell her what had happened.

I only hoped it wouldn't cause issues between her and

Asher, because Kee, one hundred percent, would stand beside me in outrage.

What a goddamn mess. I should've never gotten involved with TBK, as I'd call him from this day forward. That. Bastard. Kingcaid.

Another text came through. Penn. I couldn't see the entire message, and I had no intention of opening it to read the rest and let him know I'd seen it. No, he could stew, wondering what had happened to me and why I hadn't turned up at his place.

That meant I couldn't go back to mine, either. Penn might have thought he could get away with stringing along two women, but he was a competitive asshole who loved to win. He wouldn't take kindly to being stood up, and knowing him as I did, he'd head over to my place when he didn't get a reply.

Like a light bulb going off, an idea for payback sprang to mind. Penn *was* competitive, nakedly so. He'd never hidden his desire for victory, no matter the contest. It was one of the things we had in common that, in the early days at least, had caused so much exasperation between us.

If Penn and I were to split up, he'd want to be the one to end it, to come out the other side looking like the victor.

Well, too bad, TBK.

On this occasion, you lose, motherfucker.

You. Lose.

My phone rang. Penn again. I let it go to voicemail, then immediately deleted the message he left. I wasn't interested in his fake concern. He could work himself into a lather wondering what had happened. He could ring the hospitals and scour the streets and break into my apartment as he'd done before, hoping to find I'd overslept.

He'd find out soon enough that I was wide awake. Finally.

Tonight, I'd get my revenge.

And for that, I needed Lorenzo.

I made the call. By the time I'd finished updating him on what had happened and my plan to get my own back and emerge triumphant with my battered ego assuaged to some extent, he replied with two words.

"I'm in."

Chapter 27

Gia

Turns out revenge isn't as sweet as I expected.

"YOU'RE A KNOCKOUT! I'M SCARED TO HUG YOU IN CASE I wrinkle that jaw-dropping dress. If I didn't like penis so much, I'd totally do you, right here, right now."

"Oh, stop." I put my arms around Lorenzo and hugged him. "You're the best friend anyone could ask for."

"From the woman who has her fair share of best friends, I'll take that as a compliment." He angled his head to one side. "How you holding up?"

"I'm okay. Equal parts hurt and pissed off, but I'll survive. I always do." I hitched a shoulder in a nonchalant fashion even as my insides crumbled.

"Has he been in touch?"

I nodded. "Twelve texts, at least as many phone calls, each one ending in a voicemail when I didn't pick up."

"Have you listened to them?"

"Nope."

Lorenzo rubbed his lips together. "Might not be a bad idea."

"I don't want to talk to him. Nothing he can say will change my mind. He's shown his true colors. It's my job to pay fucking attention to them."

"The old 'when someone shows you who they are, believe them,' huh?"

"Exactly."

I slid my hand inside his proffered arm, and we set off for Theo's. My heart rattled my rib cage with each step, and my confidence wavered, but I had to see this through. After tonight, I'd have no boyfriend, and no job. There wasn't a chance I could carry on working under Pierre at Theo's after this, even if Penn didn't fire me on the spot. Fortunately, Lorenzo had mentioned to Freddo in passing that I might be available again soon, and he'd made all the right noises regarding re-employment.

One less thing to worry about.

"We don't have to properly kiss, do we?" Lorenzo pulled a face. "Like, on the lips. With tongue. I mean, you're a fox and all, but you're my friend, and it'll feel weird."

I chuckled. "No, we don't have to kiss, especially if you're going to pull that face and ruin the illusion, but you might have to squeeze my ass or something. And dial down the camp."

Lorenzo checked out my rear end. "You have a great ass. Squeezing it won't be a chore at all."

I ran my hands over my ample buttocks. "You're right.

I *do* have a great ass, one that Penn Kingcaid won't ever touch again."

My chest pulled tight, and something must've shown on my face because Lorenzo gave me puppy-dog eyes and patted my hand.

"Whoever ends up with you is going to land a real diamond, babe."

I shook my head. "No chance. If I'd stuck to my beliefs, I wouldn't be in this mess. I should've never gone near the asshole." I thought about how hard he could make me come with remarkably little effort. "Okay, I should've banged him once, twice tops, and walked away."

That way, I'd have gotten the good orgasms and kept my heart intact.

"That's my girl." Lorenzo kissed the top of my head. "Ready to show that fucker what he's missing?"

Sucking down lungfuls of air, I held it, then puffed up my cheeks as I blew it out. "I'm ready."

I wasn't ready, but I also wasn't prepared to just walk away. I had my pride, and I intended to emerge victorious from the battlefield. Penn Kingcaid was about to get his ass handed to him on a platter. I refused to let him best me. There was only one winner in this fight for who gets to keep their ego intact.

Me.

Head held high, tits out, hips swaying, I sashayed into Theo's, my arm around Lorenzo's waist, his around mine. Angie, one of the hostesses who manned reception broke into a broad grin as I approached the desk.

"Gia! Are you okay? Penn's been going crazy. I overheard him telling Pierre he didn't know where you were."

She frowned as she took in my attire. "Aren't you supposed to be working tonight?"

Ah, Angie, the woman who had her nose in everyone's business. She was the one who'd caused an issue with me and Penn when Roberto had been taken into the hospital. My heart stuttered. God, Roberto. I hadn't even thought about what would happen to his dyslexic tuition after tonight. Ah, shit. Was this just one big mistake? Maybe I should keep my mouth shut, suck it up like a good little girl, and, for the sake of my darling baby brother, carry on with the sham of my relationship.

No.

I couldn't do it.

Not even for Roberto. I'd find another way. Somehow. Maybe Kee would help me out, although asking her for financial assistance would be one of the hardest things I'd ever had to do. It'd kill me if she thought, even for a second, that I was treating her as some kind of ATM now that she'd married a billionaire.

But continuing this charade with Penn would be far harder. I wasn't that great an actress.

Lorenzo squeezed my hip, bringing me back to the present. I bestowed a broad, fake-as-shit smile on Angie.

"Change of plans. I know we keep a couple of tables free, just in case VIPs show up unexpectedly. I'm taking one."

I swished past her, towing Lorenzo alongside me. Angie shouted something, but I ignored her, strutting deeper into the restaurant as if I were the owner, rather than Penn. I scanned around. No sign of him. He must be either in the kitchen or in his office. It wouldn't be long before word got to him that I was here, not if big-mouth Angie had her way.

As I slipped into the booth of table forty-six, Angie shot past me faster than if she'd been fired from a cannon. I gave Lorenzo a nervous smile and tugged him to sit beside me rather than on the opposite side of the table.

"Prepare for showtime," I murmured, beckoning to Eric, one of the waitstaff. He came over immediately, brandishing two menus.

"Gia. Great to see you front of house for a change. I'd recommend the linguine, but no one makes it better than you, so maybe go with the sea bass."

We wouldn't get to eat the linguine, or the sea bass. That wasn't the purpose of my visit, although Eric wouldn't know that. As soon as I'd had my say, I expected Penn to eject me from his restaurant. If the tables were turned, I would. I'd drag him out by his balls and toss him on the sidewalk.

I might do that anyway.

"Sounds delicious." I leaned my head on Lorenzo's shoulder, looking up at him as if he were some kind of deity. I fluttered my eyelashes. "What do you think, babe?"

"Whatever my angel wants." Lorenzo played his part to perfection, gazing back at me with adoration splattered over his face.

"Two sea bass it is. Oh, and whatever wine the sommelier recommends this evening. Thanks, Eric."

As Eric retreated, I caught sight of Penn storming through the restaurant, on a direct collision course with us.

"Brace for impact," I breathed, my insides all wobbly

as if I'd wolfed down a whole panna cotta. I shifted closer to Lorenzo and began nibbling on his earlobe. Thank fuck I knew the guy well enough to play the part. It'd been him or Ben, and the latter was far too loved up with his new boyfriend to help me pull off a good enough performance that would fool Penn into thinking it was real.

Lorenzo turned his back, shielding me from view, and lowered his head. To the outside world, it'd look as if we were kissing without having to do the deed. He winked at me, and then he was gone, and standing in his place was a furious Penn Kingcaid, his face redder than when I'd teased him in front of Oliver Ellis on Saturday night, his nostrils breathing fire—okay, not actual fire like a dragon —elbows at right angles to his body, his chest thrust out.

"What the fuck is this?"

He waved his hand in the air, making it unclear what he meant by "this." I presumed he was referring to Lorenzo, who, somehow, had ended up several feet away. Penn must've yanked him right off the seat, his rage giving him strength, because Lorenzo wasn't a small guy.

"I've spent all fucking day calling you, and you turn up here with another man." He jerked back his head. "What the hell is going on, Gia?"

"Oh." I clasped a hand to my chest and formed my features into pure innocence. "Sorry, I must've missed the calls. I've been kinda busy." I gave a little giggle that sounded nothing like me and batted my eyelashes. "This is Lorenzo. I don't believe you've met. He's an old... friend."

Penn's eyes bulged at the not-so-hidden message, and he opened his mouth, then shut it.

Lorenzo, picking up on his cue, which, considering we hadn't practiced or talked about this as a scenario, was pretty darned impressive, muscled his way past Penn and retook his seat. He draped his arm over my shoulder, looking all alpha and possessive. In return, I ran my hand up his thigh.

"Babe, what gives? Who's this jerk?"

I leaned into him. "He's not a jerk." I giggled again. *Dear God, I have to stop with the giggling. Otherwise, Penn will smell a rat.* "This is Penn Kingcaid. You remember, I told you about him. He's the guy who's been keeping me company while you were away."

"Oh." Lorenzo ran his gaze over Penn, playing along with the plan beautifully. "Good to meet you, man. Thanks for taking care of my girl while I've been gone. But I'm back now, so she's gonna be kind of busy with me. Ain't that right, babe?" He growled and bared his teeth, and despite the seriousness of the situation and the fragile state of my heart, I almost lost it, stifling a laugh at the last moment.

I risked a glance at Penn, my stomach twisting at the confusion and pain etched on his beautiful face. And then I remembered the blonde and the way he'd held her and then shouted across the lobby that he loved her, and my heart hardened.

"It's been great, Penn. I've loved spending time with you, but you know me. I'm not the monogamous kind." I clapped my hands as if I'd had the best idea in the world. "Although, we're up for a threesome if you are. Lorenzo and I are both very broad-minded. Isn't that right, babe?"

By now, the entire restaurant was transfixed on the

drama unfolding at table forty-six. Those with a front-row seat openly stared, while other diners craned their necks to get in on the action. Given this was Penn Kingcaid, it wouldn't surprise me if the whole debacle ended up on the front page of the *New York Times*, especially as I wasn't keeping my voice down.

He deserved total humiliation after what he'd done.

"Gia." Penn's voice scratched as if he'd swallowed thorns. "I don't understand."

"There's nothing to understand. It was fun while it lasted, but I'm not the settling-down type, and, truly, you were getting a little serious for my taste." I shrugged, then when his face twisted, I let my act slip a few degrees. "The right woman is out there for you." And then I remembered that he'd already fucking found her. "It's probably best, under the circumstances, that I leave Theo's, but I hope you won't cut off Roberto's tuition until I've figured things out."

Penn's jaw flexed, anger darkening his blue eyes to almost black as his pupils blew wide.

"What the fuck do you take me for?" He looked me up and down with the kind of disdain that crushed what was left of my heart. "Roberto's tuition is secure. You think I'd punish an innocent kid because of something his sister did?" He leaned in, pressing his fingertips onto the table. "I thought I knew you, but all along you were playing me. And, fuck, you played me good."

He whipped around so fast that I felt the breeze from the speed of his movement, and calmly walked through the restaurant, disappearing into the corridor that I knew led to his office. A low hum settled over the restaurant as diners chewed over the impromptu show instead of their succulent filet mignons.

Time stopped, and my stomach lurched, a ball of nausea settling low in my midsection. Lorenzo squeezed my hand that I'd balled into a fist without recalling doing so.

"You okay?"

I tugged my hand from beneath his and set my napkin on the table. "I'd like to leave, please." My voice sounded so small and unlike me, the revenge I'd sought tasting sour rather than sweet. Regrets filled my head. I felt sick. Whatever Penn had done, I should have dealt with it in a far more adult way than embarrassing him in front of his clientele and providing enough gossip for the upper class to dine out on for years. I wasn't a child, yet I'd reacted like a five-year-old throwing a tantrum because their best friend had chosen someone else to give their chocolate bar to at lunch break.

Lorenzo stood immediately. He held out his hand, but I ignored it, sidling through the restaurant with whispers following me like drifts of fog on a chilly winter's day. I lurched onto the sidewalk, my lungs flattening as the realization of what I'd done hit me.

Penn had acted as if I'd wronged him rather than the other way around. And why wouldn't he? Easy to play the victim when you thought your secret was safe. And the worst of it? He hadn't even fought for me. He'd just let me go, discarded me, cast me aside.

And that hurt most of all.

Lorenzo offered to see me home, but I told him I'd rather be alone. My apartment felt cold despite the warm fall temperatures outside. I removed the fancy-pants dress I'd blown a week's wages on—an extravagance I could hardly afford, considering my recent unemployment status—and tossed it on the floor. I doubted I'd ever wear it again.

I flopped onto the bed, wearing only my underwear, the need to talk to Kee an urge that wouldn't quit. I checked the clock beside my bed. Nine fifteen. So six fifteen in Seattle. She could be on a late shift at work—Kee was an intern at the Kingcaid Seattle hotel—in which case I'd have to stew in my own mess until she finished, and that meant I could be in for a long wait. Not that it mattered. Doing what I did for a living, I was used to late nights.

I sent a text first.

Me: Are you busy? Could do with a chat.

I waited for a reply. Instead, she FaceTimed me.

"Hey, Gia." Kee giggled. "What the hell are you doing calling me wearing only your underwear?"

On hearing her bright, enthusiastic voice, I acted completely out of character.

I burst into tears.

"Oh, shit, Gia, what the hell's happened?"

I managed a few words, but they were incoherent, even to me, and I was fucking saying them. In the end, I laid my phone on the bed, got up to fetch a box of tissues, blew my nose and wiped my eyes, and then picked up my phone again.

"Penn's cheating on me."

Kee's jaw plummeted, her eyes shooting wide. "Say that again?"

"He's a cheating bastard, so I got my own back, and now he hates me because he thinks I'm the cheat, and I'm beginning to wonder if I handled it all wrong, but he's still going to pay for Roberto's tutoring, for now at least, so that's something."

The stream of consciousness poured out of me, words bumping into the ones that followed. Kee made a soothing noise as if she were comforting a toddler, which, let's face it, wasn't that far off the mark. The more time that passed, the greater the certainty grew in my chest that I had not come out of this looking good. That didn't change how bad Penn looked either, but Kee wouldn't have done this. She'd have calmly and serenely called him out on his shit and watched as he tried to dig himself out of a great hole.

But I wasn't Kee. I was me. Gianna Greene. Over-the-top, outspoken, rash.

"Gia, breathe for me. Slowly. Now start again, from the top."

And so, I did.

Chapter 28

Penn

Being right sucks.

I couldn't stay at Theo's another second.

My heart had shriveled to the size of a prune, incapable of keeping even the most basic functions thriving. The questions thundered around my mind over and over.

Why?

Why had Gia brought another guy to my restaurant and flaunted him in front of me when only last night, we'd had an idyllic dinner and she'd seemed just as happy as I was? I hadn't gotten a single inkling that anything was wrong.

I mean, sure, I hadn't spent the night at her place, or invited her to spend the night at mine, but after making progress on the deal with Oliver Ellis, I'd felt it important to put the wheels in motion right away.

That couldn't be it.

There was more to this than immediately obvious, but even if I had done something I wasn't cognizant of, Gia had still brought another guy to *my* fucking restaurant and let him put his hands all over her. They'd sat there, kissing, touching, making fucking goo-goo eyes at each other.

I'd thought we had something. I was in love with her. *Correction. I am in love with her.*

My heart withered a little more. This, *this* right here, was why I'd never allowed myself to get close to a woman. Whatever Sandrine had said to me Friday night about love being wonderful, it wasn't. Giving yourself that completely to someone else simply handed them power that they could use against you.

Gia had used her power against me, and I wasn't sure I'd ever recover.

I gathered my things and muttered a goodbye to Pierre and one of the waitstaff who gave me a sympathetic head tilt that did not go down well. At my glower, she bustled off, chin tucked into her chest.

Sensible move.

My penthouse smelled of her, and it made me want to burn the place down. She was the first woman I'd ever brought here, and she'd be the last, too. Tomorrow, I'd call in a cleaning company and have them bleach the fuck out of this place, erasing every trace of her.

What a shame they couldn't do that to my mind, my heart, my body.

I ached for her, yet even if she begged me to take her back, I couldn't. Not now.

But damn, I wish I knew what I'd done to provoke her to act in this way. Gia was a paradox, a complicated woman who acted first and thought later, who was mouthy and brave and funny and the best sex I'd ever had, and the woman I'd truly, deep in my soul, expected to spend the rest of my life with.

And this was how she'd treated me.

Hurt morphed into rage, a torrent coursing through me, the tide impossible to stem, the current too strong.

I broke.

Dishes shattered against the marble floor, glasses smashed until there were only shards left. I slammed my fist into the wall, the kitchen countertop. I tugged on my hair, yanking at the roots. I screamed and cursed and... fuck... I cried. I cried until my throat was raw and my eyes dry, no tears left to shed, no fucks left to give, no heart left to care.

I sank to the floor, surrounded by the mess I'd made, paralyzed, my body numb, my mind shut down.

I lost track of how long I sat there, but somewhere a phone rang. It cut off and rang again, and again.

And again.

Somehow, I found the strength to pull myself upright, crunching through broken crockery and glass to search for my cell.

Ash's name flashed up before voicemail kicked in. Almost immediately, it rang again.

"Ash." My voice rasped as if I'd smoked a hundred cigarettes one after another. "What's—"

"You cheated on Gia!" he roared. "What the fuck,

Penn? How could you? I always knew you were a player, but I dared to think, to fucking *hope*, that in Gia, you'd found someone so like yourself, your fucking soul mate, that you couldn't possibly mess it up. Kingcaids don't fucking cheat. Where's your pride?"

His tirade was so out of character, so unbelievably shocking, that it took me a while to put the pieces together, to realize that he was accusing *me* of cheating, when Gia was the cheat. I'd done nothing to deserve what she'd done to me, or the vilification from my eldest brother.

"Wait. What the hell are you talking about?"

"Gia called Kiana. They were on the phone for over an hour. She's distraught, brokenhearted. Kiana told me she's never seen her like this. I don't know Gia nearly as well as she does, but even I'm aware she's not the type to resort to histrionics. So, I ask again, what the *fuck* are you playing at?"

"I-I—" I ran my hand through my hair. "You've got it all wrong, Ash. Gia—"

Ash snorted. "Don't deflect. Who's the blonde?"

"What blonde?"

"The blonde Gia saw you with at your apartment. The blonde you hugged and professed your love for."

The truth rained down on me like great hailstones the size of golf balls. I didn't remember sitting but found myself on the floor again, holding my phone so tightly that I thought it might break.

Gia had seen me with Sandrine and had jumped to all the wrong conclusions.

Not that I blamed her. If the tables were turned, I'd have come to the same conclusions she had.

I clasped the back of my neck with my free hand. Sandrine had turned up unexpectedly, excited to tell me that she and Kyle had found a place to rent not all that far from me. Conscious of my lunch date with Gia, I'd hurried her out of there, but that had been a good thirty minutes before Gia was due. And she was *never* early.

For anything.

Why now? Why this time?

Sandrine's news that she'd soon move into my neighborhood had jolted me into action. I'd intended to tell Gia everything over lunch. About Theo, about my part in his death, about Sandrine and Corabelle and how special they were to me, and how I wanted her to be as much a part of their lives as I was.

I'd planned to tell her I loved her.

And now... everything lay in tatters, scattered at my feet, broken like the dishes strewn over my kitchen floor.

Gia had seen me with Sandrine and exacted her revenge. The conversation we'd had on the plane to Grand Cayman came back to me, how she'd been reading that article about the woman who'd left rotting fish guts in her boyfriend's apartment after she'd caught him cheating. I'd asked her whether she'd do something as awful as that, and she'd replied that if someone cheated on her, she'd do a lot worse.

And she had.

I hadn't a clue whether the guy she'd brought to Theo's tonight meant something to her or if it had all been a ruse to deliver ice-cold revenge to me, but whatever the reason, it didn't matter.

Gia had seen something she'd misunderstood, and rather than broach the issue with me like a normal person, she'd humiliated me, touching and kissing another guy in front of me, in my restaurant, surrounded by my customers and my staff.

She'd thought I was heartless enough to withdraw funding for Roberto's tutoring when he'd only just begun.

She'd believed me capable of cheating on her.

The last thought was the most painful of all.

"No one," I muttered to Ash. "The blonde is no one."

I cut the call without giving him the right of reply and instantly turned my phone off. Exhausted, I struggled to my feet. I cast a glance into the kitchen, at the mess I'd made, and I left the broken pieces where they lay, all jagged with shards missing, impossible to stitch back together.

What a stark correlation to my life.

I grabbed a bottle of twenty-year-old scotch and staggered into my bedroom. Only one way to make it through the next few hours.

Get hammered.

A noise woke me, and as I jolted upright, the bottle of scotch I vaguely remembered downing rolled off the bed and thumped to the floor, the remnants spilling onto my carpet.

Fuck my life.

One more thing for the cleaning staff to clear up today.

I should get on that. The sooner they started, the sooner I could put the last few months behind me and move on.

The noise came again, and then I realized someone was knocking seven shades of shit out of the door to my penthouse. Odd, considering you needed a code for the elevator to get up here.

Which meant whoever it was knew the code. That narrowed it down to a family member.

Groaning, I swung my feet to the floor, gripping the sides of my head as tiny hammers went to fucking town on my skull. I glanced at my phone. Five thirty in the morning? What the hell?

My mouth felt like the insides of a sweaty sneaker, and I urgently needed to shower. I thought about ignoring the unwelcome visitor, but it might be my mom or my dad, and I'd never leave them standing in my foyer, no matter how much I craved crawling back under the duvet and pretending the outside world didn't exist for a little while longer.

Although, for my parents to turn up unannounced at dawn would be a first.

I side-eyed the destruction in the kitchen as I passed, a fresh wave of pain coursing through me. Love could go suck on a wasps' nest.

Bleary-eyed, I opened the door. "Ash?"

My brother, overnight bag in hand, brushed past me. He dropped it by the couch, his eyes scanning my penthouse as if he expected to see... well, I didn't know what he expected to see, but the chaos of smashed dinner plates and crystal glasses wasn't it, given the speed his eyebrows shot up his forehead.

"What the fuck's happened here?" He whipped around, concern pulling at the skin around his mouth. "Penn?"

I hitched up my left shoulder and twisted my lips to the side. "I kinda lost it."

Ash angled his head to the side. "Fuck, brother, you sure know how to destroy a kitchen." He took three strides, bringing him to me. He clasped my upper arms. "Talk to me."

"What are you doing here?" I asked, avoiding his question. I wasn't interested in talking. I'd rather crack open another bottle of scotch and sink into oblivion.

"After the way our call ended last night, I was worried. I got straight on the jet and came here."

"Hence you dragging me out of bed at the ass-crack of dawn."

Ash glanced at his watch, eyes widening. "I hadn't even realized the time."

I trudged into the kitchen, picking carefully through the chaos in my bare feet, and reached for the coffeepot. The scotch would have to wait until Ash left. "Want one?"

"Here, I'll do it." He ushered me out of my own kitchen. "Get something on your feet before you cut yourself." He sniffed me. "Maybe take a shower first."

A smile pulled at my lips. "Is that your passive-aggressive approach to telling me I stink?"

"No. If I wanted to tell you that, I'd come straight out

with it." He flashed a grin, and weirdly, I felt better. "Now go."

After a shower, a shave, and using half a tube of toothpaste, I reluctantly rejoined the human race. In my absence, Ash had made himself useful. All signs of my meltdown had vanished, and a steaming cup of black coffee awaited me. I picked it up, sipping gratefully.

"You didn't have to clean up. I have a cleaning company coming in later." I shook my head. "I mean I'm going to call a cleaning company to come in later."

Ash pointed to the living room. "Shall we sit?"

That was Ash speak for "Get your ass in that chair and spill before I bring out the torture tactics." I trundled over to my favorite overstuffed chair and sank into it. It wrapped around me like a big hug. Thankfully, I hadn't fucked Gia in this chair. Otherwise, it'd have to go, and that would be one more thing to feel bitter over.

Silence hovered in the air like a fall mist. I cradled my coffee, conscious of Ash's eyes on me. I chose to stare out the window. A sliver of light crept over the horizon, a sign of the approaching dawn.

"Who is she, Penn?"

I gave him my eyes, my teeth worrying my lip. "I never cheated on Gia."

"That wasn't what I asked."

God, this was my worst fucking nightmare. For more than three years, I'd kept this secret, shame and guilt and hatred gnawing away at my insides, terrified of how I'd change in the eyes of my family if they knew I'd killed a man. Or as good as, whatever Sandrine said. That woman had a big heart, bigger than I deserved.

Sometimes, I edged toward her point of view. I dared to believe, only for a second, that I wasn't responsible, that the drunk driver would have hit us even if I hadn't glanced down at my phone. It never lasted, though. The old beliefs always made a comeback, oftentimes stronger than ever.

I swallowed, my tongue flicking over my lips. This story didn't have a beginning, just a horrible, messy middle and a horrific ending.

"Her name is Sandrine," I began, averting my gaze. I couldn't do this any other way. "She was married to my best friend, Theo."

"Theo?" I heard the lift in Ash's voice, the stark surprise. "Wasn't he the guy you met in college? I haven't heard you mention him for years."

"That's because he's dead." The air in my chest evaporated, leaving me hollow. I owed it to Ash to look him right in the eye when I confessed. And so I did. I lifted my head and locked gazes with my brother, the man I'd looked up to my entire life, along with my dad. "And it's my fault. I killed him."

Ash's eyes flared. He straightened, his fingers flexing around his cup of coffee. "What do you mean, you killed him?"

"Exactly that." I rubbed a hand over my mouth and set down my own cup of coffee before my trembling hand dropped it. "We were on our way upstate to meet some friends, almost three and a half years ago now. I was driving, Theo in the passenger seat." I closed my eyes. It was hard to recall the exact moments right before the accident. The doctors had said it was the brain's way of protecting itself. "My phone rang. I looked down, only for a second, and that was enough."

"You lost control of the car?"

I shook my head. "Another vehicle hit us. The passenger side of my car took the brunt of it. He died in my arms." My eyes prickled with tears. I blinked several times, and they vanished. "I promised him I'd take care of Sandrine and his little girl, Corabelle, and I have."

I dug my fingertips into my temples, the hangover I'd thought I'd beaten making a comeback. Or perhaps it was the stress of knowing that, after today, my brother would never look at me the same way again.

"I never cheated on Gia," I repeated. "She saw me with Sandrine and jumped to conclusions."

"So Gia doesn't know about Sandrine?"

"No." I rubbed my lips together. "No one knows. And I intended to keep it that way."

"But why?"

He sounded so confused, which, in turn, confused me. The why of it all seemed pretty obvious.

"Why would you keep this from Gia, from your family. From me?"

"Would you want everyone to know you're a killer?"

"Penn, for Christ's sake, it was an accident."

"No." I clenched my jaw. "It wasn't an accident. If I hadn't checked my phone, I could've done something. I could've swerved or braked or accelerated. I could've saved him."

Ash massaged his forehead. "What about the other driver? Was he injured?"

I barked a laugh. "No. Drunk, but uninjured."

313

"Drunk? You were hit by a drunk driver?"

"Yes."

"Then I'm truly flummoxed, Penn. You were the victim, not the perpetrator."

"I wasn't looking at the road. For that split second, Ash, I wasn't paying attention."

"Jesus, Penn." Ash rose to his feet and perched on the arm of the chair. He gripped my shoulder, squeezing. "And you've carried around this guilt, alone, for over three years?"

"Not alone. I had Sandrine, and Corabelle."

"And there's nothing... romantic between you?"

"No! Fuck's sake, Ash. She's my best friend's widow. She's like a goddamn sister to me. She's also met someone else. That's what she was doing here yesterday. She stopped by to tell me that she and her new man have found a place to rent close to here. She lives in Boston currently."

Silence descended once more, and when I met my brother's eyes, I couldn't read his expression.

"Say something."

"Two things need to happen, Penn. You need to stop feeling guilt for something that happened that was out of your control, and you need to tell Gia."

The guilt... yeah, that was a work in progress, although telling Ash had helped to lift this weight I'd carried around for so long. But Gia...

"What's the point in telling Gia? We're over."

"It was a misunderstanding, Penn."

"No, it wasn't. She could have asked me about Sandrine. Instead, she chose to humiliate me and think the worst of me." I shook my head. "There's no future with a woman who immediately jumps to the conclusion that I'm a cheater without allowing me the courtesy to explain myself."

"Penn—"

"No, Ash. Gia's made her bed, and she's going to have to lie in it. Alone."

Chapter 29

Gia

**Best friends tell the hardest truths,
but they're worth listening to.**

—

W<small>AKING UP AND REALIZING YOU'RE UNEMPLOYED ISN'T THE BEST</small> way to start the week, but when your jobless status is a result of your own stupidity, it makes the situation a whole lot worse.

I'd half hoped that I'd wake up this morning to find Penn beside me and I'd realize it had all been some horrible dream reminiscent of a *Dallas*/Bobby Ewing moment.

Yeah, I was a fan of cheesy eighties TV. Sue me.

Instead, I woke up alone with an ache in my heart and a head full of regrets. I'd excelled myself this time in the "Gia acts before she thinks" scenario, and the more I thought about Penn's deeply hurt expression, the more I had the creeping sense that whoever that woman was, she wasn't his lover.

I had no yardstick on which to base that belief other than an internal monologue that sounded way too logical for my liking.

Penn's comment on the plane to Grand Cayman slithered into my mind.

"I can't understand why a man cheats. I mean, if you're no longer interested in the woman, just tell her. No point in dragging things out."

By now Kee would've told Asher, and undoubtedly Asher would've called Penn. He'd know I'd seen him with the blonde, yet he hadn't called me to explain himself. So maybe there was something underhanded going on after all.

Argh!

This constant back-and-forth of good guy/bad guy was driving me insane. Despite the time on the clock reading seven oh five, which was an ungodly time of day, I threw back the covers and padded into my tiny kitchen. When desperation set in, there was only one cure.

Food.

Lots and lots of food.

In thirty minutes, I sat in front of a stack of buttery pancakes and maple bacon with extra maple syrup on the side. I'd stuffed the first forkful into my mouth when someone knocked on the door.

At this time? Couldn't be a courier because I wasn't expecting anything.

Oh, Christ. What if it's Penn?

I dropped my fork, ran into my bathroom to smooth

down my bird's nest, out-of-control hair, yanked down the top half of my nightgown to put the girls on full display, and raced to answer it.

It wasn't Penn. It was Kee.

"Nice tits," she greeted me with, and then she hugged the living daylights out of me until I gasped for breath.

I managed to shove her off of me. "What are you doing here?"

"After our conversation last night, you think for one second I wouldn't get right on a plane and come to New York? You're my best friend and you need me, and so..." She curtsied. "Ta-da!"

"God, I've missed you." I pulled her inside, motioning to the stack of pancakes. "It's as if I knew you were coming."

"Amazing. I love your pancakes." Kee helped herself to a plate and sat, piling on two pancakes and drenching the entire dish in maple syrup.

"Is Ash with you?"

Kee nodded. Couldn't do much else, considering her mouth was full. She swallowed. "Yum. Yes, we flew here on his jet." She chuckled. "How life's changed, hey?"

My chest tightened. How indeed.

"Babe, I'm sorry." Kee reached across the table and squeezed my hand. "Ash went to see Penn this morning. He called me just before I got here and explained everything." Her face took on that "brace yourself" expression. "Penn didn't cheat with the blonde woman, Gia."

"You can't know that."

"I can. He told Ash everything."

"Really?" I bit down on a strip of bacon. "Enlighten me, then."

Kee grimaced. "It's not really my story to tell, but trust me when I say it's not what you think."

"Oh, no." I waved my hand in the air. "You can't leave it at that. If you're so convinced Penn isn't a cheating asshole, then spill."

"It really should be Penn telling you this."

I looked around in a dramatic fashion. "But Penn isn't here, is he? Which leaves you to tell me."

"Well..." She sighed. "I guess now that Penn's told Ash everything, it's all out in the open."

"What is?" I huffed. "Stop talking in riddles and just tell me."

"Okay."

Kee pushed her half-finished pancakes away, then changed her mind and pulled the plate toward her again. My pancakes tended to have this effect on people. Leftovers were rarer than men who could keep it in their pants. Apparently.

"The woman is his best friend's widow."

My head jerked back. Penn hadn't mentioned a dead best friend to me. Or a widow.

Then again, wasn't that the crux of this whole mess? He hadn't told me a damned thing. Didn't mean they weren't bumping uglies, though. Maybe he'd always had the hots for her and when the friend had died, he'd just moved right in on the grieving widow, offered a shoulder to cry on, and then next thing, bam! They were fucking.

Penn's reputation was similar to mine. Before we'd

hooked up, we'd both been players, preferring variety to eating the same goddamn meatballs every night.

Problem was, I'd grown addicted to Penn's meatballs, and now I didn't want to eat anyone else's.

"And? What's to say he isn't boning her? Just because she's a widow doesn't preclude him from pursuing her."

"Oh, Gia." Kee gnawed on her lips like a mouse nibbling a block of cheese, fast and dainty. She tangled her hands in her lap. "I am not comfortable doing this. Not at all. But if the only way to wake you the hell up is to risk Penn's ire, then I'll do it. You two are meant to be together, and I will not allow your pigheadedness and tendency to act without thinking, and his stupid secret, ruin a perfect love match."

Her hand shot up as I opened my mouth to deny we were a love match, perfect or otherwise.

"Don't even. Just shut up and listen."

She then proceeded to spill all this stuff about Penn going on a road trip with his friend Theo, and a drunk driver had hit them, and Theo had died. And how Penn blamed himself because he'd glanced at his phone in the milliseconds before the other car had plowed into theirs, how he'd kept his secret from his family for almost three and a half years, taking care of his friend's wife and child during all that time, making sure they had everything they needed, providing emotional support when required.

My mind shot me back to our initial meeting, when I'd slammed into Penn on the street and spilled the fresh OJ all over him. He'd lost his temper that day, calling me out for checking Instagram even though that wasn't what I'd been doing. I'd been texting Lorenzo—rather than looking where I was going.

No wonder he'd been such an ass about it.

Every time he watched someone taking a risk by concentrating more on their phone than the world around them likely set off a trigger, gunning him right back to that fateful day.

I put my head in my hands.

Why?

Why had I found it easier to believe Penn was cheating on me instead of considering, even for a moment, an alternative explanation? Dashing headlong into action wasn't unusual for me, but I hadn't even given him a chance. I'd pronounced him guilty on the spot and then proceeded to carry out a childish act of revenge all in the name of an outrage I wasn't entitled to.

"Oh God." I lifted my head, bleakly staring at Kee. "Why didn't I just ask him who she was? Why go through this entire charade with Lorenzo just to hurt him when he'd been hurt enough already?"

"I'm no psychologist, but I think I know why."

"Because I always do shit like this? Act before thinking?"

"Well, yes, but that's not new since you met Penn." She grinned, and it took the edge off my self-loathing. "I think this all stems back to when Roberto was born." My eyebrows flew north, but Kee put her hand on my arm. "Hear me out."

I jerked my chin, interested in her thoughts. Kee and I had always enjoyed an open and honest relationship, and I knew that she'd tell me what was in her mind and her heart, even if I didn't want to hear it.

"I think the way your parents left you to your own devices to concentrate on Roberto's special needs made you feel abandoned and alone. I remember the change in you in the six months following his birth. At first, you relished the extra responsibility, the joy of not having a parent nag you every five minutes about where you were, who you were with, whether you'd done your schoolwork, or how prep for exams was going. But that euphoria soon wore off, and you found yourself without parental guidance at a crucial time in a teenager's life."

"All true. I did feel alone at times, but Roberto needed them more than I did."

Kee shook her head. "No. Roberto needed them in a different way, but his needs were no more important than yours." She sighed. "Look, I'm not blaming your folks. I love them, you know I do, and they were in a tough spot. I don't think they could have handled things any differently. Roberto was a helpless baby, while you were fifteen and, in their eyes maybe, almost an adult. I get why they acted as they did, but that doesn't change the fact that their actions had an impact on you."

"But that doesn't explain why I behaved that way with Penn. Why I never simply asked him who she was."

"Doesn't it?" Kee canted her head. "You've always been such a free spirit, Gia. Forthright, ballsy, adventurous, outspoken." She grinned. "A woman who'll turn up late to her own funeral."

"Wish I'd been late to Penn's that day."

"Trust you to finally arrive early for something only for it to bite you in the ass."

I snickered. "That still doesn't explain why I jumped to conclusions."

"Because you wanted to win, Gia. You wanted to make sure that if anyone was abandoned, it was Penn, not you. You projected your fears of not being enough, of not being worthy of attention and love onto him. And what if you had approached him and he'd admitted he was seeing someone else? You faced being told you weren't enough for him, just as you've always thought you weren't enough to earn your parents' attention. Your outrageous 'look at me' stunts all stem from your need to be recognized, to be acknowledged, to be *noticed*."

I had always been competitive. Winning was important to me, as it was to Penn. It was one of the things we'd found we had in common early on in our relationship. But I'd never connected the dots, never truly thought about why I was always so dramatic, so competitive, so in-your-face. Why I'd vehemently believed for all these years that relationships were a mistake and it was far more fun to flit from guy to guy when the truth was that I'd been afraid to commit in case I ended up abandoned again.

I stabbed a fork into my pancakes, dipping them in pools of maple syrup. "Fuck. I'm a therapist's wet dream, aren't I?"

Kee rose from her seat and shuffled her chair around to my side of the table. She put her arm around me and rested her head on my shoulder.

"You are amazing, and I love you. And so does Penn."

"Ha." I shoveled the pancake into my mouth. *Hmm,*

they aren't as good cold. Never realized that before. "Not anymore he doesn't."

"Love doesn't just disappear because one of you screwed up. Sure, he's pissed at you, but once you explain, he'll understand."

Hope prickled my chest. "Do you think so?"

She tucked my hair behind my ear. "I know so."

Admitting you're in the wrong is amazingly cathartic —and unexpectedly rewarding.

MOUTH DRIER THAN IF I'D SWALLOWED A BUCKET OF SAND, I made my way into Penn's building. My stomach felt hollow, and my heart beat at a rate far exceeding the healthy range.

Most people found apologizing difficult. Those who denied that were liars. But when you'd fucked up to the extent I had, you expected the recipient of said apology to throw it back in your face, and that made making it all the more difficult.

I could only hope that Penn would find it in his heart to forgive me.

Asher had done me a solid and texted the code for the

elevator, which would get me as far as Penn's front door at least. He might not answer, but I had to try. Asher had said he probably would, as the only people who had access to the code were family, and his advice was that if Penn shouted, "Who is it?" I'd do well to keep my big mouth shut.

I ducked my head to avoid the security cameras in case Penn had access to the lobby and saw me coming. Surprise was the name of the game, a sneak attack when he least expected it.

My backup plan was to catch him at Theo's, although returning to the scene of the crime to beg for forgiveness probably wasn't the best idea.

The backup to the backup plan was to loiter across the street from his building until he ventured outside, and then pounce.

Christ, I sound like a stalker.

The code Asher had given me worked like a dream, and mere seconds later, I found myself in Penn's foyer. I took several deep breaths to calm that thing in my chest that seemed hell-bent on leaping right out like a scene from a horror movie. Before I lost my nerve, I made a fist and knocked three times on Penn's door.

The wait for him to answer was the worst part. My breathing came fast and shallow, I had a rather unsightly beading of sweat across my forehead that I kept swiping at, and my back muscles were so tight that it'd take a chiropractor a good six months to fix me.

The sound of the lock turning came through the door, and I stiffened, bracing for rejection. I only hoped he'd give me a chance to tell my side of the story.

Debacle.

Fuckup.

Whatever.

When it opened, Penn's expression didn't even flicker with surprise. His jaw was locked up tight, and his eyes had lost the twinkle I'd come to adore. The way he looked at me was how ninety-five percent of the world greeted a cold-caller. Suspicion mingled with "Can I close the door before they stick their foot in it?"

"Hi."

Jesus. If that's my opening gambit, I might as well concede defeat right this second.

"Can I come in?"

Zero improvement.

"I'm busy."

I took the first bite of humble pie.

"Would you be able to spare five minutes to at least allow me to explain? I promise that as soon as I've said what I came to, I'll go."

"Without giving me the right of reply?" He arched a brow.

I rubbed a hand under my nose. *Classy, Gia.* "I didn't mean that. Whatever you want to say to me, I'll listen."

"What if I don't want to say anything to you? What if I said everything I wanted to last night?"

His face didn't just twist with pain. It drowned in it. And as much as his pain was a knife to my gut, it gave me hope.

If he didn't care about me, about *us*, what I'd done wouldn't have affected him this deeply.

I stepped closer, my toes inside his apartment, our

chests almost touching. The hitch of breath that caught in his throat and the flare of his nostrils as he breathed in the perfume he loved further increased my optimism. I risked touching his arm. He didn't move away.

"Penn, please." I kept my voice soft and pliable, my eyes cast a few degrees downward.

"Five minutes."

He spun on his heel and moved through the apartment, sitting on a stool at the breakfast bar. He picked up the half-finished cup of coffee he must've poured before I'd gotten here and brought it to his lips, his eyes on me as I took the stool beside his.

I inhaled a deep breath. "I know you didn't cheat on me."

He snorted. "Considering I told Ash everything, that's hardly front-page news."

"No."

Wow. This was harder than I'd thought it'd be.

"What I did was childish and stupid." I avoided using "unforgivable." I didn't want to give him a chance to agree. "Look, Penn, I have issues. So many that I can't count that high. Math isn't my strong suit."

I risked a brief grin. His icy glare chilled me from the inside out. I pressed on.

"I'm not making excuses, but when Roberto was born and my parents realized all his challenges, they poured every spare minute they had into him. I'm not blaming them or anything. I understand why they chose Roberto over me, but it left me feeling abandoned and alone. I craved their attention, but there wasn't enough to go around, so I became this larger-than-life character who seemed to breeze through life without a care in the world. But inside, I was a fifteen-year-old child in a woman's body who still needed her mom and dad. The problem with my strategy was that my parents believed I was fine. Capable and strong." I shrugged. "Which, in turn, led to even less attention."

Penn reached for the coffeepot and poured me a cup. I took it as a good sign. I murmured my thanks, blew across the top, and took a sip.

"Over the years, my abandonment issues produced several strands, all linked to that central issue. I'm big and bold and brash, and I do dramatic things, like what happened at Theo's. I have to win, to come first, to be the center of attention because it shows I *matter*."

As I said that last part, something change in Penn, a shift in attitude, a softening of his features. My belly fluttered, and I almost held my breath waiting for him to speak.

Finally, he did, and I wasn't disappointed with what he said.

"You matter, Gia."

My entire body tingled with those three simple words. I plowed on, unwilling to allow the strand of optimism to snap.

"I should have come straight out and asked you who the woman was when I saw you having coffee with her last Friday."

His eyebrows flew up his head. "You saw us?"

"Yeah. I'd just left the club and was on my way back to the subway."

"Shit." Penn palmed the back of his neck. "I should have told you about her. I meant to. But it's—"

I cut off his apology. "No. This is my fault. My responsibility. I understand why you didn't tell me about something so painful that you kept it from your family for years. I should have trusted you, but in classic me style, I jumped to conclusions. I found it easier to believe you'd picked someone else." I grimaced. "The whole thing with Lorenzo was to save face, to come out of it with my pride and, yeah, my ego, intact. By getting in there first, I won."

The skin around his mouth tightened as he flattened his lips.

"He *kissed you*, Gia. In the middle of my restaurant. He had his hands all over you. I get it, I do, but that is not on."

"He didn't kiss me. He just made it look like he had." I pointed to my pussy. "Wrong equipment. Lorenzo's the guy I went clubbing with last Friday. Remember, I told you he'd rather go down on you than on me."

"Your coworker from your last place of work?"

"That's him." I winced. "Don't blame him. I coerced him into it, and he's protective of me. When I told him you'd cheated, he agreed to help me get my own back on you. He's a great guy. You'll like him."

I'd slipped into talking to Penn as if he'd already forgiven me and we had a future together even though he'd given me no indication of that possibility.

"What you did wasn't cool, Gia."

I tucked my chin into my chest, shame a thick tar that clung to my blood vessels and nerves and ligaments. "I know."

He downed the last of his coffee, refilling his cup from the pot while my heart drifted inside my chest, anticipating a summary ejection from his home any second. I held my breath, like an accused as the foreperson of the jury stood, ready to settle their fate.

"But I'm far from blameless. If I'd told you about Sandrine from the very beginning, you wouldn't have jumped to conclusions." The edges of his lips tipped up. "At least you didn't put fish guts in my air-conditioning system."

A spark of hope lit me up. He'd remembered the conversation from the flight to Grand Cayman, and the ice-cold revenge served to the cheating boyfriend by the woman he'd wronged.

"I planned to, but the smell." I wafted my hand in front of my face. "I couldn't face it."

"Fuck, Gia." He palmed the back of his neck. "Don't you *ever* do anything like that to me again."

"I won't. Never. Nu-uh. Never ever, cross my heart and hope to die."

He reached for me. "Come here."

I almost cried, but after last night's conversation with Kee, my tears were all out of stock. Scrambling off the stool, I inserted myself between his parted thighs.

Penn curved his palms around my cheeks. "No more secrets."

He drew me in for a kiss. Lips I'd given up hope of ever tasting again roved over mine, his tongue probing, exploring, cherishing. We parted, breathless. I ran my fingers through his hair.

"I love you, Kingcaid. Even when I hated you, I loved you."

"Just as well, because you're stuck with me. Forever."

I groaned. "Not *forever* forever?"

He smiled, and I melted. He'd always gotten me with that impish grin.

"Yeah. *Forever* forever."

"I'll consider it. If you make it worth my while." I tapped my forefinger against my lip. "After all, you do still owe me for helping you devise a new menu when we were supposed to be planning Kee and Asher's joint bachelor and bachelorette party. I think I'd like to collect that debt right about now."

"Orgasms on the regular?"

I nodded. "Although, that's just the start."

"Really?" He folded his arms. "Let's hear it."

"Take me to bed and I'll show you." I held out my hand. "Proof is in the pudding and all that."

Penn couldn't stand fast enough, knocking the stool over in his haste. He ignored my hand and picked me up, one arm around my back, and the other, he slipped under my knees.

"Put me down. You'll put your back out, and what use will you be to me then?"

"Oh, shush, woman. I have lips to kiss, curves to explore, and pussy to eat."

"Well." I flashed a broad grin of my own, all teeth and scrunched-up eyes. "When you put it like that, I can hardly refuse." I pointed toward his bedroom. "To the sex cave."

He laughed, and I fell for him even harder.

"I love you, Gianna Greene. Every single brash, bold, ballsy part of you. Even if you do drive me insane."

"One thing's for sure, Kingcaid." I planted one on him, hard and fast like I hoped the sex would be. "Our life will never be boring."

Chapter 31

Penn

**Makeup sex is the best, especially
when you bring toys to the party.**

I WHIPPED OFF GIA'S CLOTHES SO FAST THAT I TORE HER SKIRT. IN
true Gia style, she got her own back by gripping both sides
of my shirt and yanking it open, scattering buttons all over
my bedroom carpet. The speed with which my fortunes
had changed made my head spin. After her betrayal had
torn my heart out, I'd truly believed we were over, yet less
than twenty-four hours later, here we were, naked,
sweaty, and about to have sex.

Fuck, I loved my life.

And I loved her. Every curvy, soft, pliable, wonderful
inch of her. We'd both behaved like idiots, risking something so precious for such stupid reasons, but with any

luck, all idiocy was behind us and we could look to a long and happy future together.

"I love your cock." Gia grinned up at me, a seductive glint in her eye. She parted her legs. "So does my pussy."

My eyes went there, as she'd expected. She glistened, ready for me without any foreplay. And as much as I'd love to go hard and fast, I intended to savor every single moment. A few short hours ago, I'd despaired of ever finding happiness again, and now I was brimful of it, ecstasy spilling over, chasing away the sadness and letting in light and joy.

"I have other ideas." I winked at her, climbing off the bed. I padded over to my walk-in closet.

"Either get out here now, Kingcaid, or I'm going in for a do-it-yourself orgasm."

I chuckled. I'd never have to wonder what Gia wanted or didn't want. What turned her off or on. I'd never be left wondering if I was touching her the way she liked to be touched or applying too much pressure or not enough. Whatever I needed to know, she'd tell me. I wouldn't even have to ask.

"Patience, Greene." I found what I was searching for and returned to the bedroom. I tossed a set of handcuffs and the clitoral suction stimulator onto the bed. I'd purchased a few things last weekend when she'd left me to go to work. Well, I had told her I'd trawl the internet for sex toys.

I gestured to her hands, and she gave them to me, a fevered smile on her lips. After handcuffing her to my headboard, I parted her knees and shuffled in between them. "Thought this might be fun. However, after the stunt you pulled at my restaurant last night, and the fact that my assistant has already messaged to tell me she's had to field calls from about thirty journalists who all want the skinny on the reason for my abject humiliation, I've decided to torture you with it instead." I arched a brow. "What I did to you in Grand Cayman was a walk in the fucking park compared to what this fun little device will do."

"Careful, Kingcaid. I exacted my revenge there, too."

"Yeah, but you've already played a different kind of revenge card. Now it's my turn for payback."

I applied a generous amount of lube to the rim, turned it on, and let it loose, so to speak. Gia gasped, then hissed through her teeth, tugging on the handcuffs. She writhed her legs, so I sat on them, stilling her. That way, she'd have to feel every single vibration without an ounce of relief.

"Jesus, Penn. Fuck, you bastard."

I laughed, watching her closely. I knew Gia's body almost as well as my own, and as she crested, I removed the toy, denying her the climax she'd almost achieved. She bared her teeth at me as I waited for her orgasm to retreat, drawing circles on her inner thighs to pass the time. And then I repeated the entire process. Again and again and again until she begged me to let her come.

"You're supposed to love me," she moaned, tossing her head from side to side.

"I do love you." I dropped the toy between her legs and bent to suck an erect nipple into my mouth. She tried to lift her hips, but I was too heavy.

"Then let me come."

"I will."

"When?" She gasped as I reattached the freshly lubed suction tip to her nub.

"When you've paid your debt to me." I climbed off her legs, and she immediately scissored them, seeking any kind of relief. "Keep moving like that and I'll drag it out all day." I gave her a wicked smile. "And all night, too."

She stilled.

"Good girl."

That earned me a growl. "I will repay you when you least expect it."

"Oh, Gia, baby. I sure fucking hope so."

I reached for the lube bottle and squirted a generous amount on her pussy, re-coated the toy, and began again. Her curvaceous, fucking wet dream of a body glistened with sweat, her tits heavy and round and fucking perfect with nipples like diamonds. My dick jerked, more than ready to get in on the action, but this wasn't about me. This was about her.

I knew Gia.

She might mutter obscenities at me, but this was what turned her on. She loved being taken to the edge and then backed away, her body peaking and falling over and over, all the while knowing the payoff would be the kind of orgasm that'd send her mind and body to a different plane. Sure, we enjoyed a quickie like most couples, but after spending last night genuinely believing I'd lost her forever, I planned to stretch out our makeup sex for hours.

I needed this.

I needed her.

I needed to make her understand she was everything to me, that she came first.

I needed to *reconnect* on a sexual level because Gia and I were both highly sexed beings, and being together like this was important to both of us.

"Penn." She groaned as I flicked a switch that reduced the pressure. "God, please. I'll do anything."

I quirked a brow. "Anything?"

"Anything."

"Will you make me pancakes with maple syrup and let me eat them off your tits?"

Despite her desperate need to come, she laughed. "If that's what you want, you weirdo, then yes. I'll make you fucking hundreds of them."

"Hmm." I canted my head. "Deal." I'd drawn this out long enough. Besides, I was close to spurting all over her belly, and I'd much rather come inside her, hold her close to me, feel her heart beating against mine. To reestablish a connection that her actions—and mine—had temporarily severed.

I couldn't take my eyes off her as she came. She squeezed her eyes closed, her expression one of bliss, of being swept up to heaven and slowly returned to the earth. I tossed the toy to the side and pressed my thumb to her clit. The little nub pulsed against me, violently at first, then slowing until there were only tiny aftershocks left.

She half opened her eyes, drunk with pleasure. I reached over her and unlocked the handcuffs, tossing them to the side. Free of her restraints, she wrapped her hand around my dick.

"Please come inside me," she whispered. "I need you close."

For the first time, I saw it. I saw the vulnerability in a

woman who was larger than life, bold and sassy and confident, yet all this time, she'd had a side to her that she'd kept hidden, so desperate not to show it to the outside world that she'd risked everything to emerge victorious.

I loved her so deeply that it physically hurt, a kind of clamp around my heart that clenched whenever my emotions peaked. They were peaking now as she opened herself up to me, let me see the real Gia.

"I got you, baby. I got you."

I caged her with my body, curving one hand around her neck to draw her to me. I lined up my dick and pressed into her, slowly, an inch at a time. Fully seated, I stilled, caressing her cheek with the back of my hand.

"You okay?"

She nodded. "As long as I've got you, I'm more than okay."

"I'm going nowhere." I pulled out and pushed back in, leisurely, in no hurry to move this along. I yearned to feel every single inch of her encasing me. "I love you so fucking much, Gia."

She drew me close, her lips at my ear, her teeth nibbling on the lobe. Wrapping her legs around my waist, she thrust upward.

"Give me everything you've got, Kingcaid."

All intentions to draw out my own orgasm scattered like fall leaves in a gust of wind. I reared back, gripped her ass, and pounded into her. She grabbed her tits and pushed them together. Fuck, I loved it when she did that. I bent over, sucking both nipples into my mouth at the same time, tasting the salt on her skin.

Too soon, my balls tightened and I came. I buried my

face in her neck, muttering some unintelligible shit I couldn't recall five seconds later, but this was what Gia did to me. She made me lose my mind.

I pressed my body into hers, only for a second, then lifted off and rolled to the side. Spent, deliriously happy, one hundred percent in love with the woman lying beside me.

"Penn?"

"Yeah?"

"Would you hold me?"

I shifted her around, her back to my front, and spooned her. Me, Penn Kingcaid, spooning a woman. My woman. Fuck, life sure threw curveballs when you least expected it.

"I'll hold you, baby. I'll hold you for the rest of our lives."

"Tell me about Sandrine."

We'd lazed around in bed all day, fucking mainly, but occasionally talking. This was the first time Gia had asked about the woman she'd thought I'd had an affair with, though. Christ, it killed me every time I thought about how close I'd come to losing her through both my stupidity and hers. We were as bad as each other.

I dug into Gia's mouth-watering ravioli. How she made something as simple as pasta taste like a slice of heaven remained a mystery to me. "What do you want to know?"

"Everything."

"She's pretty cool. I think you'll like her." I bowed my head. "She forgave me for my part in Theo's death, so I think that tells you all you need to know about her character."

Gia's fork clanked, and she stood from the dining table and plunked herself in my lap.

"Penn, stop."

She tucked a few strands of my hair behind my ear —*note to self: get a haircut*—her fingertips dancing over my skin and raising a raft of goose bumps along the back of my neck.

"It wasn't your fault."

"You weren't there." I smiled to soften words that could be misconstrued. "I don't think I'll ever fully shake the feeling that I could have done something, taken evasive action to at least minimize the impact. That belief is a part of me. But talking to Ash helped, and now, talking to you, it's helping a little bit more."

"Then keep talking. To me, to Ash, to a therapist. To anyone that will help you to see what a wonderful person you are." She pecked my lips. "Can I meet her?"

"Absolutely. She's dying to meet you. I told her all about you last Friday, but even then I was racking my brain on how to square the circle, considering I hadn't told you about her." I ran my hands over her hips and thighs, my dick stirring despite the number of times I'd come inside her today already. "You'll have to meet Corabelle, too. She's my goddaughter and I love her to bits." I flicked her hair over her shoulder. "Do you want kids?"

"Whoa, Kingcaid." She grinned, her eyes twinkling

with the kind of mischief that came easy to Gia. "Diving right in there on the heavy shit, huh?"

"It's an important question, considering you're stuck with me for life."

"Yeah, I want kids. One day. When I've achieved my dreams."

I threw my arms out to the sides. "Already done."

She palmed my shoulder. "You ass."

"Guilty as charged." I grew serious. "What are your dreams?"

"To take care of Roberto and my folks, to have my own restaurant one day." She shrugged. "To be happy and loved and accepted for who I am."

"Mouthy, opinionated, and frustrating?"

She flattened her lips, but the mirth in her eyes gave her away. "Beautiful, amazing chef, fireball in bed."

I laughed. "A complicated woman—that's who you are, Gianna Greene."

"You think you can handle that? Me in all my dramatic glory?"

I squeezed her ass. "I can handle you. Every stunning fucking inch."

"Let's put that to the test." She climbed off my lap and held out her hand. "It's payback time, Kingcaid. Prepare to beg."

Chapter 32

Gia

Well... I never expected THAT!

PENN: MEET ME IN GREENWICH.

Me: Hold on. I'll just fetch my crystal ball. Where in Greenwich, you dick?

Penn: Jesus, woman. Give me a fucking minute to send you the address.

I chuckled. I loved it when Penn and I sparred over text.

Me: Probably should have led with that. Or put them on the same message, maybe?

Penn: Grrrr.

Me: [drooling face emoji] Love it when you growl.

Me: What's in Greenwich anyway?

Penn: Me?

Me: You really are a dick.

Penn: I'm your dick. Here's the address.

I clicked on the map, frowning.

Me: What's here?

Penn: Again... me. Have you had a lobotomy?

Me: Grrrr.

Penn: [drooling face emoji] Love it when you growl.

Me: Stop stealing my lines.

Penn: [winking emoji] Get your fine ass over here, woman.

Me: A true gentleman would hotfoot it over here to Brooklyn and pick me up.

Penn: Ash is kinda busy with your bestie.

Me: [middle-fingered emoji]

I waited a few seconds, but when no reply came, I grabbed my jacket and set off for the subway. Curiosity nudged me. I had no clue what was in Greenwich that required my presence, but knowing Penn, and how he'd showered me with gifts these past three weeks since we'd fucked and made up, I expected he had something wonderful planned.

Thirty minutes later, I emerged from the subway and set off down the street, pausing every couple of minutes to check Google maps and make sure I hadn't veered off course. I spotted Penn leaning against a wall, one foot resting on the brickwork behind him, scrolling on his phone. I tried to sneak up and surprise him, but almost as if he had a sixth sense, when I got within a few feet of him, he lifted his head and grinned.

Sliding his phone into the back pocket of his jeans, he

strolled to meet me, his arms encircling my waist, his lips capturing mine in an all-too-brief kiss.

"Missed you."

"You saw me this morning before you left for work."

"I know. But I still missed you. Thought any more about moving in with me?"

Penn had dropped that bombshell on me last weekend during dinner. He'd slid a laminated card across the dining table with the code to the private elevator that only traveled between his penthouse and the lobby, and a key card that gained entry to his home. So far, I'd refrained from giving him an answer, and in true Penn style, he'd agreed to give me time, then made sure to bring it up at every opportunity.

The truth was that I'd move in tomorrow, today even, but I kind of wanted to make him work for it. Did that make me a dick? Probably. Did I care? No. Besides, Penn knew me well enough to guess at the game I was playing, and he was happy to play it right alongside me. Any day now, I expected him to withdraw the offer or place some kind of time-bound demand on my answer.

This was us. We lived for the repartee.

"I told you. I'm thinking about it."

His lips quirked at the edges. "Well, don't think too long. I'm not short on offers."

I snorted. "This from the guy who admitted I was the first woman he'd ever taken to his home."

"Doesn't mean I don't have options."

"No one would put up with you. I've seen how you leave your underwear all over the bedroom floor."

"That's because you tear them off me so fast I don't have time to drop them into the laundry basket."

I laughed, stealing another kiss from the man I'd never get enough of. "Are you going to tell me what we're doing here?" I glanced around at the busy street bustling with locals and tourists alike. "It's a little early for lunch."

"We're not here for lunch."

"Okay. So?" I made a motion with my hands for him to get on with it.

Penn reached into the inside pocket of his jacket and produced a set of keys. He cocked his head for me to follow him, then proceeded down the street, stopping outside a blue door. I frowned, peering at the frontage. Big place. A little run-down.

Penn opened the door and captured my hand. "Come on, beautiful."

He tugged me over the step, flicking on a light just inside the door. A spider scuttled away, disappearing into a dark corner in which to hide. Luckily, spiders didn't scare me. Otherwise, Penn might have lost his hearing. It took me a few seconds to take in the vastness of the space. I glanced around at the peeling paintwork, the scuffed oak flooring in a chevron pattern, a faded picture of the Manhattan skyline on the far wall.

"What's this?"

Penn released me, stepping farther into the room. He held his arms out wide. "Your new restaurant. Or what will be your new restaurant once it's had a little spruce-up."

My jaw hit the floor. I blinked, gaping at him, his

words not quite resonating. I could have sworn he'd said "restaurant."

"I-I." I shook my head. "Say what now?"

"This is yours. I bought it, and before you open your sassy mouth and give me all that bullshit about independence and wanting to make your own way in the world, it's a loan. I know how proud you are, but we all need a leg up every once in a while, and this is me, giving you yours."

"Makes a change from a leg over," was my chosen comeback. *Must be the shock.*

Penn burst out laughing. "God, I fucking love you."

He took my hand, towing me through a doorway that opened into another room, just as large. There were also a couple of smaller rooms that led off that bigger one. My mind began to whirr with possibilities.

Knock down this wall. Put in an open kitchen back here where the diners can watch the chefs cook, fancy restrooms, a large pantry, cozy booths, and intimate lighting.

God, this could be amazing.

Tears pricked my eyes. I turned my back to Penn, dashing them away. Before I'd met him, I'd dreamed of owning my own restaurant one day, but I'd expected to be well into my thirties or even early forties before I could ever afford to run the kind of business that swallowed cash faster than I swallowed Penn's dick. I'd dreamed of it for me, of course, but also for Roberto. To ensure his future as well as my own.

And now, Penn had given me a chance to turn that dream into a reality years before I'd expected it to happen.

"Are you crying?"

"No." My voice broke, a sob breaking free without permission, goddammit.

"C'mere, baby." Penn drew me into his arms, kissing the top of my head. "There's a lot of work to do, and I expect you to manage that. I have enough fucking businesses to run. I've also set a budget, so don't think you're getting a free-for-all." He winked. "And I've had my lawyer draw up a contract that lays out a repayment plan, including market-rate interest, and also gives me shares in this place until you've repaid every penny."

This man... he knew me. He knew that charity wasn't something that interested me at all. I might have landed myself a super-rich boyfriend, but success only meant something to me if I earned it. But help... I wasn't so proud that I'd throw this kind of gesture back in Penn's face. He'd opened a door for me, and I planned to walk through it. My repayment for his faith in me would be to work my ass off and make this place a massive success.

I threw my arms around him. "Kingcaid, you're a legend." I peppered his face with kisses. "I'll pay you back. Every single penny. I promise." I let him go, dancing around what would soon be my very own dining room. And then reality hit. How would I cope with working at Theo's and managing this project? I had to work. I needed the money, and even when I moved in with Penn—because, let's face it, I'd already made the decision—I refused to sponge off him.

"What's wrong?"

"I can't do this."

Penn's eyes crinkled in confusion. "What do you mean?"

"There aren't enough hours in the day to manage the refurbishment of this place and all the work that comes with setting up and launching a new business *and* cover my shifts at Theo's. It's one or the other, and I have to work. I need the money."

"Gia." Penn's sigh came from somewhere around his feet. He crooked his finger, then pointed it at the floor. "Come here."

I trudged over, already knowing what he'd say and equally conscious that I couldn't accept his offer to bankroll my life. I stared at the floor. He clipped me under the chin.

"One of these days, you're going to trip on that pride of yours and smash up this beautiful face."

"Don't, Penn. Don't make fun of my principles."

"I'm not." He caressed my face. "Y'know, when you grow up rich, it's hard to trust people. There's always that niggle. Are they here for me or for my money, for my connections, for what I can do for them? But with you... I never had that thought. Even when our relationship evolved into something far deeper than either of us had expected, that niggle never came. If it were up to me, I'd give you the world, but I know you want to earn your place, and I respect the fuck out of that. I respect the fuck out of *you*."

He dragged his teeth over my bottom lip, drawing a needy groan from my throat.

"You can do both, Gia. When you're driven, as you are, as I am, you find the extra hours in the day. But the problem with that approach is that it's all-consuming. And I'm a selfish bastard. I want time for us."

"So do I. And I don't want this to come between us. What you did... Penn this is wonderful, and I'm choking up over here, but the thought of sponging off you for the months it'll take to get this place ready for opening... I just can't do it."

Penn rubbed his lips together, his eyebrows dipping inward, deep in thought.

"Y'know, if you move in with me, then you'll save on rent. That way, you wouldn't need as much income, and maybe you could reduce your shifts at Theo's to three nights, which would free up extra time to manage the refurb of this place."

I narrowed my eyes at him. "You'll try anything to get your own way, won't you, Kingcaid?"

He chuckled, pulling me closer to him. "I'll do anything if it means I get to wake up next to this body every morning." He kissed me. "I'm serious, though. This way we both win."

"Wow... both of us?"

"It's called compromise, baby."

"Compromise means everyone loses." I grinned. There was a time both of us had believed that. Not anymore.

"Yet here we are, both winners."

I grew serious for a moment. *Odd, I know.* "This could work."

"It will work. We'll make it work. Oh! I almost forgot." He released me, darting into one of the other two rooms. He returned holding what looked like a sign.

"It's only a mock-up, and it's easily changed, but..."

He turned it to face me, and I choked up for real. My throat clogged, my eyes stung, and my heart expanded.

"Oh, Penn."

He'd had a sign made. *Gianna's Italian Kitchen.*

I took it from him, my vision blurred. This might have been the most thoughtful thing anyone had ever done for me in my entire life. It was up there for sure.

"Like I said, if you don't like it, we can—"

"I love it." I propped it against the wall, making sure it wouldn't fall, then threw myself at Penn. "I love it, and I love you."

"So that's a yes to moving in?"

A chuckle rippled through my throat despite my best efforts to contain it. "You are irrepressible."

"Irresistible, you say?" He nuzzled between my breasts. "Want to christen the place?"

I released a soft, contented sigh. "Thought you'd never ask."

Chapter 33

Gia

Sometimes, dreams do come true.

<small>Six months later...</small>

"Do you think there's enough food?" I set down another plate of bruschetta on a table already groaning under the weight. "I'm worried there isn't enough food."

Penn snagged me around the waist, drawing me into his body. "Gia, breathe, okay? You're going to give yourself an aneurysm or some such shit. There's enough food to feed lower Manhattan. There will be so much left over that we'll be able to stock up the homeless shelters."

"That's a good idea. Shame to let any go to waste when it could do some good."

I wriggled out of Penn's hold and dashed into the kitchen, where Lorenzo was putting the finishing touches on dessert—a forty-portion tiramisu. He jerked his chin at a basket of freshly made garlic breadsticks.

"You're a lifesaver!" I kissed his cheek. "Seriously, I don't know what I'd have done without you today."

I'd tried my hardest to persuade Lorenzo to join me at *Gianna's Italian Kitchen*—still struggled to get my head around that—but Freddo had moved on and Lorenzo had bagged the head chef's job at my previous place of employment. I couldn't blame the guy. It was a real step up for him, and one he deserved more than almost anyone I knew.

"It's a big day. I wouldn't have missed it."

"Do you still think buffet style was the way to go?"

I'd gone back and forth on this so many times, driving Penn to the edge of madness. In the end, he'd come to me with both fists clenched and told me to pick a hand. I'd chosen the right one. Inside, written on a piece of paper in Penn's neat handwriting was the word "buffet." I made him show me the other hand just to ensure a fair fight. I laughed at what he'd written.

"Sit-down shenanigans, which means Gia will be too tired for sex."

I still swore he'd fixed it somehow.

The last six months had passed by in a flurry of activity. On multiple occasions, I'd worried we wouldn't open on time, which would suck considering half of Penn's family had made the trip to New York to help celebrate my big day. Even Johannes had agreed to come, although

Penn had his reservations about whether he'd actually turn up. I hoped he did. For all his broodiness and scarce smiles, I had a soft spot for him.

Penn popped his head into the kitchen. "My parents are here, with Ash and Kiana."

I squealed, yanked off my apron, tossing it at Lorenzo, and dashed into the dining room. I threw myself at Kee, hugging her until she squeaked that she couldn't breathe. I let her go, accepted Asher's kiss on the cheek, and then flipped the behavior switch to "Decorum" to greet Penn's parents. I'd only met them twice before. Once at Kee's wedding and then again a few weeks ago, and as much as Penn had told me to be myself, I doubted they were ready for the full-blown Gianna Greene experience just yet.

"Mr. Kingcaid, Mrs. Kingcaid, I'm so pleased you could make it. Let me take your coats."

Penn snickered from his position behind me, and I kicked out with my foot. Fortunately for him, it missed connecting with his shin.

Penn's mom put her arms around me and gave me a warm hug. "It's so lovely to see you again. And this place." She motioned with her hand. "It's beautiful. I know it'll be a great success."

"I hope so. I'm in debt to Penn up to my eyeballs. Your son strikes a mean deal."

Penn slid an arm around my waist, his thumb brushing my hip in an attempt to calm me. "You wouldn't have had it any other way."

"No, I wouldn't." I leaned my head on his shoulder, catching a soft smile from his mother.

Guess I got her approval. Thank fuck.

The rest of the guests began arriving, and from that moment on, I didn't get a second to myself. My parents and Penn's parents were locked deep in conversation, and Roberto, my amazing, wonderful, funny little brother, charmed the pants off everyone in the room. I even caught Johannes—yep, he'd come—laughing at something Roberto said.

Boy, laughter changed that guy. He should attempt it more often.

"Gia."

At hearing my name, I turned. I broke into a smile, hugging the new arrival. "I'm so glad you could make it, Sandrine."

From the moment Penn had introduced us, Sandrine and I had clicked. Kind of in the way Kee and I had clicked when we were five, and although Kee was and always would be my best friend, it was kind of nice to have a close female companion living in the same city as I did. Someone I could call up when I needed a girls' night out, or I wanted to bitch about Penn leaving his socks on the bathroom floor, or a million other things women shared that made the female-to-female relationship a special one.

"Sorry I'm late, but Corabelle decided she wasn't happy with her momma going out for the evening. She insisted I stay with her until she fell asleep. Poor Kyle. I hope, for his sake, she stays that way until I get home."

I adored Kyle. While I hadn't known Theo, Kyle was the perfect match for Sandrine, a true life partner. The four of us regularly went out to dinner or to the theater, and I knew how relieved Sandrine was that Penn and Kyle had grown close. She'd worried that Penn would constantly compare the two men she'd given her heart to and decide Kyle wasn't worthy of her affections.

A good few months had passed since Penn had last mentioned his guilt or culpability in Theo's death, and it wasn't something I brought up. Maybe he'd finally put that awful time behind him.

I could only hope.

"He'll manage. And by 'manage,' I mean he'll call you and order you straight home."

She chuckled. "Amen to that, sister."

I pointed her toward the food, which had taken a serious beating. Looked as if there wouldn't be much left over for the homeless after all. Glancing around, pride swelled in my chest. Tomorrow, we'd open to the general public, and then the real work would begin. We were fully booked for the next six weeks, and while I suspected some of that was curiosity, New York's elite wondering how Penn Kingcaid's girl would fare running her own restaurant, it didn't matter to me. All publicity was good publicity when a business first started out, and I had confidence in the menu I'd meticulously designed, the staff I'd hired—with Penn's welcome input—and the kind of ambience I wanted to create.

"Gia, honey." Mom made her way through the crowds, murmuring apologies and doling out smiles at everyone she passed. "We're going to head out shortly. Roberto is tired, and he has an appointment with Mrs. Hunter at nine in the morning."

Mrs. Hunter had worked wonders with my brother these past few months. He'd come on in leaps and bounds, rising from the lowest in his school year to the one of the highest. Just another thing I owed to Penn's generosity.

"No problem, Mom. I'm just so glad you could come."

Mom waved Dad over. "I was just saying to your father, wasn't I, Simon, how immensely proud we are of you and all you've achieved."

Dad's eyes glimmered, and I could have sworn his chest was a little puffed out. "Very proud of you, love. Then again, we always have been."

I couldn't hide the shock at his admission. I searched my mind for another occasion where my parents had told me of their pride in my achievements, but I couldn't come up with a single time. There might have been some, before Roberto had been born, but I struggled to think of one.

"Darling, we know we weren't always able to give you the attention you deserved, especially after Roberto was born, but you clearly didn't need us." She gestured around. "Look what you've achieved. We're so happy for you. Happy your dreams are coming true. Happy you've found a good man who is perfect for you."

I bit my lip, loath to spoil a perfect evening, but sometimes, holding back was the wrong approach. Such as now.

"I did need you, though, Mom. And you, Dad. Sometimes, I felt so alone. Abandoned. Cast adrift without an anchor." I rushed on. "I adore you both so much, and Roberto is the center of my world, but I missed your guidance, your advice." I shrugged. "I guess, I missed you."

"Oh, love." Dad hugged me tightly. "I wish you'd told

us how you felt. Even before Roberto was born, you had an independent streak a mile long, but if we'd had any idea..." He shook his head and touched Mom's arm. "Tell her, Bianca."

"Gianna, come here." She held out her arms, and I tucked myself into her embrace. "We just thought you were fine, darling. Like your dad said, you've always been independently minded and grown-up. But you're right. We should have made more time for you." She leaned back, stroking my face. "Forgive me?"

Tears sprang to my eyes, stinging like a swarm of wasps had set up home behind my eyeballs. I blinked to prevent them from falling. Instead, the opposite happened, and the next thing I knew, the three of us were hugging and crying and exchanging words of love. Not to be left out, Roberto muscled his way in between the three of us, his innocent "What gives?" turning our tears to laughter.

I told Penn I'd be right back, and walked my family to the subway station across the street. For the first time, it truly felt as if we were a family of four, rather than a family of three plus one. Tonight might have been the culmination of a long-held dream to own a restaurant—although I swore I'd be eighty before I'd repaid the loan to Penn—but I'd also achieved another dream. My parents were proud of me. My parents loved me. My parents had *always* been proud of me, had *always* loved me. And while I'd known that to be the case, hearing it had validated my sense of self and made me a true part of this wonderful family of mine.

"Love you." I kissed Mom first, then Dad, and finally

Roberto. "Jeez, kiddo, it won't be long before you're towering over me."

"I know."

His grin, bursting with confidence, gave me this inner glow. Fuck, I loved this kid. He'd changed so much since receiving extra tutoring that I hardly recognized the child who would lose himself to angry outbursts and frustrations he had struggled to comprehend.

"Look after Mom and Dad now, y'hear? I'll be along to see you next week."

"Penn, too?"

I ruffled his hair. "Yes, Penn, too."

"Excellent." He fist-bumped me. "He's way better than you at gaming."

"Hey!" I pretended his comment had offended me, then laughed. "You're right, Roberto. I suck."

I waited until they disappeared into the bowels of New York's subway system, then turned to make my way back to the party. Penn greeted me outside, his arms waiting for me. I tucked my head against his shoulder and stuck my hands in the back pockets of his pants, giving his muscular ass a good squeeze.

"My parents are proud of me." My breath hitched, and I swallowed past a thick throat. "They love me and they're proud of me."

Penn eased me back, tucking a few stray strands of hair behind my ear. "Who couldn't love you and be proud of you? You're amazing."

"Thank you," I whispered, overcome with gratitude for the man who'd made all my dreams come true. "I couldn't have done any of this without your support."

Penn kissed my forehead. "I think you'd have found a way. You're meant to reach the stars, Gia. I'm just glad I'll be around to see it."

Chapter 34

Penn

Nerves suck, but the payoff is worth it.

"Have they gone?" Gia sank onto a nearby chair and kicked off her shoes. She lifted her foot and massaged the sole. "Please tell me there aren't any stragglers hiding in the kitchen, hoovering up the last of Lorenzo's caramel profiteroles."

I chuckled. "They're gone. It's just us."

Pulling a chair close to hers, I brought her foot to my lap. I dug my thumbs in, eliciting a groan that turned my mind to sex. What was it about this woman that meant no matter how many times I buried myself inside her, it wasn't ever enough?

I hungered for her.

I thought of little else other than having her in my

arms, kissing her delicious mouth, stealing her breath and her words of love.

Every morning, I woke with her beside me and thought about what a lucky fucking bastard I was.

Time hadn't diminished the passion I had for her; it'd escalated it. Even at work, a place I'd always managed to throw myself into with gusto, shutting off all interruptions, she crept into my mind at least a hundred times a day.

"God, that feels good." She rolled her head on her neck, eyes closing as she released a slow breath through pursed lips. "It went okay, I think."

"Okay?" I shook my head. "When did you start underplaying events? No, it didn't go 'okay.' It went fucking superbly."

"But the guest list consisted of only family and friends. They're hardly going to rip me a new one if they thought the fettuccini Alfredo had too much butter in it, or the garlic bread wasn't crusty enough, or the—"

I cut her off with a kiss. I'd discovered that, oftentimes, it was the best way to shut her up when she went off on a tirade. She shuffled her chair closer to mine, curling her toes around my cock.

The last thing I wanted to do was pull away, but if I let her carry on, I'd end up fucking her on the tiny couch in her office. And while I'd make it work, I had other plans to execute first. Plans I'd fussed and worried over for weeks, and now here we were, and I had to get this right.

"You're insatiable," I muttered against her lips. "And although I like where your mind is going, I must remind you that this is a busy street, and those are some big-ass windows at the front."

She wrinkled her nose. "True." Then she said, "Screw 'em."

Straddling my hips, she rocked against me. *Ah, Christ.* My dick sprang to life from half-mast in less than a second.

"Gia." I gripped her waist. "Fuck."

"Yes, fuck, Penn. Good plan."

She did this figure-eight thing with her pelvis and pushed her tits in my face. I had about three seconds to stop her before my resolve crumbled.

"At this rate, your first review will be along the lines of 'No idea what the pasta tastes like, but the sex show was top notch.'"

"Ah, crap. You're right. Must be professional." She stood, taking me by the hand. "Let's go home."

"Wait." This wasn't going at all like I'd planned. When it came to Gia, I was nothing more than a ball of putty for her to mold in whatever way she saw fit. "First a drink and a toast." I pointed to the chair. "Sit. I'll get them."

Confusion drifted over her face, but for once, she didn't question me. "No more champagne for me. I'm all bubbled out."

I grinned, sauntering off as if I lived a stress- and care-free life, which, most of the time, I did. But the second I disappeared into the kitchen, a herd of stampeding buffalo rampaged through my insides, or that was what it felt like. This wasn't nerves; it was far, far worse. Nerves were what happened before a big presentation to investors, or at the opening of a new hotel, or telling my father I'd started a rival restaurant under a different name.

I'd never come so close to puking without imbibing copious amounts of alcohol.

I poured orange juice into two champagne flutes, the memories of our first coming together—literally—tugging a smile out of me. I left them on the counter and ducked into Gia's office to grab my jacket. Reaching into the inside pocket, my fingers closed around the small, square box. I kept my back to the door in case my nosy girlfriend decided to come look for me, and opened the box.

Perfect.

Exquisite.

One of a kind, just like her.

My hands shook as I plucked the ring from its housing. This was, no contest, the scariest thing I'd ever done in my entire life, and I'd done some crazy stuff, especially during my college years. Skydiving, bungee jumping, flying helicopters and planes, sailing down a mountainside on a bike that had faulty brakes.

But proposing to my girlfriend—now *that* was some terrifying shit.

I slipped the ring into my pants pocket and returned to the kitchen to pick up the OJ. I found Gia where I'd left her, massaging the soles of her feet again. If Gia in stilettos didn't give me a hard-on, I'd question the purpose of women wearing high-heeled shoes at all.

Then again, Gia in sweats and sneakers gave me a hard-on, so my observation didn't stack up.

"Here." I handed her the flute and pulled up a chair.

She took a sip and grinned. "Orange juice? Aren't you afraid I might spill it all over your expensive shirt?"

I smiled, too. "I was so pissed at you that morning."

"Really?" Sarcasm filled her tone. "You hid it so well."

My chest squeezed. The last six months had seen a reduction in the guilt I carried over Theo, which, in part, I guessed, was down to Sandrine finding love with Kyle, whom, while he wasn't Theo, I liked enormously. But on occasion, that thread inside me tightened.

Gia leaned forward to caress my knee. "When Kee told me about Theo, I thought back to that day and wondered if that had triggered you in some way."

"Yeah, it did, although at the time, my annoyance was centered around a ruined shirt ahead of an important meeting."

"Hey, what can I say? I'm a girl who makes a memorable first impression."

"I'll say." I canted my head. "Wonder if we'd be together if you hadn't thrown a cup of OJ all over me?"

"Half a cup," she corrected, her eyes twinkling. "Either way, we'd have met ahead of Kee's wedding, but maybe those first few occasions wouldn't have been quite so fraught without 'OJ-gate.'"

"Fraught? That was pure lust manifesting itself as indignation." I held out my glass and touched it to hers, astounded that my hand didn't shake. "To you, Gia, and all the success coming your way. Enjoy it. The first installment on your loan is due at the end of the month."

She burst out laughing. "What happens if I default?"

I ran my fingertip up her thigh. "I take no prisoners in business."

A shudder ran through her. "Let's go home, Penn."

"Not yet."

I steadied myself. *This is it.* Originally, I'd had the idea to drop the ring into the glass of OJ, but then she'd have to fish it out and it'd be all sticky—although not as sticky as cum, as we'd discovered. Instead, I removed her glass, set it on the table next to mine, and picked up her left hand.

"I'm so fucking proud of you. These last few months, you've astounded me with your work ethic, your creative eye, and your amazing cooking, which I've had the pleasure of tasting as you developed your menu. I know, with a hundred percent certainty, that this is only the first of many restaurants you'll open, and I am honored to be here at the very beginning."

I filled my lungs through my nose, blew out slowly, and then dropped to one knee. Fishing the ring out of my pocket, I held it in front of her. Her free hand flew to her face, her eyes widening.

"Oh my God."

"I love you, Gia, in all the ways that matter. Neither of us is perfect, but we're perfect for one another. I never imagined falling for a woman who drives me crazy inside and outside the bedroom, but you tick all my boxes, including those I wasn't even aware of." I slipped the ring over the tip of her finger. "Will you be my wife?"

"Christ, Penn, yes. Yes!"

I pushed the ring the rest of the way on, drew her to her feet, and kissed her until we were both breathless.

"I just had a thought," she said when we broke apart.

"As long as that thought isn't 'I've changed my mind,' go ahead."

She grinned. "Brides are supposed to turn up late on their wedding day. For the first time in my life, I'll be able to be late without pissing anyone off." She ran her palm down the front of my shirt. "Would an hour push my luck?"

I caught her hand, bringing it to my lips, where I kissed the ring. "A minute, an hour, a day. It doesn't matter to me. I'll wait a lifetime for you."

"I don't deserve you."

"No, you don't, but you're stuck with me anyway."

I captured her lips, drowning in the way her body melded to mine. Whatever life threw at us, it'd never be dull, not with this outrageous, outspoken, messy, crazy girl by my side.

I relished every single moment, for with Gia beside me, I'd struck gold.

A Thank You from Penn

Thank you so much for sticking with me and Gia to the end. You deserve a medal!

Seriously, though, as much as she drives me crazy, I love every single inch of her, even if I sometimes wish I had a ball gag to hand.

Hmm... maybe a trip to the sex store is in order...

Anyway, I digress.

I hope you're enjoying getting to know my family. There's a lot of us, and many more stories to come. Next up is *Wrecked By You* where my broody, sullen brother Johannes will finally be forced to face up to his demons, thanks to a spirited, wonderful woman named Ella. Well, that's what he thinks her name is anyway.

Argh... I've said too much.

If you can't wait for *Wrecked By You* to release, then have you read the ROGUES series yet? You met Oliver Ellis when Gia and I had dinner with him (I'll never be able to look at pumpkin pie the same way again -thanks Gia!), but why not start at the very beginning with Entranced. Available on Amazon.

Or, if you'd like a free prequel to the ROGUES series, all you have to do is join Tracie's newsletter and your copy of Entwined will magically arrive on your device of choice. Go to her website at www.authortraciedelaney.com and click on "Claim My Free Book" on the home page.

The longed-for story of the middle brother, Johannes, a tortured hero with a deep-rooted distrust of women.

But walls are made to be toppled, and the beautiful, if secretive, Ella Reyes has all the tools she needs to reduce Johannes's defenses to rubble.

Coming Soon on Amazon!

Acknowledgments

They say it takes a village to raise a child... well it takes this group of amazing people to help me birth a book. I don't know how I got so lucky to have this team around me, but I'm never letting any of them go. (Team, let this be a warning - I will stalk you!)

To my amazing hubs who somehow still puts up with me after too many years to mention. Thank you for everything that you do.

To my brilliant, dirty-minded, kind, generous, amazing PA, Loulou for your unending support and love for me and my writing. You're truly one in a million.

To my critique partner, Incy. Your support means the world. I still brace every time that email drops in my inbox, but I wouldn't have it any other way.

Lasairiona, my wonderful Woo friend - thank you for reading an early copy and for your loud and effervescent enthusiasm for Gia and Penn and for all you do to push me forward and make me strive for excellence at every turn. On to the next!

Bethany - thank you so much for your brilliant editing and wonderful suggestions. Next up Johannes... prepare yourself!

Jean - you are in my thoughts constantly. Love you to the moon and back.

Katie - Gah... I run out of superlatives when it comes to you! I adore our chats, our laughs, our plotting sessions. Here's to many, many more (see note above about stalking if you ever try to leave me.) I truly will never forget the orange juice/cum conversation!

Jacqueline - ZERO CONTINUITY ERRORS! I swear, I smiled for a week when you told me that. We'll keep your other feedback between us LOL.

Virginia - Given how many amazing authors you proof-read for, I had to steel myself to send this one to you. Imagine my relief when you messaged with "OMG! It was amazing!" Phew!

To my ARC readers. You guys are amazing! You're my final eyes and ears before my baby is released into the world and I appreciate each and every one of you for giving up your time to read.

And last but most certainly not least, to you, the readers. Thank you for being on this journey with me and taking a chance on a new series. I'm damned lucky to do this for a job, but without you, I wouldn't be able to. I hope you carry on and devour the rest of the Kingcaid series. There is plenty more to come.

If you have any time to spare, I'd be ever so grateful if you'd leave a short review on Amazon or Goodreads. Reviews not only help readers discover new books, but they also help authors reach new readers. You'd be doing a massive favor for this wonderful bookish community we're all a part of.

Books by Tracie Delaney

BILLIONAIRE ROMANCE

The ROGUES Series

The Irresistibly Mine Series

The Kincaid Billionaire Series

PROTECTOR/MILITARY ROMANCE

The Intrepid Bodyguard Series

SPORTS ROMANCE

The Winning Ace Series

The Full Velocity Series

CONTEMPORARY ROMANCE

The Brook Brothers Series

BOXSETS

Winning Ace

Brook Brothers

Full Velocity

ROGUES Books 1-3

SPINOFFS/STANDALONES

Mismatch (A Winning Ace Spin Off Novel)

Break Point (A Winning Ace Novella)

Control (A Driven World/Full Velocity Novel)

My Gift To You

About the Author

Tracie Delaney is a Kindle Unlimited All Star author of more than twenty-five contemporary romance novels which she writes from her office in the freezing cold North West of England. The office used to be a garage, but she needed somewhere quiet to write and so she stole it from her poor, long-suffering husband who is still in mourning that he's been driven out to the shed!

An avid reader for as long as she can remember, Tracie was also a bit of a tomboy back in the day and used to climb trees with her trusty Enid Blyton's and read for hours, returning home when it was almost dark with a numb bottom and more than a few splinters!

Tracie's books have a common theme of women who show that true strength comes in all forms, and alpha males who put up a great fight (which they ultimately lose!)

At night she likes to curl up on the sofa with her two Westies, Murphy & Cooper, and binge-watch shows on Netflix. There may be wine involved.

Visit her website for contact information and more www. authortraciedelaney.com

Made in the USA
Middletown, DE
05 January 2023

21386228R00234